I0561886

Midnight!!

Midnight!!

by
Claude Vignon

Translated, annotated and introduced by
Brian Stableford

A Black Coat Press Book

English adaptation and introduction Copyright © 2021 by Brian Stableford.
Cover illustration Copyright © 2021 illustration by Aurélien Maccarelli.

Visit our website at www.blackcoatpress.com

ISBN 978-1-64932-084-1. First Printing. August 2021. Published by Black Coat Press, an imprint of Hollywood Comics.com, LLC, P.O. Box 17270, Encino, CA 91416. All rights reserved. Except for review purposes, no part of this book may be reproduced or transmitted in any form or by any means, electronic or mechanical, including photocopying, recording, or by any information storage and retrieval system, without permission in writing from the publisher. The stories and characters depicted in this novel are entirely fictional. Printed in the United States of America.

TABLE OF CONTENTS

Translator's Introduction

Minuit!! récits de la veillée, signed "Claude Vignon," was first published in Paris by Amyot in 1856. The copy reproduced on *gallica* bears the contemporary stamp of what was then the Imperial Library, and gives no indication that there was anything unusual about the publication, but the collection was reissued the following year under the title *Contes à faire peur,* with a prefatory note saying that the edition was licensed for distribution in Belgium and elsewhere, but prohibited in France, implying that the first edition had been belatedly suppressed after being brought to the attention of the censors.

If that were the case, it would not have been particularly unusual; censorship under the Second Empire, which had been severe since 1851, was beginning gradually to ease in 1856, but it did so incompletely and rather uneasily, and the censors often found themselves embroiled in controversy, most publicly and most loudly in such celebrated cases as those of Gustave Flaubert's *Madame Bovary* (1856) and Charles Baudelaire's *Les Fleurs du Mal* (1857). The fact that the partial suppression of *Minuit!!* attracted no such publicity is not proof that it was not successfully carried out. The text is readily available today, being reproduced on *wikisource* as well as on *gallica,* but the almost total lack of secondary references to it suggests that it was very difficult to access for a century and more. That is a pity, because it is a

7

very interesting work and represents a significant landmark in the development of French fantastic fiction.

The mystery with which the work appears, in retrospect, to have been surrounded is not limited to its rather ghostly presence in the annals of French literature; its signature appears to have remained mysterious for some time. The name "Claude Vignon" had already been employed on several items of art criticism, including reports on the Salons of 1850-51, 1852 and 1853, and in 1861 it reappeared on a second collection of short fiction, *Récits de la vie réelle*, which forsook the fantastic but showed an evident continuity of interest in its themes. It then appeared on a series of further works, mostly novels, whose publication extended into the early 1890s. Even then it does not appear to have been generally known that "Claude Vignon" was actually the artist—primarily reputed as a sculptor—baptized Marie-Noémi Cadiot (1828-1888), who had married the "Opportunist" politician Maurice Rouvier (1842-1911) in 1872. Rouvier's political career subsequently advanced through the stages of député, minister and senator, reaching climaxes when he served two terms as Président du Conseil (i.e., prime minister) in 1887 and 1905.

The brief biography contained in the catalogue of the Bibliothèque Nationale dutifully notes that Cadiot's first husband, whom she had married in the 1840s—the BN catalogue has "1848?", but other sources give the date as 1846—was Alphonse-Louis Constant (1810-1875), who subsequently became famous, or notorious, under the assumed name of Éliphas Lévi, the most celebrated occultist in France and a key figure in the French Occult Revival. Unusually, the BN catalogue takes the trouble to assert—apparently mistakenly—that it was after Constant's death that she married Rouvier, thus implying, without actually saying so, that she might not have been divorced before being associated with the Marquis de Montferrier (presumably the son or grandson of the most famous holder of that title who died in 1829 and who was the father of the artist Julie Hugo, 1797-1865, Victor Hugo's sister-in-law), with whom she lived after leaving Constant, representing herself as his wife. Other sources express no doubts about the legality that second marriage. All sources agree that she did not stay with Constant long; Cadiot's Wikipedia entry records that they had one child, a daughter who died in 1854 at the age of seven, but does not give a reference for that datum; the allegation made in the *wikipedia* article on Constant that they had several children and numerous descendants is probably fanciful.

All easily-available sources agree that Cadiot adopted her pseudonym from a novella by Honoré de Balzac ("Béatrix," 1839) and not from the famous seven-teenth-century painter Claude Vignon; that is perfectly plausible, the Balzac character being an art critic alleg-edly modeled on the contemporary critic Gustave Planche (1808-1857), whom Cadiot must at least have met when she similarly began reporting on the annual Salon, and probably knew quite well. As to whether she also knew Balzac—who died in 1850—we can only speculate, but his influence on her work is obvious and acknowledged. She was evidently well-connected in the artistic and literary society of Paris even before 1850, while she was married to Constant, and she might have introduced him into that society, in which he is known to have been avid to make his mark. He is widely alleged to have associated himself, at least briefly, with Théophile Gautier's coterie, and it is not difficult to find possible influences of Gautier on *Minuit!!,* as well as apparent influences of Charles Baudelaire, whom Constant and Cadiot might have encountered in Gautier's salon. While the acquaintances remain hypothetical, however, appearances suggest that Cadiot read Baudelaire's translations of Edgar Poe avidly, before their assembly in *Nouvelles histoires extraordinaires* (1857), and took considerable inspiration therefrom; no other French writer showed the apparent influence of Poe at such an early date and so extravagantly.

While Cadiot and Constant were together Constant was also closely associated with socialist organizations, and it is important to note that they would inevitably have come under close police scrutiny after the *coup-d'état* of December 1851, when several leading Romantic *littérateurs* were exiled from France and many others subjected to severe restrictions with regard to publishing their work. The Marquis de Montferrier is unlikely to have been immune from such scrutiny. If *Minuit!!* did, indeed, attract the hostile attention of the authorities in 1856 it would not be in the least surprising, and it is not surprising either that the stories collected therein do not appear to have been published previously. There is no way of knowing when they were written, but some of them, at least, were probably written some time before the publication of the book; the stories show a progressive development of method and theme that suggests that, with one possible exception, they were written in the order in which they appear in the volume, that exception being "Isobel-la-Ressuscitée" (tr. as "Isobel the Resuscitated") which might well have been written before any of the others.

The last story in the book, "La Dalle" (tr. as "The Slab") was presumably the last to be written, and if the allegation that Cadiot's daughter died in 1854 at the age of seven is true, there is an inevitable temptation to see a certain significance in the fact that the story deals with the mysterious disappearance—and death—of a six-year-old girl, who appear to be reincarnated thereafter (although the fact that the girl's stepfather is an ambitious politician named Rouvières can only be a pure accident.) Within the collection, the story forms the final element of a curious sequence, all dealing with mysterious and unorthodox reincarnations, and the internal pattern of that sequence suggests that its relationship with the other items might be why "Isobel-la-Ressuscitée" was relocated in the order of presentation if, indeed, it was.

In calling the supernatural element of the stories in *Minuit!!* "unorthodox." the reference is, of course, to a kind of nascent literary orthodoxy, which had already undergone a marked evolution within the fiction of the Romantic Movement, and which Cadiot's collection appears to be consciously continuing and attempting to extrapolate, In common with German and English Romantic fiction, French Romantic fiction had gone through a "Gothic" phase of the production of what Jane Austen famously called in *Northanger Abbey*, "horrid novels." Many of the early examples originated in Germany, but their lurid horrors were copied in England by such novels as Horace Walpole's *The Castle of Otranto* (1764) and Matthew Gregory Lewis's *The Monk* (1796) before being largely displaced in fashionability by more subtle accounts of exaggerated menace by such writers as Ann Radcliffe and Charlotte Smith, who deliberately desupernaturalized their plots, explaining away any seeming supernatural apparitions. In Germany too, the crudities of the early "horrid novels" was superseded to a considerable extent by the subtler and more various hallucinatory fantasies of E. T. A. Hoffmann. In France, Radcliffe and Smith became the most popular English writers in translation among general readers, while Hoffmann became a particular favorite of the writers who participated in the Romantic *cénacles* originated by Charles Nodier and Victor Hugo, and carried forward by Théophile Gautier. It is not surprising that French prose writers, who joined the game a trifle belatedly, not only followed the trend but did so self-consciously, often intent of seeking originality within it. The stories in *Minuit!!,* which are obviously the work of an intelligent, well-informed and thoughtful participant in the Movement, are remarkable in mapping out an evolutionary spectrum of Gothic and post-Gothic fantasies that exemplifies certain key phases within the evolution of Romantic fantasy.

Two of the stories are set in Germany, one in the Middle Ages and one in the sixteenth century, and are described in subtitles as "legends," thus advertizing their own tacit obsolescence. "Le Convive des Trépassés" (tr. as "The Guest of the Dead") is pure Gothic melodrama, deliberately brutal in its supernatural improvisations and their deployment in an unusually stark moral fantasy. It is a "horrid" story through and through,[1] and there are few examples in French Romantic fiction that are as forthright. Although it introduces its revenants in a conventional manner, as insubstantial spirits who might well exist entirely in the mind's eye, it proceeds uncompro-

---

[1] We have no way of knowing why *Minuit!!* was banned in France, if, in fact it was, but it is unlikely to have been because of the horrors featured in this story and the next one, and it is more likely to have seemed suspect because of sensitive political references in the author's introduction.

misingly to the material manifestation of a resurrected corpse that is exceedingly solid as well as exceedingly violent—an unusual move that might seem crude, but is quite deliberate in its crudity, and not at all unthinking. The materiality of revenants was to become a central and fundamental theme of Cadiot's supernatural fiction, and the subsequent stories in the collection are scrupulously arranged so as to illustrate its logical problems as well as progressively exploring its narrative potential.

The similarly gruesome "Les Morts se vengent" (tr. as "The Dead Avenge Themselves") is a subtler story, in spite of its use of physical horror, which belongs to a distinct subcategory of ambiguous fantastic fiction, whose inclusions feature endings in which victims of horrific visions wake up, to their great relief, only to find that their "hallucination" has left behind evidence of its reality. That narrative twist was by no means as familiar in 1856 as it subsequently became, but Cadiot does not employ it, as many later writers were later to do, simply as a narrative twist; she does not deal in such "narrative ambushes"—indeed, she sometimes goes to considerable lengths to make sure that her reader knows exactly what is happening in her stories, even though her characters are completely at sea. ("La Dalle," for instance, is only given that title—a far more natural title would be "Pâquerette"— as a deliberate "spoiler" intended to tip the reader off as to what has happened long before her characters find out.) In "Les Morts se vengent" the primary focus of the author's interest is not so much on the material reality of what happens to the protagonist, notwithstanding the lurid physiological detail that she provides, as the long term psychological effect that the experience has on him—and that is the direction in which Romantic fiction in general, and Cadiot's particular contribution to it—was headed, as is made very evident by "Les Dix mille francs du Diable" (tr. as "The Devil's Ten Thousand Francs").

For most of its length, "Les Dix mille francs du Diable" does not appear to be a supernatural story at all, and it could very easily have been concluded without becoming one. It is, in essence, a character study in a vein elaborated and popularized by Balzac—who was, of course, one of the writers who had made a key contribution to the gradual general desupernaturalization of Romantic fiction, abandoning the explicit supernatural devices of such stories as *La Peau de chagrin* (1831) and "Séraphita" (1834) in order to concentrate on the intense social and psychological naturalism of *Le Père Goriot* (1835) and its numerous quasi-sequels within his sprawling account of the "human comedy." There was, in essence, no need for "Les Dix mille francs du Diable" even to become a hallucinatory fantasy, let alone for the hallucination featured therein to be credited with an unusual and uncompromising materiality, and a thoughtful reader might be inclined to wonder why the author made that narrative move. There is, of course, no way to know what she was thinking, but it is certainly an interesting puzzle to contemplate, especially in the context of the collection as a whole and the subsequent development of the author's career.

The question of solidity becomes particularly problematic in the second "legend," "Isobel-la-Ressuscitée," where, again, the materiality of the eponymous *femme fatale* seems more than a trifle odd, not to say perverse. It is not at all clear exactly what she is supposed to be; she is variously described as a *fée*, a *vampire*, a *Loreley*, a *sorcière* and a *willie*, all terms attributed to *femmes fatales* in various classic Romantic fantasies penned by

members of Théophile Gautier's coterie, but the myste-
riously resurrected Isobel does not fit the standardized
image of any of those legendary entities. The story does
not permit her to give her any explanatory account of her
own nature and is careful never to offer the slightest
glimpse of her motivation. One term that is not used
with reference to her, even by analogy, is *doppelgänger*,
perhaps understandably, as fictional *doppelgängers* are
almost always employed to confront their doubles, and
very rarely depicted as replacements for a person who
has died, as in this story—although Cadiot was to employ a variant of the same motif in "La Dalle," and it is
also arguable that "Le Reflet de la conscience" (tr. as
The Reflection of Conscience") is a posthumous *doppelgänger* story of sorts, albeit an even more unusual one.

It seems highly likely that the initial inspiration for
"Isobel-la-Ressuscitée" was provided by Théophile Gautier's "La Morte amoureuse" (1836; tr. under various
titles, including "Clarimonde" and "The Amorous Revenant"), a similarly enigmatic story in which the conventional decoding of the mystery, which represents the
amorous revenant as a vampire, does not really solve the
problem of her peculiar materiality. Cadiot follows the
fundamental pattern of Gautier's story, in which a wiser
older man makes a determined attempt to save the young
hero of the story from the clutches of the *femme fatale*
but it is arguable that the dutiful replication is counter-
productive in terms of enabling an interpretation of the
story, logical or morally. The import of the plot-structure
is further confused by the decision to make the would-be
savior a disciple of a reputed magician rather than a
priest. In the final analysis, it is difficult to comprehend
exactly what the author of the story was trying to do, and
why—but a case might be made that the confusion does

not detract from the impact of the story, and that its failure to make any kind of common sense merely becomes an aspect of its mystery.

In view of her difficulties in grappling with such logical problems, however, it is perhaps not surprising that Cadiot soon decided to concentrate her narrative methodology on the psychological effects of guilt and remorse, at the expense of metaphysical assumptions regarding the reality of revenants, thus removing the import of "Le Reflet de la conscience" and "La Dalle" a long way from that of the anecdote featured in her introduction. A modern reader is bound to suspect that she took her imaginative prompt for those two stories from some of Baudelaire's translations of pioneering works by Edgar Poe, most obviously "Le Coeur révélateur" (*Paris Journal* 1853; tr. of "The Tell-Tale Heart") and "Le Chat noir" (*Paris*, 1853; tr. of "The Black Cat." If the similarities between her works and those stories are coincidental, the coincidence is certainly remarkable.

Cadiot was far from being the only French writer to take significant influence from Poe, of course, and those two stories were particularly frequent sources of inspiration, but it is significant that most of the French writers who compiled such psychological melodramas in later decades aimed their stories (as Poe usually did himself) at the newspaper market, and that their work reflected the inevitable effects of the limitation of available narrative space, whereas Cadiot, to whom no such market was readily available in the difficult years of the early 1850s, felt free to expand the theme and to offer greater detail and complexity in her psychological studies. That might seem to make her stories a trifle prolix by comparison with Poe, and far more akin methodologically to Balzac, but that is not injurious to the quality, and certainly not to the sophistication, of her work.

In parallel with making her work more "Poesque" Cadiot apparently decided to forsake the explicitly supernatural entirely, even when the "reflections of conscience" developed in her stories retained their solidity, as in "La Dalle." The same logical problem that afflicts the character of Isobel-la-Ressuscitée also afflicts the character of the resuscitated Pâquerette, of course—how does she come to exist? what kind of hidden forces were involved in her genesis?—but the lack of answers to those questions does not seem as obtrusive or as confusing in the latter story, as a matter of narrative construction, and it certainly indicates the way that the wind of change was blowing within the evolving narrative of French fantastic fiction. By virtue of that internal development—and, indeed, the gathering of the stories into a collection—*Minuit!!* is a unique volume within the tradition of French fantastic fiction, and modern aficionados of the genre ought to reckon it fortunate that the censors did not succeed in suppressing it entirely, even if they did banish it from France for a while.

"Claude Vignon" is rarely listed by modern critics as a significant contributor to the development of the French *fantastique*, and *Minuit!!* is not extensively annotated in bibliographies or critical accounts of the genre—although Jean-Marc and Randy Lofficier's *French Science Fiction, Fantasy, Horror and Pulp Fiction* (2000) scrupulously mentions it in passing as an early work influenced by Edgar Poe—but that relative neglect is a pity, because the volume really is a remarkable one, and its contents remain very readable, unaffected by their antiquity. There is a certain irony in the fact that interest in Noémi Cadiot's work seems to have been recently renewed primarily because she was once briefly married to "Éliphas Lévi," because it is very difficult, judging by the very different directions that their careers took after 1850, to detect any influence he might have had on her,[2] and their publications suggest that she was a more intelligent person and a considerably better writer than he was. If, as seems to be the case, *Minuit!!* really was suppressed by Napoléon III's censors, successfully if not completely, that is one more black mark among many to be placed to their discredit; the temporary suppression certainly left a considerable scar on the history of French fantastic fiction, which is long overdue for healing, or at least masking.

Brian Stableford

---

[2] *Minuit!!* appeared five years before the publication of Constant's historical fantasy novel *Le Sorcier de Meudon* (1861; tr. as *The Wizard of Meudon*), and the fiction he had published earlier—most notably the Biblical fantasy *Les Trois malfaiteurs, légende orientale* (1847)—is very different in kind.

There exists in the human heart a string ever ready to vibrate to fantastic and mysterious tales. The soul seems to precipitate itself in haste into the supernatural world, as if it were searching there for a revelation of existences to come, or recovering a memory of anterior existences.

Does an imperceptible bond attach our terrestrial life to the uncomprehended life of otherworldly spirits? Or does our capricious imagination love to follow that of the poet into unknown regions uniquely to launch itself tremulously outside the habitual circle of its reveries, impassioned for the splendid, terrible or impossible types of a creation beyond our reality?

Whatever the primal cause is of our attraction toward marvelous stories, it is no less true that the attraction in question exists. By the fireside in winter, during the vigils of Christmas or Candlemas, we huddle around the hearth, our eyes fixed on the magician who draws our thoughts toward fantastic regions and our ears alert to the slightest creak in the woodwork and the slight whistling of the wind in the eaves or the corridors.

And it shall not be said here that simple and naïve minds are the only ones to tremble and squeeze together close to the fireplace; all are equal before the same emotion; superior intelligences, in the presence of inexplicable facts, are attained by terror like others, perhaps even more than the others. They experience all the sensations of the vulgar, and it is precisely among those elite organizations that one finds the least incredulous to supernatural events. That recognized verity is easily explained, moreover, for at the bottom of those poetic, gracious or terrible stories there is something other than a nurse's superstitions or a grandmother's fanciful tales; there is the Unknown.

The Unknown! On our part, that word expresses neither superstition nor incredulity, for it reserves all the rights of confounded reason and responds to all the aspirations of faith toward the world of eternal things.

What do we know, in fact, of our primitive existence and our final existences? Felicity or misfortune, according to our conduct down here, that is what all religious dogmas inform us; but by what steps does one rise on the holy ladder, or descend toward the portal of the accursed city?

Does one remember, beyond life, those whom one loved or hated on earth? The innate sentiments of the soul render doubt almost impossible. In any case, religions are in accord in honoring the dead, and the Catholic religion, in particular, teaches us that we have over them, and that they have over us, a direct and omnipotent influence.

If one remembers them, can one see again those whose memory one retains?

Can one communicate from one world to the other by means of sensible signs, as one can by prayer?

Is it easier for the blessed or the reproved still to be manifest to those who mourn them, or to those who have ceased to fear them?

Is it God or the Evil Spirit who allows souls to return to earth?

Do apparitions exist elsewhere than in wounded imaginations, and is the marvelous the obscure revelation of a supernatural world or only the poetry of exalted sentiments?

At all these questions, vulgar philosophy smiles, without being able thus far to justify the temerity of its smile, and faith responds to us by numerous passages in the Holy Scriptures and the history of the Church.

The Gospel tells us that when the Savior died, resuscitated cadavers showed themselves in the holy city; and Christianity, by its doctrine of the resurrection, vulgarizes such prodigies, in a sense. Bishop Spiridion is seen to consult, even in the tomb, his daughter Irene, with regard to a deposit he had confided to her and to receive a response from the very bosom of death;[3] possessions by evil spirits, the plaints of souls in torment, and visions of the other world fill the ever-poetic pages of legend. But is not profane history itself full of supernatural and marvelous events?

The Greece of Homer and the Rome of the Caesars have their unexplained traditions. The demon of Socrates and the spirit of Brutus have had apologists and adversaries. The school of Alexandria opposed to the miracles of Christianity the prodigies of theurgy; Julian evoked the visible forms of his gods and saw them appear old and decrepit, while voices in the sky announced the imminent end of the Apostate. Strange lamentations were heard over the sea deploring the death of pantheism when Christianity had appeared in the world. "Let us leave here!" incorporeal voices had cried in the temple of Jerusalem, abandoned by its angels to the fury of the gods of Rome.

---

[3] The reference is to the legend of Saint Spiridion (or Spyridon), Bishop of Tremithous in the fourth century.

The commencement of all histories is full of marvels. There are few ancient families that have not conserved their singular memories and fantastic traditions, the stories of which generate both fear and pleasure when one listens to them in the evening, to the sound of the wind and the rain.

But frightening apparitions of phantoms or otherworldly spirits do not only have the privilege of awakening astonishment and terror within us; certain sentiments of the soul, certain intimate dramas of human passions often produce a more profound effect and a more ineffaceable impression than lugubrious or supernatural visions.

As we said above, it is the Unknown, above all, that attracts imaginations amorous of the marvelous and inquiring minds; an unexplained fact, or even a sentiment that does not enter into the class of generally understood sentiments, summons the study of elevated intelligences, just as a reputedly insoluble problem in geometry summons the research of mathematicians.

What is more gripping than a temptation?

What is more fearful than a remorse?

What is more terrible than a mental illness?

In any case, in all the branches of human knowledge, the circle of our knowledge is quickly traveled, and the secrets of nature are posed so rudely as boundary-markers at all points of our horizon that it is a need for the mind to cross the pillars of Hercules and efface the inscription of ignorance: *Nothing beyond.*

These reflections we have often made; and before extraordinary events and certain universal traditions of humankind, Montaigne's redoubtable "What do I know?" has come to stop them short. Every fantastic story evokes them anew, every supernatural event gives them pasture.

A little while ago, during a long Candlemas vigil, they returned more tenaciously than ever on the occasion of a curious and almost contemporary anecdote.

There were five or six of us sitting around a modest hearth drinking tea, nibbling cakes and chatting in the fine French manner that is encountered above all in intimacy.

Our host—or, rather, hostess, for we were in the home of a lady—belonged to that almost-extinct species in which the women are able to be as lovable at sixty as at twenty-five, and still find the means to retain an eager court around them when the beauty of youth has long vanished.

Madame J. L. is the daughter of an influential former Conventional. The position of her father and the literary reputation of her mother, who counted among women of intellect in the time of the Directoire, furnished her with the opportunity to make the acquaintance in her childhood of the majority of the illustrious or eccentric individuals of the end of the eighteenth century and the commencement of the present one.

Inheriting the talent of her mother, she continued to live in the literary world of the Empire and the Restoration, and she owes to that existence, even fuller than long, being today one of the rare women that intelligent young men like to frequent and to know well.

Such women are like a living repertoire of unpublished anecdotes, which form the underside and the lining of contemporary history. They know, as one says vulgarly, the hidden faces of cards, and are able to indicate to you the strings that activate the great puppets of transcendent politics and the hidden intrigues that sometimes raise them aloft and enable them to climb the Capitoline hill and sometimes precipitate them from the Tarpeian rock. In a word, they know life, and blessed are those who consent to learn from them, to profit at twenty from sixty years of experience; they become strong men.

We were chatting, then, about this, that and the other, mingling randomly the criticism of fashions and that of philosophical theories, foreign politics and the latest novels. In due course, when the hands of the clock were in the environs of midnight, we got on go the eternal theme of long vigils and began to talk about ghosts.

As always, some denied their reality and others affirmed it, some confused the question and others tried to explain it, and we were falling into utter chaos when Madame J. L. intervened in the conversation.

"Oh," she said, "if you're embarking on the chapter of apparitions, don't expect me to sustain any thesis. We children of the eighteenth century are scarcely of a time when marvelous stories have much credit. Romantic traditions go back much further than that and there's no good tale without a somber manor, a ruined keep and a legend in which noble knights are mingled with the sinister amours of Imogine and Alonzo,[4] or some other macabre couple.

"For myself," she continued, with a thin smile, "I've never haunted by moonlight the Gothic ruins of blonde Germany, the tenebrous lairs of verdant Erin or

---

[4] The reference is to a narrative poem by Matthew Gregory Lewis, separately published as "Alonzo the Brave and the Fair Imogine" but originally inserted into the third volume of the famous Gothic novel *The Monk* (1796). Imitations of it include one by the great pioneer of French Romantic prose, Charles Nodier.

even the poetic heaths of our Bretagne. In sum, I'm not at all superstitious, and I only believe positively in political revenants, for good reason.

"I have, however, from my mother the most inexplicable story that has perhaps ever been told; although I wasn't an eye-witness I've at least been an auricular witness, for this story is now the most striking memory of my childhood."

What is it?

That question no mouth pronounced, but all gazes expressed it simultaneously, with a vehemence that did not permit any evasion.

"Good," she said, "now the children are asking to be afraid of the wolf or the bogey-man. Well, you'll be very disappointed, for what I'm talking about is neither a tale or a drama, nor even a legend; it's quite simply and brutally a fact."

"All the more reason for establishing it," I exclaimed.

"Well, then," said Madame J. L., "know first that Madame P , my mother, fleeing the racket of Parisian celebrity, had come to stay with me in a pretty little house in Montrouge. That first point is perhaps not very interesting for you, but it serves as the basis of my story.

"In a house nearby Monsieur Sylvain Maréchal[5] was living tranquilly with his wife, his sister-in law

---

[5] The atheist poet and essayist Sylvain Maréchal (1750-1803) was a utopian socialist, one of the forefathers of Anarchism, who was jailed for publishing an "honest man's Almanac" in 1788, which proposed a new secular calendar, and published his work anonymously thereafter; an enthusiastic Revolutionary, he edited the newspaper *Révolutions de Paris*, and was fortunate to avoid the guillotine when the members of the

Agathe Desprez and Madame Gacon-Dufour,[6] a relative of the famous Marquis de Brumois and woman of letters. Let us take note, in order not to age me unduly, that I was then only five or six years old. Do you all know the role and the doctrine of Sylvie Maréchal?"

It is necessary to admit, to our shame, that the youth of today is so ignorant of events, things and men of old that two or three responded with an uncertain gaze, and almost as many by a tentative shake of the head.[7]

"Sylvain Maréchal was part of the school of atheist philosophers who were like the tail of the first encyclopedist school. A friend of Chaumette[8] and an enthusiastic partisan of the goddess Reason, he played

---

Convention turned on one another; his later works include a fanciful account of *Les Voyages de Pythagore* (1799).

[6] Marie-Armand Gacon-Dufour, known as Madame Humières following her first marriage and then (after 1794) as Madame Dufour de Saint-Pathus (1753-1835) was a pioneer of feminism who wrote essays on history, agricultural economics and women's rights as well as practical manuals and several moralistic novels; initially a severe critic and later an ally of Sylvain Maréchal, she assisted in the publication of several of his works,

[7] Author's note: "Recently, M. Amadée Achard has resuscitated in two witty feuilletons published in the *Assemblée nationale* the name and doctrines of Sylvain Maréchal." Louis-Amédée Achard (1814-1875) was a prolific journalist, satirist and novelist, best-known for swashbuckling *cape et épée* novels. He was still at the very beginning of his career in 1856 and had not yet published any novels.

[8] The ultra-radical Revolutionary Anaxagoras (previously Pierre-Gaspard) Chaumette (1763-1794), one of the architects of the Terror, who organized the Festival of Reason in November 1793 but fell victim to the guillotine shortly thereafter, on a charge of treason that was probably trumped up..

an active part in the main events of the Revolution. A good man nevertheless and very helpful; in spite of his outré principles, during the Terror he saved several friends of the throne and religion. In private life he always seemed simple, confident, laborious and modest, A good man, then, but believing himself conscientiously obliged, in order to contribute to the progress of his century and the wellbeing of his contemporaries, to profess atheism and to publish from time to time little pamphlets such as *Le Dictionnaire des Athées, Le Code d'une societé d'hommes sans Dieu,* etc.

"Neighborly relations were gradually established between my mother and Madame Maréchal, which began with greetings at the window and ended up with exchanges of information on the most propitious terrains for growing resedas and methods of making jam. Soon, those insignificant relations reached as far as Sylvain Maréchal.

"They chatted, and found themselves to be in the same society and the same social zone. If their opinions were different, at least they belonged to the same intellectual current. In brief, by chatting, they linked themselves more intimately and soon almost formed a common household.

"Short, of an appearance that was not advantageous, and hesitant, Monsieur Maréchal was certainly no handsome cavalier, but when he did not fall into the mania of atheism, he had an accurate, facile, benevolent and almost cheerful turn of mind. He was, moreover, exceedingly laborious, sometimes working up to fifteen hours a day, and he scarcely took any other recreation than his trips to Paris to fulfill his functions as a librarian at the College Mazarin.

"In the evenings, we gathered together. In summer we went for walks in the green valley of Arcueil, in the meadows of Cachau, or climbed up to the park of Sceaux and the woods of Aulnay. In winter we played cards and chatted. To begin with we were occupied with current affairs and the news that Monsieur Maréchal brought back from Paris; then we talked about poetry, art, literature, philosophy and religion... Oh, then the discussion became heated; theses for and against the immortality of the soul were defended with an equal ardor; arguments were deployed like projectiles, and we ended up agreeing to disagree. Then we shook hands and bid one another a cordial bonsoir, accusing one another mutually of sophistry, bigotry or impiety and cursing one another for all eternity.

"'Get away, my dear neighbor,' cried my mother, 'leave the good God alone. All the darts you unleash doubtless have their merits from the intellectual viewpoint, but all pure hearts admitted a long time ago as the best of arguments the finest of the beautiful lines of Voltaire: *If God did not exist it would be necessary to invent him! If he still existed, it would be necessary to forget him!*'

"'Oh, truly, beautiful lady. I believe that my poetry responds to Monsieur Voltaire's and I request mercy for the rhyme...'

"'In favor of the reason?'

"'No, in favor of the improvisation.'

"'Well, your improvisation has neither rhyme nor reason, so there!'

"'Beautiful lady, worthy daughter of Moses, your reflection is insufficiently amiable to emerge from a pretty mouth and insufficiently charitable for a Christian soul—for you are a Christian and therefore have a soul... an immortal soul, even, thankfully! As for my-self, one thing consoles me for your sermons, which is that I do not have the same advantages; when the malady that torments me has carried me away, I shall at least sleep tranquilly, and will have no more arguments to sustain against devotees.'

"Anger commenced to take hold of the two champions

"'For myself,' replied Madame P***, 'I submit to the insults of atheists in the hope that they will not cost me as many years in purgatory.'

"'Yes, yes, that's right, dear neighbor; say right away that for having recruited me to your party you'd go straight to paradise. I don't know whether you've read Rabelais, but it seems to me that you'd do better to say to me frankly, like Panurge to Brother Jean: *Then you would be an filthy beast, damned like a malevolent serpent, and I would be like a harp, saved to the cheerful paradise...* But as my illustrious friend Monsieur de Lalande[9] says...'

"'Don't talk to me about that man,' cried my mother, violently, putting her cards on the table with a decisive gesture. 'I'll never take the advice of a man who eats spiders with nothing but salt.'

"And for once, an inclination of Madame Maréchal's head indicated that she agreed completely with that judgment, to the scorn of marital authority. The formidable attitude of the two ladies announced the closure of the discussion."

---

[9] The atheistic astronomer and freemason Jérôme Lalande (1742-1807), who dropped the *particule* from his name in honor of the Revolution, although the participants in the reported conversation retain it.

"Lalande ate spiders!" we all cried in unison, challenging our story-teller.

"Yes, truly, and he was very fond of them," replied Madame J. L. "I have the fact from several of my contemporaries."

"Ah! Ugh!"

"What diabolical appetite can he have had for spiders?" asked the most curious among us.

"I can't tell you in knowledge of the matter, having never tasted one, but when a similar question was put to Monsieur de Lalande he had the custom of responding with the appreciation that, as you must have remarked, fits the most various eccentric tastes: *they taste like nuts.*

"While still young, Sylvain Maréchal had been cruelly afflicted by a disease of the liver, and his friends were not unaware that it was necessary to anticipate his imminent demise. It was, however, prompter than ought to have been expected, for he died on 18 January 1809, in the middle of the incessantly renewed discussion of the immortality of the soul.

"The mildness of his character was only belied on those occasions, but for once, it did not abandon him for an instant. He sensed death approaching and limited himself to responding: 'My friends, battle as much as you please, but I can't go on. Night has come for me.'

"He had acquired the habit, as a kind of game, of having conversations with his friends in blank verse. After a pause, he added at that moment: 'If we sleep until the good times, we'll sleep for a long time!' Then he wanted, before expiring, to give his wife information regarding the state of their modest fortune. He reminded her of a few sums lent to friends or deposited in various houses, and indicated the places where she could find the documents of those loans and deposits. Then he leaned toward Mesdames P*** and Gacon-Dufour, who were nearby, as if to speak to them privately; but suddenly, a coughing fit interrupted him, not to quit him again, in the middle of the sentence: 'Don't forget, above all, that there are fifteen...'

"Sylvain Maréchal was mourned for several hours by his intimate friends. His wife, his sister-in-law, Madame Dufour and my mother took care of his burial, and all was said. As soon as he was deposited in his grave, his disciples had to forget him, since, according to him, nothing any longer remained of the celebrated atheist.

"My mother did her best to console the poor widow, whose grief was better proof of the need for immortality than any reasoning. She tried above all to have reborn in her heart the doctrines that her husband had expelled, and to render her cares and consolations more efficacious, and also to enable Madame Maréchal to avoid the heartbreak that one experiences in finding oneself alone under the roof where one had previously been two, she took her temporarily, with her sister and her friend, to stay with her.

"Those ladies received importunate visitors during the day, who came to bring banal condolences, crueler than blessings, to their genuine grief. Let alone in the evening, they occupied themselves with a few feminine tasks, while communicating to one another, punctuated by sighs, their melancholy reflections on the brevity of life and the eternal separation that suddenly breaks apart the most united existences. My mother then hazarded a few doubts about the desolating maxims of the deceased, and Madame Maréchal yielded to hope. The ladies concluded their vigil at about ten o'clock and each retired to her apartment.

"Madame P*** had retained the first-floor bedroom and had put Madame Maréchal in a small room next door. Madame Dufour had been lodged on the second floor with Madame Desprez; Madame Dufour occupied the room directly above my mother's.

Those ladies went to bed as soon as they were in their rooms, and, depressed by dolorous shocks, did not take long to fall asleep. My mother also went to bed, but, as was her habit, she picked up a novel and commenced reading. The work was probably interesting, for midnight chimed while she continued turning the pages, without thinking of going to sleep.

"My mother was romantic; also, in addition to the part she took internally in the misfortune of her friend, her imagination also traveled far from the house of the atheist, on the track of the heroes with whom she wanted to identify. The most absolute silence reigned around her; people go to bed early in Montrouge, and the neighbors did not have the habit of making the pavement resonate after nine o'clock.

"Suddenly, she distinctly heard the key turn in the lock of her door. She thought at first that it was one of the ladies, unable to sleep, who was coming to spend a few moments with her, having seen that the light in her room was on, and she opened her curtain.

"The door had just opened slowly, and Sylvain Maréchal, in person, came toward her.

"He was dressed in his habitual costume, and his pose and gait were so true, so natural and entirely similar to his ordinary pose and gait, that Madame P*** needed to close her book and co-ordinate her memories in order to be persuaded that she was not seeing her living neighbor.

"The atheist approached the alcove and saluted my mother courteously. 'I beg you, beautiful lady,' he said to her, 'to be kind enough to recall that I was unable to finish what I was saying to you yesterday—which is to say that there are fifteen hundred francs in gold hidden in a secret place behind my desk in the library. I had saved them in order to surprise my wife agreeably by adding an extra story to our house, in accordance with her intentions. There are also letters from a woman— you know from whom. Burn them...'

"Madame P***, who was neither visionary nor fearful, quickly recovered her composure. 'Well, my neighbor,' she exclaimed, 'I'm glad to see you, now that you have to believe in the immortality of the soul.'

"The atheist looked at her without responding, as if, the goal of his appearance having been fulfilled, he had nothing more to say to mortal ears; then he went back to the door and disappeared.

"At the moment when my mother leapt out of bed in order to follow the phantom and convince herself of her vision, she heard precipitate footsteps in the corridor. The door opened and Madame Dufour threw herself recklessly into her arms. 'Oh!' she cried, in a tremulous voice. 'My dear friend, I've just seen Monsieur Maréchal...'

"My mother took a step back and stood there, stupefied. 'You've seen him?'

"'Yes.'

"'Did you also hear him?'

"'I saw and heard him as I can see and hear you.'

"'How was he?'

"'Exactly as we had seen him a few days before his death.'

"'What did he say to you?'

"'He said to me… oh, but my dear friend, it's in-credible…it's impossible… he told me that he had hid-den fifteen hundred francs in gold in a secret place be-hind his desk at the College Mazarin, with the intention of adding another story to his house...and that in the same hiding place there were letters from a woman, which it was necessary to burn.'

"'Well, dear,' said my mother, seized by vertigo, 'I've also seen Monsieur Maréchal, and he said exactly the same thing to me,'

The two women were frightened; they looked at one another, nonplussed, without daring to impart the tumul-tuous thoughts that were upsetting their souls.

"The night passed in prayers; the next day, they went to Paris and asked to visit Monsieur Sylvain Maréchal's study.

"The fifteen hundred francs in gold were in the hid-ing place, as well as the letters. They took the gold and burned the letters.

"Those letters...I shall not say whose they were. There are characters that history has consecrated and that it is necessary to leave stainless. What point is there, an-yway, in criticizing a woman who, in our stormy days, was young, beautiful and unfortunate?"

Madame J. L. had concluded her story.

As for us, we remained plunged in endless reflec-tions. The redoubtable and solemn UNKNOWN loomed up before us, with a finger on its lips, like the statue of Hermes; we sensed insoluble problems put to the torture all the coverts of our thought and all the springs of our intelligence...

The Guest of the Dead
Legend

The emperor Frederick Barbarossa, duly reprimanded by the Grand Council of Venice, came after many refusals to render homage to the sanctity of Pope Alexander III,[10] who, as penance for his rebellion and a host of other detestable sins, sent him to the Holy Land to fight the infidels.

When he had decided to depart, Frederick sent throughout his empire a large number of heralds-at-arms to summon, first all of his high barons and liege-men, and then all the good burgers of his good cities, and finally all his loyal and faithful subjects: nobles and commoners, burgers and villeins.

Many came at the first call and took the cross with great heart in order to follow their emperor to Palestine; but many required the summons to be repeated, because they liked sowing their fields and cleaving to their hearth better than riding over mountains and valleys in unknown lands, and preferred to earn indulgences by saying *Ave Marias* under the porches of their churches rather than pursuing the Saracens toward Damascus and Saint-Jean-d'Acre.

Gradually, however, whether they liked it or not, all good Germans in a condition to bear arms were brought under the orange and black banner of Barbarossa and

---

[10] The Holy Roman Emperor Frederick I, nicknamed Barbarossa, acknowledged Alexander III as the true pope—having previously supported the antipope Victor IV—in 1177

took the road to Asia, to go and be decimated by famine, plague and Greek fire. And in the meantime, during the long years in which Germany waited for her children and her emperor, who was never to return, everything went from bad to worse in the empire.

To begin with, strong arms were lacking in the fields to labor the earth, and the crops cultivated by the old men and the children did not grow well; in the towns and in the fortresses the lords, always at war with one another, destroyed edifies and ruined commerce; on the Rhine, communications were cut everywhere and navigation was interrupted. To complete the misfortune, it seemed that all the maleficent spirits that haunted the Germanic lands in those days, without any regard for the pious devotion of the crusaders, had redoubled their rage and skill in order to torment the infirm old men and the poor widows.

Never, perhaps, had the gnomes and sprites of the forests of the Hartz and the Niederwald showed themselves so restless and played such malevolent tricks on the housewives who had sole care of their cottages or on travelers delayed on the roads; never had the fays and the loreleys been crueler and more deceptive to fishermen and boatmen; never finally, had the phantoms, stryges and vampires of the banks of the Danube slept less tranquilly in their tombs. In sum, there was a veritable desolation.

Fortunate still were those housewives neglected by their spouses who saw growing beside them some handsome lad, already strong, and soon capable of being the head of the family! Those gathered their courage, in the hope that better managed affairs and a more firmly conducted plow would soon bring back ease to their house. But what dolor, also, was there if those sons, the last hopes of an entire family, showed bad sentiments or gave themselves to vice and idleness, for want of a powerful hand to support or chastise them.

And that is why two poor women of the village of Arnsberg, situated in the confines of the Black Forest, were weeping and lamenting.

"Ah, Barbel my friend," said one of them, wiping her eyes, "What have I done to Heaven to have a killecroff [11] in my family; for, God forgive me," she added, making the sign of the cross, is it not evident that Fritz is a killecroff, on seeing the manner in which he eats, drinks and beats his brothers, and all the children of the village?"

"Margareth, my good Margareth," replied the other, sobbing, "Don't blaspheme God and don't curse your son. Alas, if Fritz were a killecroff, my son Hermann would also be one, for throughout the country he alone is capable of matching Fritz in the matter of brutality and gluttony; but everyone knows that killecroffs, or changelings, are the spawn of the devil born of possessed girls and introduced into families by henchmen in place of veritable children. Now tell me, what have you and I, poor widows whose husbands are in the Holy Land fighting the infidels, done to see our sons exchanged by the devil for his own?"

---

[11] As the text explains, a *killecroff* is a kind of changeling; the term had apparently been introduced to French Romanticism by Gustave Brunet in his 1844 translation of Martin Luther's table talk; it was subsequently recycled in X. B. Saintine's oft-reprinted collection of *La Mythologie du Rhin* (1862; tr. as *Myths of the Rhine*) but was still esoteric when *Minuit!!* was published.

Margareth sighed. "Oh, my dear Barbel, perhaps never have so many killecroffs been seen in Germany as at present! Do you remember the one in D*** who ate as much as two workers, cried and beat the neighbors all day long, and was only able to laugh when misfortune struck the house?"

"And the one in K*** near Halberstadt, Margareth, who, from birth didn't leave a drop of milk in his mother's teat for his twin, and dried up another five nurses! But, thank God, we were soon rid of that one, for his father took the good advice of his friends and relatives, and took him to Halberstadt to devote him to the blessed Virgin Mary. And as he passed over a bridge devils started to dance on the water and to call 'Killecroff! Killecroff!' The child, who was in a basket and had not moved or proffered a word until then, being scarcely six months old, started to agitate and to cry 'Oh! Oh! Oh!'

"'Killecroff, Killecroff where are you going?' shouted the devils.

"'I'm going to Halberstadt to have myself cradled,' replied the infernal nursling—on seeing which, his father, who was a good Christian, recognized the genealogy of the brat, signed himself devotedly and threw the basket into the water, infant and all. Then he returned to do penance."

The two devotees signed themselves in their turn and raised their eyes to the heavens.

"Ah, Lord God," murmured Margareth, picking up her spindle, which she had dropped, "no, my dear Barbel, it's necessary to hope that our children aren't killecroffs…!"

To be sure, if some sage rector had initially found the judgment of the two prudish women regarding their children severe, he would have ended up thinking like them merely by seeing the surly and grim faces of the two boys, occupied at that moment in administering forceful slaps and punches.

They really were the two most frightful fellows that one could see and the two most diabolical scoundrels in the entire country. They were fighting then over the cadaver of a vulture, which each of them claimed to have killed, and blows fell as thickly as hailstones, accompanied by insults and blasphemies.

The elder was sixteen years old and the younger fifteen; but they were singularly strong for their age—which did not make them any better, said the two poor mothers, for they only employed their strength and skill in wringing the necks of their neighbors' chickens to make a meal, in stealing pitchers of beer and playing nasty tricks.

Fritz was a big, strongly-built and bony fellow with a flat head and twisted, almost limping, legs. Thick red hair fell over his forehead and mingled with his bushy eyebrows, which only allowed a glimpse of the wild pupils of two wandering eyes of different colors. Beneath those eyes a nose like the beak of a bird of prey surmounted a twisted mouth with overlapping teeth, which completed giving poor Margareth's son a horrible physiognomy.

Hermann, the young of the two scapegraces, was a stout boy, square from top to bottom, whose face was more bestial than grim. His heavy head, supported by a thick neck, was illuminated by two faience-blue eyes shaded by a magnificently tangled shock of coarse hair. He had bulging highly-colored cheeks, pale blond eyebrows and lashes, and thick lips. Gluttony and drunkenness were his principal vices, and for a pot of beer and a slice of bacon he sold himself body and soul to Fritz the bandit.

On an empty stomach, when he saw his mother weeping and his little neighbor Ketha, Fritz's sister and his own promise, he swore to mend his ways, but that repentance did not last long, for that miscreant Fritz, who had never been able to touch holy water without swearing, taught him to profit from that moment of confidence to steal coins and victuals and drown the repentance in some frank mouthful.

When the two mothers, having run out of sermons and weary of tears, had recognized their total impotence to put their sons on the right path, and when Ketha had begged her mother to send her as a novice to the convent rather than give her in marriage to Hermann, the parish priests of the neighborhood got involved, and with a great reinforcement of holy water adjured the devil to abandon the killecroffs. But Satan held tight to his property, for neither prayers nor exorcisms changed the miscreants. Every year they seemed to become more prolific drunkards, more prolific thieves and more malevolent.

Often, strange noises had been heard in the hovel where they made their lair, ill-sounding for a Christian son of a good mother; so everyone in the village desired ardently to be rid of the killecroffs..

They poached, pillaged and started fires. They pursued young women, threw excrement into the holy water and profaned cemeteries. But seigneurial justice was finally stirred by so many crimes. Fritz was seized by the Baron of Halberstadt's men-at-arms after killing a gamekeeper, and shortly afterwards his body, hung high and short, was swinging on the gibbet, to serve as an example to his companion.

After the execution, Hermann judged it prudent to decamp and to give some proof of repentance. That is why he went to the town to learn his father's trade, who had been a weaver before departing for the Holy Land.

Fritz's cadaver was left suspended from the gibbet for a long time, as evidence of the power of the lord of Halberstadt, but the executioner finally took it down and buried it, with neither benediction nor prayers, in an old abandoned cemetery.

When Hermann came back with his mastery as a weaver, the memory of the execution was still vivid in all memories; he understood that it was necessary not to attack people or property if he did not want to rejoin Fritz. He had, in any case, passed his nineteenth year and he knew that the doctors affirmed "that killecroffs, or *suppositii*, never attained the age of twenty."

On his return, therefore, he passed himself off as best he could for a good, tranquil and adroit weaver, and quickly produced his aune of cloth. He seemed to have forgotten in the town his habits of violence and rapine; but he was incapable of containing himself in confrontation with a pitcher of beer, or of seeing the sign of a tavern without going in to sample the Rhine wine, and he hardly ever came out before his troubled head and his tottering legs had lost their power, the former to guide him and the latter to carry him.

In spite of those appearances of conversion, Ketha did not decide easily to marry her fiancé. She wept a great deal, but it was necessary to provide a support for her mother; it was, moreover, pious work to complete the conversion of that strayed soul.

The marriage took place discreetly, and the young couple went to set up home in the house of Hermann's father, who had died in the Holy Land. That house, constructed some distance from the village, was constructed on piles and only had a very narrow entrance on the ground floor, which formed the cage of the staircase and a kind of dark cellar where provisions were stored. At the top of the staircase was the unique living room of the poor dwelling. A large four-poster bed, a dresser, a broad fireplace, above the mantel of which a few rusty weapons were hung, and a loom formed the entire furniture. It was there that Hermann's ancestors had lived, father and son, all weavers by profession, and it was there that Ketha and her husband were to live and work like humble manual laborers.

All went well for some time. The mothers had enriched the young household with all that remained to them, and the weaver earned a few écus making cloth; but such good conduct could not last long on the part of the former companion of Fritz the hanged man.

Soon, Ketha remarked that the loom remained motionless for entire days; her husband went to the town to obtain thread or take cloth, spending more in one day on drink than he had earned in a week. Gradually, penury replaced ease, for remonstrations exasperated the weaver instead of converting him.

In the meantime, Margareth, Ketha's mother, died and Barbel came to take a place at the hearth. Then Hermann, seeing one more mouth to feed in the abode, took his house and his family in horror; he only came there to drink and eat when he had no more money, and to carry away anything that he could sell to pay for new orgies.

The poor women prayed and wept.

When Hermann came back, drunk, staggering and brutish, after entire weeks of absence, it was to pass through his house like a scourge, to beat Ketha, who had no money to give him, to insult his mother, and to make the entire village curse because of his debauchery and his depredations.

One evening, Barbel, old and stooped, less by age than by chagrins, counted the family's last resources, groaning. "Oh, my dear child," she said to Ketha, "the Lord has reserved rude proofs for us, and his hand has been heavy upon us. Consider your good mother Margareth, who died of chagrin for having seen the body of her killecroff son suspended from the gallows for six months, and am I, great God, destined to die too of shame and dolor? For if Hermann continues to live as a miscreant, I shall certainly see his cadaver too swinging in the wind at the tip of the gibbet."

"Dear mother, don't despair thus," said Ketha. "God will touch Hermann's heart once again. May God protect him! For seven days and seven nights I haven't seen him, but when he returns, do you believe that he can be without repentance, on hearing out plaints and seeing our dolor?"

At that moment, a hoarse and winy voice became audible in the distance; that scarcely distinct voice was soon recognized by the two women. It was intoning nasally an old Bacchic song, a sort of drama with two characters, one a penitent and the other a drunkard, who, having met, were trying mutually to convert one another, one to the virtue of anchorites and the other to the free expansion of the swine of Epicurus.

> *"Who are you, you who are singing?"*
> *"Who are you, you who are bored?"*
> *"I am a penitent,*
> *Who goes through life weeping."*
> *"I weep endlessly!"*

"You motives are pious?"
"I mean when the wine
Emerges through my eyes!"

Barbel and Ketha made the sign of the cross, weeping; they sensed that the hoarse, trailing, halting voice belonged to the ultimate degree of drunkenness; that the weaver's unsteady legs were following an uncertain route, and that the ignoble song was often interrupted by hiccups.

Gradually, however, the voice approached and the words became more distinct.

"Do you know that it's necessary to die?"
"I want to die...at table!"
"Dread a sad future,
That isn't a fable!"
"I only dread thirst!"
"You ought to dread death."
"I drink as long as I'm thirsty
And when I've drunk, I sleep!"
"Dream, then, about dying!"
"I dream of it when I think of it."
"You ought to remember it
And do penitence."
"I very often do it..."
"You never do it!"
"...When I have no more money
Penitence I do!"

Soon the poor women, trembling, heard heavy and unequal footsteps striking the pavement of the courtyard, and the door screeching on its hinges.

"I fast every day."
"That's why you're so pale."
"Should one not always
Fast during lent?"
"I only have one meal!"
"You do your duty, then?"
"I commence in the morning
And I finish in the evening!"

Hermann climbed the stairs. He shoved the door rudely and made his entrance staggering; then, without seeing his wife and without saluting his mother, he went to fall like an inert mass on to a stool. His garments were ragged and soiled with wine and mud; his tearful eyes darted a vague gaze around him.

"Hey, wife," he cried, cursing, "Where's my supper? I want my supper! Haven't you had time to set the table, Madame Lazybones?"

Ketha wiped away her tears and tried in vain to find the strength to respond.

"What, preachy beauty, have you the pip? Or has the Devil done me the favor of tying your tongue so that you can't say a word?"

"My son," said Barbel, finally, after an effort, "Shut up and let your wife be. You've supped too much, and far from home, where you don't worry about filling the bread-bin!"

"Hum! What's this?" growled Hermann, without paying much heed to the maternal admonition. "Am I or am I not the master of the house? No cackling, women, and serve me a drink!"

"Shut up yourself, my son!" cried the indignant Barbel. "Your wife and your mother are ruining their health spinning all day long, and can't succeed in earn-

45

ing the daily bread. The time has finally come to resume work and make a few good aunes of cloth! This isn't a drinking den, and there's no cause for rejoicing, since, far from becoming a good Christian, you persist in remaining a filthy drunkard without pity or respect for us."

"To the devil with the mother and the wife!" shouted the furious drunkard, making the entire house shake with a formidable thump of his fist on the massive table that occupied the middle of the room. "Now, which of you is going to fetch me a drink, you old hags?"

That exclamation was followed by a moment of silence, and that silence had something solemn about it; the old woman was rotating her spindle beside the fireless hearth with a feverish movement; Ketha was trembling and weeping, hesitating between obedience and revolt.

"Will you obey me, finally, instruments of Hell?" roared Hermann "Obey me, or I'll thump you!"

Old Barbel raised two glaucous eyes to the heavens, in which two bloody tears were pearling. "Don't move, daughter!" she said, in a tremulous voice to Ketha, who was rising to her feet.

Herman bounded like a ferocious beast, launching himself at his mother, seized her by the shoulders and threw her on to the stone staircase.

"Thunder! It's you, then, old fay, old witch, who teaches insubordination to my wife! Get out! Get out, and quickly! Run to the Sabbat and may Satan roast you, you and your broomstick!"

And as the poor mother got to her feet, with difficulty, he lifted her up again, dragged her down the steps, half-dead, and threw her outside, cursing; and, in spite of the cold and the darkness, he slammed the door shut.

"To the devil!" he said.

He went back up to the room.

"You, now, pretentious beauty!" her said, seeking Ketha with his gaze. "Obey, and find the route to the cellar for me, quickly! But damn it, has she gone already? I'll have to make those spouters of paternosters feel the bit! I can't see her!"

At that moment, the drunkard's foot collided with an inert body; that was Ketha, who had fainted with horror, on the tiles.

Then Hermann, alone in confrontation with his inanimate wife, felt himself marked with the sign of Cain; fear enabled him to see through the fumes of drunkenness, and he fled like a man accursed.

Some distance from his abode he encountered his mother, exhausted, bruised and bloody, who was hanging on to the brambles by the roadside in order to go to die outside the house of the village pastor. The poor old woman lifted a hand toward the heavens on seeing Hermann, and in a voice full of prayer she murmured: "God forgive you, my son."

The drunkard wandered for a long time in the countryside, prey to a kind of delirium in which images of reality were mingled with phantoms engendered by the vapors of drunkenness.

Sometimes, it seemed to him that a thousand demons were pursuing him with discordant cries and hideous grimaces; sometimes it was his mother and his wife, pale victims who were imploring his pity or, weary of praying in vain, were asking God to punish their torturer; sometimes, finally, it was the gibbet of Halberstadt that loomed up menacingly before him, and Fritz's cadaver that was writhing at the summit, as if in the anguish of an eternal agony.

Soon, that last hallucination achieved a strange empire over his mind. It seemed to him that the fatal gibbet was attracting him invincibly, and that, in spite of his will and his efforts, every step was bringing him closer to it.

Then, when he was very close, he saw Fritz suddenly detach himself therefrom by dint of his gesticulations, and he felt the hand that had struck his mother grasped by the stiff, cold hand of the hanged man, as if by a vice.

Then he was dragged into an immense round in which thousands of fantastic and terrible figures were dancing furiously. It was as if all the dead people that the gibbet had borne had arranged a rendezvous for an infernal orgy by the dubious light of the moon, which was about to set.

All the bandits were there who had once desolated the country, and whose skeletons were rattling with the grating sound of horrible laughter; and also the murderers, whose bodies were utterly fleshless, while their arms and hands retained the appearance of life, still soiled by ineffaceable blood; and also infanticide girls, who seemed to be condemned eternally to give their living breasts to their dead children.

All those specters vomited by Hell were dancing with rage an irregular, mad, jerky dance, as if convulsive.

Hermann was dragged away by the killecroff, without the strength to resist, devoid of will and energy. Screaming, he followed the vertiginous round, which unfurled in a spiral at the foot of the gibbet.

Exhausted, bruised and out of breath, he finally fell. Then it seemed to him that there was nothing but specters around him, dancing and sniggering. He thought he could see their bony, livid fingers designating him as

48

a victim or a prey, and the circle tightened to envelop him completely. They spun without stopping or slowing down, as if moved by a mechanism. Herman soon sensed space and air lacking, for the cold limbs of the specters were pressing upon him and choking him. There was something like a circle of ice around his head, something like a horrible weight upon his breast. He lost consciousness.

The cool of daybreak calmed the anguish of the weaver. He opened his eyes painfully and found himself, with horror, lying under the gibbet of Halberstadt.

His first impulse was to flee far from that sinister place, without choosing his direction and without looking ahead.

Gradually, however, his senses calmed down and he disengaged from the visions of the night the frightful reality. Far from being seized by repentance, however, and a need for expiation, he only experienced a brutal horror for everything that reminded him of his crime. From the place where he was, he could still perceive his house and his village in the distance. That sight was odious to him, and, only listening to his bestial instinct, he drew away from the locale rapidly.

This time, as he was hungry, he followed a direct route and did not make detours to avoid seigneurial justice.

In spite of his haste to arrive at the goal of his journey and the precipitation of his march, Hermann only reached the edge of the Black Forest toward the middle of the day. He engaged in a dark path vigorously hollowed out by diluvial rain, where the shadow was so dense, even in broad daylight, that he could scarcely see far enough to recognize a traveling companion at ten paces.

After a few moments of rapid march, he stopped outside a wretched woodcutter's hut and knocked vigorously on the door three times. A decrepit old woman with glazed and squinting eyes stuck her head through a hole lined with straw, which served as a window.

"Come on! Hurry up, my dear!" he cried, as soon as he perceived her. "Open up, and quickly, if it pleases your cousin, the devil!"

The old woman came down the few steps that separated her from the ground as quickly as her age and her infirmities permitted; then she lifted the wooden latch that barred the door internally, and Hermann precipitated himself into the room.

His first movement was to sit down at a big table soiled with wine and bordered by benches, and as he found that the old woman was not hastening enough to serve him, he struck it with a vigorous blow of his fist.

"Thunder! Get the rust out of your old carcass, firebrand of Hell, and serve me a good meal! I've been marching quickly and I'm hungry."

"Lord! Master Hermann," said the old woman, terrified, "how agitated you are! But don't get angry, for here's the remains of my men's soup; the bacon is sliced, the beer's in the pots and I can hear my Antoine calling out from the entrance to the sunken path. He's your good companion, and you can wait for the time of an *Ave Maria*."

While making that speech, the old woman took a few pewter pots from a large dresser and a few wooden spoons, and set the table, in order to assist her guest to be patient.

During those preliminaries three men arrived, and after having rid themselves hastily of their weapons and their cloaks, they sat down by Hermann's sides, cursing the ingratitude of the weather.

Those three men were Antoine and his two sons. Perhaps Master Antoine and his sons feared God and said their paternosters, but they had a strange reputation in the region. To begin with, for charcoal-burners, they were more often seen hunting and marauding than cutting wood, and their house, kept by an old woman who was half-witch, had become a rather ill-famed drinking-den, where the bad lots of the neighborhood got drunk during the day. It was said in low voices that several foreign travelers who had gone astray in those parts had never seen their homelands again, and that their cloaks had sometimes been recognized on the shoulders of the charcoal-burners.

At any rate, fairground merchants and traveling peddlers did not like to stop after nightfall at Master Antoine's inn; but no one accused the charcoal-burners out loud, for the father and sons were reputed to be redoubtable to their enemies and made them pay dearly for ill-sounding words.

Hermann maintained his habits of idleness and debauchery in Master Antoine's house. To continue that life, the weaver was capable of anything, and Antoine had understood that, so he helped him obligingly to spend the last coins that remained to him, knowing full well that once he was hungry and devoid of a frederick, the drunkard would belong to him entirely.

When, therefore, after copious draughts, Hermann dared to boast about his exploits of the previous night and recount how he had put his house in order, Antoine applauded that energetic action wholeheartedly

"A plague upon weeping and moaning women," he said, "who don't know how to do anything but complain and recite paternosters! You'd have done well, my master, while they were going on, to clear out the place completely by throwing the wife out with the mother. It would have been good riddance."

"And I dare say," said Hans, his elder son, "that with a pretty maidservant, very mild and very obedient, which I'm holding in reserve for you, it would be a pleasure to make your house into a nice inn like this one, where, by feeding your guests, you'd be able to feed yourself, drink for free and make merry for the rest of your days!"

"Damn! Advice has its price, and the proverb is right that says that a good mother's son doesn't lie!" Antoine put in "Hey, old woman! Something to drink, and better! There, Master Hermann, my colleague, drink, and don't forget not having supped at home yesterday!"

Hermann swallowed a full goblet of *eau-de-vie* in a single draught. "Damn!" he cried. "You're right, fellows! Out with the wife! And we'll soon be hanging the cooking-pot over a bright fire, for my old trade as a weaver is up in flames, I swear to you,."

It was with a good heart that the charcoal-burners lavished wine and *eau-de-vie* upon their guest, for they had dreamed for some time of forming an association of rapine with him; in fact, his house, transformed into an inn, would make an excellent subsidiary of their own. In addition, Herman had broad shoulders and solid fists; they could lend one another a strong hand if the occasion arose.

The old woman seemed to have divined the intentions of her masters, for while distributing Rhenish wine and cherry brandy around the table she did not neglect to fill Hermann's goblet twice rather than once.

As the weaver's drunkenness was augmented, his head was excited further against poor Ketha, His ignoble passions, over-stimulated by the drink and the encouragement of the charcoal-burners, drew him toward new crimes, and he was now yearning to return to the house that he had fled with so much horror, in order to throw his wife out.

Antoine's sons continued to design and excite his brutal instincts; suddenly, he got up and tipped over his goblet, still full, cursing.

"Damn it!" he cried. "No need to wait any longer to be master in my own house! It'll still be daylight for another hour; in any case, I know my route, and if you please, my good companions, we'll sup together tomorrow in my place!"

Upon which, the old woman having brought a good flask of *eau-de-vie*—for, she said, it was a lantern to light his way—he picked up an iron-tipped staff, staggered out of the hut, and advanced into the country.

At first he followed the route traced by a winy but rapid stride, as if a determined will had dominated momentarily the fumes of drunkenness.

Although it was already late, as the day had been fine, the last rays of sunlight were shining with a splendid glare, and the country was still illuminated by the fugitive light that gilds the atmosphere for a few moments before sunset. Crimson-tinted clouds, mingled with yellow and leaden hues, enveloped the star ready to disappear over the horizon, seemingly presaging an imminent storm, but until then the gold of its rays only made the shadows stand out more darkly.

Gradually, the action of the air completed the weaver's drunkenness; his ideas become confused and he stumbled over the stones of the road.

It was in vain that he tried to remember his route and to follow it with a firm stride; his unsteady legs seemed only to be lending him their service regretfully, and his mind no longer had any but a vague perception of exterior objects.

In the meantime, dusk enveloped the earth entirely in its gray veils; the blue mountains on the horizon were only separated from the sky by a line of fire, and the accumulated clouds were colored by coppery reflections, while the distant rumble of thunder announced the storm.

Hermann tried to increase his pace, but al his efforts only ended in making him turn about in the middle of a road that he no longer recognized. By the fugitive gleam of lightning flashes he perceived the towers of Halberstadt in the distance and the bell-tower of his village, but when he tried to orient himself in order to go in that direction, the towers and the belfry immediately changed location and appeared on the opposite side, as if to mock his efforts. The whole surrounding country, of which he had known every corner and viewpoint, every field and roof, since childhood, seemed to be spinning around him in order to multiply his uncertainties and astonishments.

It was like a vast circle shaken by an inexorable movement of rotation, and as darkness descended more thickly over the earth, the circle shrank, the more distant or less obtrusive objects faded into obscurity, and nothing any longer remained standing around the weaver but the fantastic silhouettes of pointed steeples, high keeps or gigantic oaks.

The storm was approaching with desperate rapidity; the clouds were crowding together and the lightning flashes were ever more frequent in their torn flanks. The wind chased dry leaves along the roads with strange noises, and swirled, whistling, in the high branches. At every turning and corner of the hedges a thousand fantastic forms appeared to the drunkard, which agitated in all directions to bar the route he traced, leading him astray in the long grass and laughing at his efforts.

Hermann became irritated against the obstacles, and swallowed further mouthfuls of *eau-de-vie* at regular intervals in order to sustain the futile struggle. He struck out angrily with his iron-tipped staff at all the real or imaginary barriers that hindered his progress.

"By the dead God!" he cried, furiously, "the devils have made a pact against me! Can't I finally find my house?"

And while stumbling, he went astray between the stunted trunks of a few old willows that bordered a stream, whose gnarled crowns seemed to make the hideous faces of gnomes appear periodically behind elder and privet bushes. At every step he hurled another horrible oath at the sky and made a more desperate effort, until, battle-weary, he returned toward another exit in order to search for his route. And it was pitiful to see him, tottering, marching at random, turning painfully in a circle that he had already explored twenty times over.

Sometimes, stiffening himself by means of a residue of lucid will, he launched himself at a run and crossed a large space with a single bound; sometimes, he fell, exhausted and bewildered, at the foot of a tree or into the mud of a ditch. He stayed still for a moment and then, brutalized and stupefied by ever thicker vapors of drunkenness—for at every pause he had recourse to his flask of eau-de-vie—he got to his feet again in order to search for his route through the paths that divided up the countryside and seemed to him to be multiplying infinitely and intersecting in an inextricable tangle, like the confused threads of a ball of silk.

Suddenly, without knowing how, he found his legs hindered by long grass, and stuck from time to time, as if by barriers hidden under creepers of terrestrial ivy and climbing plants.

The storm was imminent. The clouds intercepted the moonlight completely. The thunder, coming closer and closer, formed the dull rumble that precedes a downpour. The wind was swirling furiously in the trees and curbing them like reeds, and the earth exhaled the bitter odor that announces rain.

By means of a last effort of will, Hermann tried to hasten his steps and to free his legs from the bushy and tangled grass; but at each of his movements he seemed to receive a violent blow of a stick against his legs, and the more he agitated, the more the blows multiplied.

"May Satan come to my aid!" he cried, finally, in a paroxysm of fury. "By Fritz, my old friend, who danced so well for me yesterday, does Sire Lucifer not have in his domain a poor little blue flame at my service, to light my route?"

At that moment, large raindrops began to fall. Suddenly, a little blue flame, which cast no light, shot forth from the ground and described unknown forms on the wet ground. It danced with a magical rapidity, circling the weaver, licking his garments without burning them, and touching his feet without enabling them to feel any heat.

Hermann repeated horrible oaths a hundred times over; he struggled like a madman, but, soon embarrassed by the creepers, he fell face down on the ground. As he fell, he tore up violently one of the sticks that was striking his legs with redoubled blows. He raised it swiftly to eye level, and uttered a cry of malediction.

It was a black, worm-eaten cross. He had gone astray in the middle of an abandoned cemetery.

"Thunder!" he cried. "You're bad jokers, Messieurs the dead! By the devil!! Since the fires of Hell give no light, isn't there one of your old carcasses that wants to get up to show me my way?"

The rain was falling in torrents,

Hermann's foot struck a grave still freshly dug.

"Hola, all of you! Is there no kind companion here who wants to help me? If some good son of Satan will come with me, I'll keep him to supper! I'll slake his damned thirst with my last bottles of Rhenish wine, and then guide him back politely to his lodgings, in order that he can offer me as much!"

And the drunkard accompanied those blasphemous words with cynical bursts of laughter. But suddenly, a malediction expired on his lips and the laughter caught in his throat. He had just felt himself gripped by an icy hand.

That stiff, bony and hooked hand sank into his flesh by means of a horrible pressure and shook him with a superhuman violence.

His head cleared as if by magic, and all the blood flowed back toward his heart.

In the midst of the horrors of overturned nature, the fury of the storm, the claps of thunder and sinister lightning flashes that embroidered the clouds with fiery festoons, a specter loomed up, motionless and terrible.

Hermann raised his eyes swiftly, and suddenly closed them again. A lightning flash that had just lit up the sky from the orient to the occident had struck the hideous head of the specter; it was the weaver's old companion, the killecroff accursed throughout the land, Fritz the hanged man!

Hermann fell to his knees, chilled by horror, paralyzed by fear.

The blue flame, having vanished momentarily, had just returned; it launched forth, bold and incompressible, before the specter and enveloped it like an infernal circle. Its faint light only projected phosphorescent reflections over it, and Fritz stood out against the thick darkness like a pale blue silhouette.

It really was him, such as the inhabitants of the region had seen him for a long time, attached to the gibbet of Halberstadt. His stiff, long and green-tinted body was dislocated at the joints. His horribly contracted features mimed the grimace of the scaffold; his red hair stood up over his forehead as if by virtue of a supreme anguish, and his round and bloody eyes protruded from their orbits.

But so much hideousness, once attenuated by the dull reflection of death, now contained the flame of a supernatural and diabolical life. His limbs agitated, as if put to work by a spring, and slowly bent at the joints with an automatic movement. The ardent color of his hair was heightened by gleams that resembled jets of fire, and his eyes, veiled by his thick eyebrows as if by a necessary shadow, resembled carbuncles and launched flashes of lightning.

He was motionless. and he plunged that terrible gaze all the way to the utmost depths of the weaver's soul. The latter remained fascinated, as if by an invincible power; a muted gasp exhaled from his throat; his teeth chattered; he remained nailed to the ground by a supreme terror.

This was not the nightmare of the day before but a terrible reality!

By means of a slow movement, the phantom lifted his right arm and extended it toward the horizon. Far away, in a straight line from the end of that arm, a light was shining, like a star in the night. By the intermittent reflections of the storm, Hermann recognized his house, where Ketha was still awake.

Completely sobered up by terror, he bounded out of the cemetery and started running desperately through the countryside.

He ran with a prodigious rapidity. Neither the beating rain that lashed his face nor the gusts of the west wind that almost lifted up the earth stopped his hectic course. Launched forward by the omnipotent force of terror, he traversed woods and precipices, in spite of the obscurity, without collision, without drawing breath and without looking behind him.

And the further he went, the faster his flight seemed. One might have thought him, not a man traveling over the ground, but a demon flying to the sabbat on the clouds of the sky.

Finally, the rain ceased momentarily and the clouds parted, letting a few rays of moonlight escape. Harassed, out of breath, exhausted, unable to do any more, Hermann let himself fall like a mass at the foot of a tree.

He propped himself up in the wet grass and lifted his eyes to see where he was.

Great God! He was at the foot of the gibbet of Halberstadt, and Fritz, the hideous specter with the green-tinted limbs, the twisted mouth and the flamboyant eyes was before him, upright and impassive, his arm extended toward the horizon.

Horror rendered the weaver a new energy; he resumed his desperate flight.

The fields, the meadows, the mountains and the valleys disappeared in turn behind him, mute witnesses of distances crossed.

From time to time he turned round, vanquished by fatigue; then he saw Fritz, who was still following him, always at an equal distance, always at the same measured and automatic pace.

In vain he took more forceful strides, in vain he leapt across unusual spaces; in vain, in his superhuman course, he scarcely skimmed the ground. The specter, in spite of the slowness of his march, did not lose an inch of ground. Sometimes, Hermann even thought that he was on the point of being overtaken and seized once again by the terrible hand of the hanged man. Then fear lent him wings. He ran without looking back for instants that seemed to be hours, and when strength failed him and obliged him to catch his breath, he still found the phantom behind him, and there was not one pace more between them, nor one pace less.

The night had advanced; the rain, having become finer, was still cold and penetrating; a mortal silence reigned in the region. But the infernal voyage continued its course relentlessly. The weaver was still traversing woods and fields, and yet he never reached the end of his journey. It seemed that distances all took on fantastic proportions and extended immeasurably.

The unfortunate man, within sight of the village, shouted and called for help, but his voice expired in his throat, stifled by fear, and his teeth were chattering with a violence that did not permit him to formulate a prayer.

Finally, exhausted, dying, at the end of strength and courage, Herman arrived at the threshold of his house, seized the door-knocker and agitated it frenziedly, uttering howls of fright.

Ketha recognized her husband's voice and came down the stairs, recommending her soul to God.

Hermann struck redoubled blows; he heard the inexorable march of the specter behind him, and the seconds appeared to him to be centuries of anguish.

Finally, the bolts emerged from their sockets and the door opened.

Hermann leapt into the house, his head lost, his eyes haggard, like a madman. He pushed the bolts again with all the force that he could still find and looked around.

But the specter had not come into the house.

"Wife!" he cried. "Quickly, quickly...! Bring everything here... everything that we have... quickly... quickly... the furniture, the casks... everything, everything!"

And, tottering, he leaned on the wall.

Ketha remained immobile, not understanding. Hermann opened the judas-hole in the door and showed her Fritz, who was still advancing.

The poor woman uttered a scream of horror.

"My brother!"

Then, understanding her husband's idea by means of a rapid intuition, she launched herself into the cellar.

In an instant, the ladders, the vats and the barrels were snatched from their places and heaped up before the door in a formidable barricade.

In the common room, at the top of the steps, they closed the door, bolted it again and forbade access by means of a pyramid of furniture that they prepared to sustain with their bodies.

When the last fortification was complete, the weaver collapsed, exhausted; Ketha threw herself to her knees beside him and implored God.

But the footsteps of the accursed killecroff approached continuously. Soon they were heard making the pavement of the courtyard resound under their sonorous impact.

Ketha seized Hermann in her arms and said a supreme prayer. She had forgiven, and prayed to God to forgive also.

Suddenly, the footsteps stopped; there was a moment of silence, and the door-knocker, slowly lifted, fell back again with a dull thud.

They both leapt to the interior door and stiffened themselves, sustaining the furniture that defended it with all the force of their taut limbs. Then, motionless, their respiration halted on their lips, they waited.

After a few seconds, a second blow was repeated by the echo.

A solemn silence reigned in nature. A third blow, stronger than the first two, made the exterior barricades tremble.

Ketha felt faint.

"My God, what does he want?" she asked her husband, in a voice so faint that he only divined by the movement of her lips what he could not hear.

"I blasphemed…I invoked Satan… I challenged the dead to show me my way, to send me a guide… I invited a damned soul to come and sup here… I promised to follow him thereafter. And Fritz came…"

The weaver's voice expired in his throat, for the hammer struck the door three times, at equal intervals, and at the third stroke, the first barricade shook, while two barrels rolled on the floor.

There was an inexpressible anguish; the patients felt their hair stand up on their heads and all their blood froze in their veins.

The blows were still resounding, and at every impact an item of furniture fell, clearing the entrance to the house. Soon, the bolts themselves opened without resistance.

Then the specter's slow footsteps struck the steps of the staircase at regular intervals. When he reached the last one, his bony fingers struck a dry rap on the panel of the door, and the wall trembled.

As at the first barrier, every blow overturned an obstacle; as at the first barrier, when the last obstacle fell, the door opened by itself, and Fritz the hanged man appeared on the threshold.

At that horrible sight, Ketha fell in a faint; Hermann fled into the darkest corner of the room and huddled against the wall, as if he hoped go find a refuge there. But the pitiless specter marched straight toward him, gripped him with steely fingers, lifted him off the floor and sat him down facing him at the dining table; and when they were both seated, he darted his flamboyant eyes at his former companion and struck the table with a curt blow to demand the promised supper.

Hermann uttered a despairing cry and shook his head in a sign of refusal. "In the name of God, go away!" he murmured feebly, trying to make an impossible sign of the cross.

But the killecroff remained immobile, maintaining his funereal rictus and keeping his damned soul's eyes fixed on the weaver. He struck the table a second time, more imperatively

Then, in a choked voiced, the weaver appealed to his wife: "Ketha…!"

The poor creature lifted herself up painfully and opened her eyes slightly.

At the sight of her husband and the specter of her brother, she let out a shrill cry and fell back, broken, like someone emerging from a horrible dream only to enter into a reality even more terrible.

The killecroff rapped for a third time.

"Ketha," murmured Hermann, "fetch us something to drink."

Moved by a supernatural force, fascinated by the terrible gaze of the hanged man, she got up, took a few dried fruits and a piece of ham from the dresser, and placed them on the table in front of the two diners; then she rinsed out two pewter goblets mechanically and put them alongside; then, still followed by those two eyes, which resembled torches lit by Hellfire, she went down to the cellar in order to fetch the last bottles that Hermann had left there.

When the bottles had been deposited in front of him, Fritz took his goblet and raised it in the air. Hermann filled it to the rim and replaced the bottle on the table.

But the specter's arms remained motionless and extended until Hermann had also poured himself a drink and had approached the wine to his lips, blue-tinted by fear.

Then the golden liquid seemed to descend the killecroff's throat as if through the plug-hole of an empty barrel; and while drinking, he still directed his fixed gaze at the weaver. Under that insupportable pressure, the unfortunate weaver was also forced to drink.

When Hermann put down his goblet, he found the extended arm of his guest before him again, requesting more wine. It was necessary to fill the empty cup again and renew the funereal libation.

And when the first two bottles were finished, Fritz, still pitiless, thumped the table to demand moiré.

Still under the killecroff's infernal domination, Ketha obeyed his signs without being conscious of herself..

Fritz did not eat, but he kept drinking. The wine seemed to circulate in his veins as in an avid and desiccated torrent, without animating his face, and without warming his rigid limbs or rendering them any more supple.

Finally, when the last bottle had disgorged its last drop of liquid, when the last goblet had been emptied, the specter stood up, and with a inflexible gesture, made a sign go the weaver to follow him in his turn.

With a bound that contained a supreme energy, the unfortunate launched himself to the back of the room and hung on with the force of his most powerful grip to the columns of the bed. Then, with a heart-rending cry, he invoked Ketha one last time as a protective angel.

With a movement more rapid than thought, the poor woman had thrown herself upon her husband to try to shield him with her body; but the killecroff ground out his sinister laugh and plunged his hooked fingers into the weaver's thick hair; with a single effort he lifted him away from that feeble aegis and threw Ketha far away.

Between the dead man and the living one there was a horrible combat, devoid of pity and mercy. Sobbing, Ketha clung on to her husband's garments; she invoked God and even begged on behalf of the dead man.

Hermann clung to the furniture, the walls and the steps of the staircase with all his strength; but the frightful specter did not seem to hear the prayers or feel the resistance. Having reached the exterior door, Hermann grabbed the doorpost and clung to it with his fingernails and teeth; Ketha threw herself across the path. Fritz kicked her away and went past, dragging his prey, without looking back.

Ketha remained unconscious on the threshold of the dwelling.

When she recovered her senses, the night allowed her to glimpse the first glimmers of morning, and a funereal bell was ringing the knell of the dead, for Barbel had just expired in the house of the rector of Arnsberg.

Then she went up to the upper room and knelt down to pray next to the open window.

The rain had stopped, the clouds were dispersing in the sky, and on the horizon the pale tints that announced the day were enabling the silhouettes of bell-towers and keeps to emerge from the blackness.

Far, far away in the countryside, Ketha was still able to recognize the phantom of the killecroff, dragging the inanimate body of her husband through the brambles and the stones.

And, so the legend says, Hermann was never seen again down here.

The Dead Avenge Themselves

A numerous society had gathered in the home of Madame M***, who resides for six months in her château, situated in one of the most beautiful regions beyond the Loire.

It was All Saints' Day; it was already cold and the yellowed leaves were falling, impelled by the north wind blowing through the pathways of the garden. People were no longer thinking of long walks under the hornbeams; the grapes had been trodden and the fruits picked. In the large hearth a bright fire was crackling, around which the young and old folk gladly clustered; and as it was evening, card tables, each bearing a lamp coiffed with a green shade, had been set up in the four corners of the drawing room.

However, boston and whist scarcely amused the grandparents, and even mistigris[12] only had a limited power over young minds. Near the fire a sulky or morose group had gathered, whom the mistress of the house had to strive to distract. Unfortunately, it is often when one searches for an idea that one cannot find one. She was therefore quite embarrassed when her partner, divining her perplexity, exclaimed:

"We're being very selfish, we old people, with our cards! The children are bored, and I can see my young friend Pauline, gazing at the boston table with a expression that says clearly how little she is interested in heart

---

[12] Mistigris was a variety of poker employing a wild card, usually the joker.

tricks. Come on, Madame M***, we need a game for all ages. Let's arrange ourselves a little in the corners and make room in the middle of the room for playing innocent games."

The proposal caused inclined heads and heavy eyelids to lift

"Will you play with us, Doctor?" asked the girl designated a moment ago by the name Pauline.

"Oh, not me, dear child; I'll watch you, and that will be my greatest pleasure. I no longer have wit enough to reply to 'What shall I put in my basket?' or 'Monsieur le curé doesn't like bones,' and my movements aren't sufficiently agile to defend myself at Blind Man's Buff or Warm Hand."

"Oh, but yes, Doctor," said the mistress of the house, "since the young folk are playing, it's necessary to play their games with them if we want them to play ours afterwards. What age are you anyway, my dear contemporary, to play the old man? Fifty years old, perhaps?"

"Eh! But isn't that the age of serious ideas? You, dear Madame, can play with your daughter; that's always good for you; you're young and cheerful, and Pauline resembles your sister. My humor has always been severe, as you know. I bounced Pauline on my knees when she was a little child, but I've never taken part in the girl's games. All of you play, then, and leave me in my corner, as is customary, to chew the pommel of my cane, remembering the past or thinking about the future. Ten years sooner or ten years later, isn't it always necessary to learn that role?"

The individual who said that, while going to install himself in an old wing-chair by the fire, was a tall, thin man who had once been blond but was now gray-haired, whose hollow temples, sparse hair and stooped figure made him an old man, although he was scarcely fifty, as Madame de M*** had said. He had a high and intelligent forehead, and a gaze that was both keen and soft. His left cheek was marked by a profound scar that resembled the mark of a bite.

For twenty-five years Doctor Maynaud had been practicing medicine in the town neighboring Madame de M***'s château, and although he had been a young man when he settled in the locale no one remembered seeing him without white hair and wrinkles, so invariably severe was his forehead and so calm and retired had his life remained.

Nevertheless, he had become the friend of all the families in the neighborhood, and in Madame de M***'s salon, partly composed of Parisian visitors and partly of neighbors, there was not a single person who was not honored to have him as a fellow guest.

This evening his brow was even more pensive than usual. While the games were organized around him, and as they became noisier, he seemed to isolate himself in order to give audience to reveries or grave, almost dolorous memories. Perhaps the bells that were ringing to announce the festival of the dead were conducting his thoughts toward another world or making him think of beloved tombs. Perhaps he was seeking the answer to a scientific or moral problem. Whatever it was, he was certainly a hundred leagues from Madame de M***'s salon when, after a game, it was a question of settling the bets.

The doctor's absorbed expression struck everyone. As Pauline de M*** was liable to a penance for a pair of gloves that she had left as a hostage, someone thought it amusing to send her to wake the morose old man up with a kiss.

Pauline looked at her old friend maliciously and advanced on tiptoe. Then, when she was before him and she had shown the unblinking doctor's impassivity to the players, she took his neck abruptly in her hands and applied a noisy kiss to his left cheek.

Doctor Maynaud uttered a terribly scream, bounded as if at the detonation of a firearm, looked around madly and, in the midst of general astonishment, ran out of the drawing room.

Madame de M*** ran in pursuit of the unfortunate doctor, called her domestics and ordered that someone must catch up with him, take him to his room, render him all possible aid and find out what had provoked that sudden attack. Everyone set forth on campaign and searched the courtyards, the gardens and the corridors; but it was in vain; he could not be found.

The general consternation suspended all games. People wondered fearfully what pain could suddenly have gripped Doctor Maynaud and caused that fit of madness. A real anxiety soon replaced astonishment, for the character and temperament of the doctor were equally opposed to such violent scenes. The domestics sent forth in all directions returned without having been able to catch the fugitive.

The next morning, naturally, that event was the subject of all conversation. People were sent in search of news all the way to the nearby village, to the doctor's home; but they could not obtain any information from his aged housekeeper, and it was in vain that each of Madame de M***'s guests tried to reach him that afternoon

In the evening, after dinner had been dragged out, and after slowly savoring all the enjoyments of a dessert as opulent as a provincial dessert can be in the autumn, and the coffee drunk even more slowly, everyone went into the drawing room and all possible and impossible explanations for the doctor's flight were discussed again. Everyone gave his opinion and defended it, and the final result was that the thing remained quite incomprehensible.

The conversation finally lapsed for want of fuel, and became sad because it was raining, because it was cold, because it was the day of the dead, because no one had anything else to say, and, finally, because no one knew what to do to pass the time.

The old men were beginning to fall asleep in their armchairs and the young ones to count exactly how many sections there were in the parquet. For the hundredth time, the regulars in Madame de M***'s salon engaged in long silent conversations with the chubby amours above the doors while following the episodes of the eternal hunt that ran over the tapestries of the walls. How blessed the Melusine would have been that evening who could finally have made the stag leap, set the dogs barking and the hunters running! What would they not have given to see the swings of flowers break under the weight of the plump and joyful amours!

Toward ten o'clock, when everyone was thinking of slipping discreetly out of the drawing room to go to their bedrooms, the door opened and the doctor appeared.

He was still the same man as the night before, and yet they hesitated momentarily to recognize him. Ten years of dolor could not have changed him more than those twenty-four hours. His forehead was creased with new wrinkles, his eyes had hollowed out their orbits and his gray hair had turned white.

"I have apologies to make to you, my excellent friend," he said, in a voice that was still emotional, advancing toward Madame de M***. "I owe them above all to our dear Pauline, for the disagreeable scene that I rendered to her in exchange for the good child's caress. I doubtless appeared to you to be mad, and perhaps I am; but you sensed a horrible dolor under my cries, did you not?

"Doctor, we here are all your friends, all incapable of experiencing anything but a sincere trouble at the sight of your suffering. We didn't know..."

"You didn't know that I was subject to such fits? Reassure yourself, dear soul," said Doctor Maynaud, striving to smile, "it was the first time, and doubtless the last—for," he added, "you can see in my face, my dear Pauline, that another kiss like that would no longer leave anything but a cadaver."

"In the name of Heaven, Doctor, what's the matter with you?" cried the young girl, even more frightened by the doctor's expression than his words.

"I owe you an explanation for that strange scene, my dear child, as well as your mother and all our friends. You're very kind to be interested in the health of a poor old man, who will doubtless no longer sadden you with his presence this time next year."

"My friend!"

"Doctor!"

There was a general cry of sympathy, and yet, no one dared to contradict Monsieur Maynaud, so much had his face changed since the day before.

"I'm old, my friends," he began, "but in 1806 I was twenty years old and a student in medicine with the Faculty of Montpelier. On All Saints' Day that year the weather was magnificent for a day in late autumn. The last sunlight was gilding the leaves that remained in the branches of the trees and dressing the grayest walls of Montpelier with a joyous mantle. We were on vacation, for naturally, there were no lectures on feast days; that's why I departed with three of my friends, three students who enjoyed fresh air and liberty as much as me, to explore the surrounding area.

"Toward evening, after having spent our day wandering though the countryside, we were approaching the town again in order to find a small tavern in one of the outlying districts appreciated by students. We encountered a few of our companions, struck up a conversation, and ordered a copious supper from the landlord.

"The wine was good, the liqueurs exquisite; we talked in the lively fashion that verve sustains, argument stimulates and which throws the mind into a slightly incoherent world of ideas, because all subjects have been touched upon in turn, all questions investigated, and all theses sustained. Half wine and half chatter, perhaps, at eleven o'clock in the evening, when we tried to get up to return to our lodgings, we were stumbling and bumping into walls. Some of us were drunk, the rest tipsy.

"Those of us who were drunk stayed in the tavern on their benches or under the table. Those who were only tipsy, of whom I was one, steadying themselves as best they could, went back into Montpelier in a group.

"The route was settled by common accord and the conversation continued, scattered with interrupted phrases; but there were periodic defections, some recognizing their way home and returning, and a few others dropping behind, leaning on walls and interrogating belated passers-by.

"Personally, I was neither one of those who retained enough intelligence through the fumes of alcohol to guide myself nor one of those who had lost it entirely. Soon, I found myself in the center of the town and was uncertain which way to go.

"First I went straight ahead, without worrying any longer about my goal. The weather was fine and my head was spinning, but gradually, the turbulence of my thoughts calmed down and I tried to recognize the streets and intersections.

"That wasn't easy, for the moon was invisible and the town of Montpelier scarcely suspected, in those days, that it would one day be illuminated by gas. Street-lights of any sort were absent except outside the mairie, the prefecture and the schools. I was therefore groping my way, trying to penetrate both the darkness and the effects of drunkenness.

"Eventually, I thought I recognized a quarter that was familiar. I got my bearings and, my mind floating between wakefulness and dream, I turned into a tortuous little street that I was accustomed to taking. Mechanically, I felt all the doors of the street because it seemed to me that I would eventually find mine and discover the lock into which I had to insert my key. The more I searched, the more I crossed the street from right to left, the more the idea that I was in the vicinity of my house took root in my mind.

"I bumped into a door that was familiar, and without noticing the flag floating above it to designate a public establishment I inserted my key in the lock. It turned with difficulty at first, but with the aid of a few jerks the door ended up opening.

"I went in, advancing like a blind man with my hands before me, and took a few steps in various directions in order to find the staircase. After a few moments I found an interior door that yielded to the simple pressure of my hand. I pushed it, and scarcely had I crossed the threshold than it fell back heavily, striking the wall.

"My first impulse was to look around, but the obscurity prevented me from distinguishing anything. I only felt that I was not in my own room. An impression of cold made me think that the place was uninhabited, and by the sonorous sound of my footsteps on paving-stones I understood that the enclosure was vast and scantly furnished.

"For a moment, I thought I was in a church, but in churches the lamp of the sanctuary burns night and day, and there was no illumination in that silent and chilly place.

"I wanted to get out and I retraced my steps in the direction of the door, but, either because intoxication rendered my steps uncertain or because the door was not obviously detectable from inside, I could not find it again.

"Then I wanted to know exactly into what place I had wandered, and as I distinguished though the darkness, at the far end of the hall, a large sheet of glass covered by a curtain, I advanced in that direction in order to obtain more light.

"Scarcely had I taken a dozen steps than I collided violently with the corner of an item of furniture or a ledge. I made a slight detour and continued my route with more precaution, but did not take long to be halted by a second impact.

"I extended my hand and felt the cold of marble; then, when I made a second movement, a more intense, more penetrating chill, more repulsive to my flesh froze the blood in my veins. What I recognized, as a student of medicine and surgery, was the chill of death.

"Suddenly, the fumes of drunkenness fled and all my presence of mind returned. I was in the amphitheater where the people who died in the hospice were deposited on marble tables in order to be delivered to study and dissected. I was, however, habituated to finding myself in that place; I was not a debutant to be frightened by the sight of a cadaver. But surprise, the darkness and perhaps the time of year—for I could hear the knell of the dead sounding—all contributed to cause me an invincible sentiment of dread.

"Fear gripped me by the throat and agitated my limbs with a convulsive tremor. I circled those inflexible walls like a prisoner around his dungeon; I applied my hands to each panel, hoping eventually to find the door and make it yield under my pressure, but all my efforts were in vain. The paneling seemed to repel me. Perhaps fear had rendered me impotent even to open a door.

"The bells were still ringing, slowly and inexorably.

"My teeth were chattering; a cold sweat was pearling on my forehead. The moon, which had risen, filtered its pale light through the red curtain of the window. Gradually, objects began to emerge from the darkness. I distinguished the bizarre shadows of surgical instruments extending along the walls, then the black marble tables, whose ridges caught rays of light, then the dispersed scalpels, and then the cadavers.

"There were two—only two.

"One of them was an old man already labored by our hands; I recognized him. The other was a young woman who had died the day before, still fresh.

"The old man, bloody and butchered, his limbs partly detached from the body, was horrible to see.

"The young woman, beautiful with the fascinating beauty of death that consumption leaves its victims, attracted my gaze invincibly.

"Midnight chimed, and each stroke mingled its solemn timbre with the funereal song of the bells. The day of the dead was commencing. My terror became even more intense, it seemed to me that the cadavers were about to hold me to account for my profanation, for on the second of November, in all Faculties of Medicine, the amphitheaters are closed; the dead are respected, as if their souls were watching over their bodies on that day.

"Immobile, frozen, I remained crouching at the foot of the enclosing wall, without being able to take my eyes off the young woman.

"Suddenly, I shivered; it seemed that I heard a stifled groan.

"I listened, my ears pricked, with the terror that makes the senses acquire an unusual acuity. A more prolonged sound troubled the silence.

"I looked around, and I thought I saw the head of the old man shift slowly on its marble bed. I was mad with fear; blood rose to my head and whipped my temples violently.

"I wanted to flee at any price, but my insensate efforts always ended up making me turn in the same circle.

"The bells, as slow at first as the plaints of an invalid, now began to ring at full tilt, their hasty coups resembling gasps of agony. The shaken windows repeated their sound with lamentable notes. At moments, one might have thought that the dead were weeping, asking for mercy and pity, at other moments that they were waking up, lifting themselves up in dense cohorts, filling the air with a warrior hurrah.

"I fell to my knees, devoid of strength and reason, my sight troubled, my head lost.

"This time, I really had heard a sigh nearby; this time, I really had seen the cadavers stir!

"And while I felt myself dying, the old man uttered lugubrious cries, for he could not succeed in moving his head, the top of his skull having been removed, nor in moving his limbs, lacerated by the scalpel or sliced by the saw. He was making extraordinary efforts to lift himself from his marble slab, and each movement shook his bloody brain. Finally, he succeeded in sitting up, and his eyes, half-extracted from their orbits, interrogated the darkness.

"'Today is the day of the dead,' he said, in a voice that resounded in my entrails. 'The dead wake up and avenge themselves! Who is there, with me, in this horrible charnel-house...? A young woman! Get up, child! Get up, for you still have limbs, and you're reposing in ignorance of the torture that awaits you! Today is the day of the dead, and the dead wake up and avenge themselves!'

"Slowly, in her turn, the young woman lifted herself up and opened staring eyes.

"'Poor girl! Oh, you've scarcely expired, and you have no idea of the tortures that the odious living reserve for us! The dead, they say, what are they? Inert flesh of which the earth will make a dung-heap. Insensible matter good for the experiments of the scalpel! And yet, this icy flesh, which no frisson causes to tremble, it suffers, it feels...until the hour of its complete dissolution. When the trenchant implement cleaves the flesh, we feel its sharp and agonizing tip; when our entrails are spread outside our abdomen, we would like to be able to retain them in spite of the sacrilege that is stealing them; when our brain screams under the trepan, when our heart bleeds under the lancet, the most intense dolors tear us apart: dolors of which the executioners, those who can still die, have no idea.

"'Oh, my skull is open! I'm suffering horribly! What are they searching for in my head? Thoughts, perhaps? It's in the name of science that the barbarians slice us up, butcher us and rummage around inside us! Ha ha!' he added, with a snigger that made echoes resonate. 'But they'll be dead in their turn! Today is the day of the dead, and the dead wake up and avenge themselves!

"'Go on, quit your marble couch and come close to mine... that's it! Come closer, since you can walk... good... sit down now and look at all these instruments of torture around us. Poor child! Scarcely being dead, you think you're asleep, don't you? Well, they'll come, they're going to come... they'll open your breast in order to search there for the phthisis that killed you. They'll part your bones and you won't be able to scream...They'll rummage in your heart and your heart will feel the sharp lancet plunge again and again, a thousand times, to the sound of their laughter...for they laugh, the wretches, as they rip us apart! They talk about their orgies! They talk about their mistresses...

'And then, when it's all finished, when a part of your being has been thrown on to the rubbish dump, when your hands and your feet, so pretty now, have been cut off and carried away by them to make playthings of them, they'll roll up the remains in a gross sheet—the charity sheet—put them in a box, scarcely joined up, and throw them in an ignoble ditch... at random... on top of me, on top of yesterday's dead, under tomorrow's, between an old beggar and some debris of shame or crime.

"'You'll feel all that; and the heavy earth, and the pressure of another coffin on top of yours, and the frost and the snow, and the damp of the rain.

"'Then the suffering will last for a long time...a long time...until the worms have gnawed your bones; until the arid sand has drunk the juice of your flesh in order to make grass and flowers with it.

"'That's what the dead suffer under the tyranny of the living who reign over the earth. But today is the day of the dead...and the dead wake up and avenge themselves!'

"And the cadaver, proud of his royalty of an hour, straightened terribly, parading a fixed gaze around himself.

"'But what do I see? Look! Who is hiding over there, under the shadow of a table? A dead man must be with us...how those two eyes burn! Perhaps he's alive...! A living man? A torturer? Yes, yes, it's a living man! She how he's folding himself up...how he seems to be requesting the walls for a refuge...listen to the rattle of fear in his throat...Ha ha! It's our turn! Go on, girl, go on! I give the prey to you! Put your hand on his heart and you'll feel it beating... Is it beating? Oh, then avenge yourself, dead woman!'"

The doctor shuddered, and his lips went white; words expired in his throat.

People hastened around him; he was made to inhale salts; but his faint only lasted a few seconds. His eyes opened again; he recovered the power of speech and he added, in a strangled voice:

"Then I felt the dead woman's two hands enclose my neck in an icy circle...and on my cheek—here, where you see this scar, where you kissed me, Pauline...I experienced a pain so sharp that thought can't imagine it. First there was a bite, made with teeth that seemed to be diamonds of ice, then a horrible suction that drew in my life.

"I lost consciousness.

"When I opened my eyes again it was daylight and I was in my bed with an ardent fever. My friends and comrades were crowded around me.

"'Well,' they said, laughing, 'What the devil were you doing by night in the amphitheater with the subjects? Do you mistake the dead for grisettes when you're drunk?'

"'Today is the day of the dead,' I repeated, mechanically. 'The dead wake up and avenge themselves!'

"'Get away! Have you gone mad? We're going to make a few applications of cold water to your skull.'

"I told them the horrible story, but the students only saw my account as an echo of delirium. 'Vision!' they said. 'Fumes of drunkenness mingled with nurses' tales.'

"Then they strove to demonstrate to me, in the name of reason, the impossibility of the events. They told me all the stories of hallucinations since the remotest antiquity, and for a moment I was ready to believe that I had had a frightful nightmare engendered by wine and fear.

"As I hesitated between their reasoning and my memory, something disturbed an apparatus that I had on my head, and I felt a sharp pain in my cheek. All my terrors returned to me; I demanded a mirror, and removed the bandage and the compresses. On my bleeding cheek there was a gaping wound and the marks of teeth.

"'And this?' I cried. 'Is this a dream too? If my head in delirium heard the dead speak, if the power of my overexcited imagination alone showed me that funereal drama, have I also bitten myself?'

"They had nothing to respond to that terrible proof. My friends doubted, and fell silent.

"They cared for me; I healed—but since that epoch I have never gone into an amphitheater, and I have defended all my dead against autopsy. Young girls, too, when they are pale and tall, like Pauline, have a strange effect on me.

"You understand now what the dear child's unexpected kiss caused me to experience yesterday, on a date and at an hour on which, for thirty years, I've been unable to free myself from my terrors. For a second, it gave me the illusion…Pauline, I won't repeat it!"

Madame de M*** and her friends hastened around Doctor Maynaud in order to reassure him. Multiple protestations of sympathy reached him from all directions. There was talk of cure, forgetfulness, of the future…

But the following year, the eve of All Saints' Day passed sadly in Madame de M***'s château. At the customary gathering of friends and neighbors, the doctor was missing, and no one could avoid a constriction of the heart in remembering him.

The Devil's Ten Thousand Francs

I

Reader, you know your Balzac and, in consequence, the *Maison Vauquer*, too well for us to undertake a pale copy of that scene.[13] However, it is there that it is necessary to conduct you in order to find the beginning of our story. It is, alas, in a bourgeois boarding house that our hero lodges, and a bourgeois boarding-house is always the *Maison Vauquer*!

Take yourself back in memory for a moment, then, to the stinking cloaca of the Rue Neuve-Sainte-Geneviève. Imagine once again the damp dining-room that conserves in perpetuity a fetid odor formed of incessantly present aromas of hash and stewed prunes; the old furniture, the chipped crockery, the stained napkins; and then the staircase with worn steps, the cold bedrooms devoid of furniture. Evoke, above all, the personnel of the establishment: old men without families dragging out the final days of a miserable life painfully, or hiding an unforeseen deprivation; fallen creatures living like mollusks because they are not dead and no one has killed them; young provincials whom parsimony or the poverty of their families has obliged to resolve the problem of

---

[13] The *Maison Vauquer*, in which Eugéne de Rastignac lodges in *Le Père Goriot*, is described at considerable length in the book as a representative exemplar of a slice of humble Parisian society.

living in Paris and completing their studies there on twelve hundred francs a year.

Good. Now take all that down a step. Make the house even more ignoble and the poverty even more repulsive. Transform Maman Vauquer into a dirty old man who lives with his cook. Place the establishment in the Rue Copeau[14] at the back of a courtyard and imagine Poiret more brutal, Madame Michonneau older and more withered, Rastignac more disinherited. You have the bourgeois boarding-house, "for the two sexes and others" kept in 1840 by Monsieur Buneaud.

People pay six hundred francs a year to board there—judge it by that!

The table is served, and all our familiar characters are arranged around it, in the various attitudes that reveal their habits, their character and their infirmities. However, there is a new face among them, a head less withered than the others, but sad and devoid of expression.

One senses that the individual in question is the destined brother of his companions, doubtless with a similar past and surely a similar future. He is another Poiret, but a younger Poiret, Poiret at the precise moment in which the transformation of man into mechanism is taking place.

Monsieur Naigeot is only fifty years old. He is small, plump rather than thin, and balding. The hair that remains to him is not yet white, but indecisive in color, in which blond, chestnut and gray participate, doubtless because of mixtures. Below it he has a square face, fleshy and sensual lips, a large and deformed nose, and small, dull eyes. His prominent forehead, furrowed with thick wrinkles, is one of those unfortunate foreheads that

---

[14] The former Rue Copeau became the Rue Lacépède in 1853.

express stubbornness rather than determination, fatigue rather than labor; it is the degraded brow of an ox that has carried the yoke for too long; the brow, in sum, of beings who read on the threshold of their future, like Dante's damned on the threshold of their Inferno: *Abandon all hope here*.

At the moment when we perceive him in the midst of the boarders, the soup has been served, and Buneaud is delivering to circulation the plate on which he has just divided into portions the thin slices of the eternal boiled meat.

The initial fury of the appetite is appeased; the boarders are beginning to exchange between them, and with the master of the house, the usual polite remarks. They are asking one another for their news, enquiring about one madame's catarrh and her neighbor's walk.

"Have the monkeys in the Jardin des Plantes come out today?"

"No, it's not warm enough yet."

"It's said that the little female capuchin is dead."

"But the chimpanzee has arrived."

"Poor beast!"

"And you, Monsieur Naigeot, have you seen the chimpanzee?"

"You know that I haven't had the time, Monsieur Buneaud. I have my affairs to attend to! I don't have my bread ready baked, like these messieurs."

"That's true. Oh, lack of money! It's always the same... By the way, while you weren't here a letter came for you. A famous letter, too, with thirty-six stamps and I don't know how many addresses on the envelope, because it's been running after you for two months! It's come from America. But don't worry, I refused it. Three francs to pay! No thanks!"

"You've refused a letter from America!" cried a student at the extremity of the table, while Naigeot limited himself to raising a gaze upon Buneaud in which astonishment and indifference were mingled. "From a country where one can always have an uncle! Well, you wouldn't have had to refuse a letter from America for me—and I say it with regret, Papa Buneaud," he added, with a comical gravity, "but I'd have immediately divorced your shack."

"One can always reclaim it from the postman. Do you have relatives in America, Monsieur Naigeot?"

"I believe so," he replied, without emerging from his torpor.

"You believe so? Damn it, you ought to know!"

"I once had a brother..."

"In America?"

"I don't know...but he might be in America. A lot of water has flowed under the bridge in thirty years."

"A brother! For thirty years you haven't know what has become of him, and a letter arrives from America with a great many forwarding addresses! What a drama, Papa Naigeot!" the student went on, striking the table with his fist. "But it's an inheritance falling to you from the sky! You're going to become a Croesus! You're going to regale us, Papa Naigeot!"

"Good!" exclaimed another student. "It's not too maladroit to have refused the letter—thanks to this affair Buneaud might lose a boarder! That wouldn't suit him, whose nurslings enrich him. Can you see the Pactolus traversing the courtyard? Crack! No more paying guest, right away!"

The young men clapped their hands; a stupid smile wandered over the lips of the less brutish old men. As for the others, outside the movement and indifferent to the conversation, they were cutting up their meat with the same automatic regularity. There were people in the Buneaud boarding-house whom even the noise of a cannon or the tocsin would not have caused to raise their heads.

"Finally, Monsieur Naigeot, is it necessary to reclaim the letter?" asked Buneaud.

"Er..."

"What! You're hesitating? A fortune arrives for you, and you're refusing to welcome it! You have a brother in America—a brother who writes to you!—and your heart doesn't beat any faster than one pulsation an hour! Papa Naigeot, oysters have more passion than that!"

"A fortune! A fortune! Perhaps, on the contrary, it's to borrow money from me! Dominique was once a wastrel...while I've always been a man of order and economy...and three francs, after all, is three francs!"

The young men looked at one another from all the ends of the table, making signs to one another to exhort the fellow to recover the famous missive. Then there was a fusillade of comments and gibes.

"Say, Naigeot, cede your rights to me, and if the patron will give me three francs' credit until next month, I'll pay for your epistle and your heritage. What do you say?"

"Hey, an American uncle for three francs isn't dear! I'd give thirty sous to have my share of it—still on credit, you understand."

"And me twenty sous—on condition of a share of the inheritance in proportion to my contribution, as is only fair."

"Well, that would be four francs—twenty sous too many; enough to pay for a grog. To Papa Naigeot, our benefactor!"

"Come on, Messieurs—no stupidities," put in Monsieur Buneaud, in a quasi-paternal tone mingling authority and bonhomie.

"Stupidities? But it's very serious. We want that letter, and we'll pay for it!"

"Perhaps Monsieur Naigeot finds our pretentions too elevated. Let's reduce them. Let's content ourselves with an interest of a thousand per cent on our contribution..."

Naigeot remained impassive.

"I propose that we all chip in, to retrieve the letter tomorrow morning, on condition that it's read aloud in an intelligible voice by the patron!" cried the one most irritated by that stupid indifference.

"I'll subscribe for fifty centimes," said another throwing a ten-sou piece on to a carafe-stand—a tin-plate carafe-stand once painted red but now completely chipped. "Come on, Messieurs et Mesdames. Hands in pockets! Three francs! It's three francs! We need three francs! That's another two francs fifty."

The student stood up and circled the table, tapping his coin on his wooden bowl, like the acrobats who take collections in front of the booths in the Champs-Élysées. The young people each hastened to throw in their offering. Even the old boarders, solicited in their turn, donated their sou mechanically.

"Noël, Messieurs! We have the blessed three francs! Here, patron. I'm placing them in your hands. A thousand per cent, Naigeot, that makes thirty francs for you to pay tomorrow from your succession."

"Talk about virtuous men, economical men, who understand business! Here's Naigeot, a cashier, a bookkeeper, a dealer in figures, a master of making reports and balancing accounts, who's mortgaging his property for twenty-four hours at thirty thousand per cent per month. At that rate, old chap. I'll offer you a year's credit!"

Buneaud's boarders listened to these calculations with bewildered expressions, laughing at the students' joke. None of them would ever have been able to take seriously a calculation by means of which three francs could produce in a year's time three hundred and sixty-five times thirty francs.

As for Naigeot, he had followed the students' operation as an amateur, and had recompensed them with an approving nod of the head.

"At that rate, Messieurs," he said, "You'd be the inheritors! Unfortunately, it will be three francs lost, and that's all. But at least it's you who will have wanted it!"

"Is that Naigeot disillusioned enough?" said one of the students, folding up his napkin, for the dinner was over and everyone was getting up to go to his business or his pleasure. "What a mollusk, resigned to living and dying stuck to the same rock! But Papa, you're scarcely fifty years old! You still have a future, after all! And when one has an annual income of three hundred francs, and one keeps books from morning till evening to make six hundred more, when one lives from the first of January to the thirty-first of December in the comfortable maison Buneaud, it's necessary to take refuge in the future to resist the present, and to mortgage one's hopes on hazard, if one can't do any better!"

"Pooh! Hazard! A bad debtor, Messieurs."

"Not always, Papa. There's no other who pays a thousand per cent interest in twenty-four hours. Until tomorrow, and good luck!"

The students went out; the old men went back upstairs to their rooms, alone or in groups, some to go to bed, others to play a few hands of piquet or bézique. Buneaud went into the kitchen. The addressee of the famous letter picked up his hat as if to go out, for, after dinner, he always returned to balance the inputs and outgoings in the establishment of a petty merchant of the quarter. In spite of himself, however, he became pensive, and while dreaming he strode back and forth in the deserted dining room.

After all, he said to himself, *more extraordinary things have been seen. What if I were to become rich? Me, François Naigeot! What would I do?* he asked himself, mentally, darting a circular glance around.

As he was trying to respond to himself, eight o'clock chimed on the hospice of La Pitié.

"Good!" he cried, running outside. "I'm going to be late now! These young people are all mad!"

That speech put an end to the whim of ambition born in Naigeot's brain. He ran to his work, concluded his daily task and returned to go to bed with the mechanical regularity of a one-eyed horse that has been turning the same capstan for ten years.

He was, in fact, a wretched creature, that man with a yellowing cranium, a bleak gaze and a heavy tread. Never, perhaps, have beings disinherited by the mediocrity of their intelligence, the narrowness of their minds, bad luck and a thousand other causes, condemned to drag out a tedious existence with the aid of incessant and fruitless labor, been personified in a more complete type specimen.

However, François Naigeot was endowed to the highest degree with all the social virtues that acquire or conserve fortune: patience, economy and the complete absence of passions. Only one thing had agitated his life, only one motive had made him act; that was the fear of failure, the horror of poverty.

And by a strange contradiction, but more frequent than one might be disposed to believe, Naigeot had condemned himself all his life to the harshest privations, in order to shelter himself from need. Never, even during the years of his youth, had he given himself to the satisfaction of a desire. Never had he forgotten the future in the traction of the present. At twelve years of age he had hoarded the money that his father had given him for his meager pleasures. At twenty, after three years of apprenticeship in a house of commerce, when he began to receive a salary as a sales clerk, he deposited it with his employer and left it to accumulate interest. He scarcely dared to take out the sum indispensable for his maintenance, so much was he consternated by the fate of his older brother—who, after having consumed his patrimony and run up debts, had been reduced to embarking on a ship in order to seek his fortune.

The frugal family table, and that of Monsieur Gobain, his employer, had limited the circle of his gastronomic excesses. He had never lost more than an écu gambling, on his days of folly, and he had always reproached himself bitterly for it. As for women, he had always considered with horror those who might have provided an opportunity for expenditure, and had forbidden himself to think of marriage before possessing a certain fortune. To marry without having an assured existence seemed to him the most culpable of impetuosities, for one could fall into poverty with a family—and to fall into poverty was, in his eyes, the most horrible of misfortunes, the most shameful disgrace, almost a crime!

However, sitting at a counter, his quill behind his ear and the pages of a ledger open on his lectern, he considered with an admiring eye the wife of his employer, enthroned facing him in all her finery.

To have such a wife, to dress her in lace and silk, to take her to the theater, and twice a year to the Hôtel-de-Ville ball, appeared to him to be the ultimate in happiness. He counted his savings, added the small sum that the paternal heritage would give him, and calculated the number of years that he would have to wait before arriving at the Pillars of Hercules of prosperity. Unfortunately, even adding in the interest on the capital, fortune would still take a long time to arrive, and he despaired of attaining before old age that joy reserved for others luckier than him.

Then, he reflected the dreams of his youth, desperately, upon his employer's wife. He adorned that face, majestically framed by a cockleshell bonnet, with a thousand graces; he admired that waist, tightened in a well-buckled corset, continually. Although the good woman was less than pretty, she became for the unfortunate cashier a Beatrix ornamented with all beauties as well as all virtues, a criterion who served Naigeot as a term of comparison every time he tried to form an opinion for himself or someone else regarding a person of the female sex. She was agreeable or ugly, stupid or intelligent, according to whether or not she resembled, Madame Gobain, that was all!

And the years went by for the clerk, between the routine of his stultifying work, his constant preoccupation with economies, and his mute admiration for his employer's wife, whom time did not wither in his eyes.

A day came when Naigeot was forty, lacked two teeth, had a paunch and gray hair. He could have married then, for he had become his employer's associate to the tune of twenty per cent, but he let a long time go by before making a firm decision; then he waited longer before choosing, among all the women who were offered to him, the one that appeared to resemble Madame Gobain most closely. In brief, he only made up his mind on the day when an unexpected terrible, disastrous event overturned the edifice of his hopes and annihilated at a stroke that little fortune acquired with such difficulty.

Monsieur Gobain, who doubtless had, like his clerk, an ideal of fortune, secretly engaged in hazardous speculations and went bankrupt. When the concordat was signed, all that remained to the unfortunate Naigeot was an infimal dividend, which bought an annuity that gave him an annual income of three hundred francs. Thus, after thirty years of labor, after having refused himself all wellbeing and all joys, he found himself reduced to the poverty that he had dreaded so much.

Henceforth, his privations would no longer be voluntary but obligatory. Henceforth, it would be necessary to work to earn his daily bread and not to amass what was necessary in order to live, eventually, an idle and comfortable life! At first Naigeot thought of dying; then he calculated that he no longer had the means to maintain his active despair for long and thought about earning enough to augment his income of three hundred écus. He therefore made arrangements with two or three second-order establishments that had no special accountant, that they would give him so much a month to come every day to put their books in order. In that manner he earned six hundred francs, which paid for his board in Buneaud's house, while the other three hundred suffced for his maintenance, his laundry and his meager expenditure. Again, he found the means of capitalize a considerable part of it.

And those were the very simple events, in a life exempt from excess and shocks, that had made a of man born with all his limbs and a well-organized brain the brutish creature that we encountered at the beginning of this story.

The next morning, when the breakfast bell had brought all the boarders together again in the dining room of the Buneaud house, the letter from America was solemnly brought on a tray and placed in the middle of the table by way of a centerpiece—or, rather, a *pièce de résistance* destined to deceive the appetite of the most voracious students.

"Who's going to read it?" they cried, all at the same time. And everyone examined it, sniffed it, and counted the stamps and the forwarding addresses.

"Say, Naigeot, what if it's a simple invitation to your brother's marriage, eh?"

"Oh, my God, that's quite possible," said the piteous bookkeeper. "As long as it's not a request for money! I'm very much afraid that poor Dominique might be in penury!"

"Let's go! We'll soon know," cried the one who was holding the envelope, breaking the seal. "Papa Buneaud, in your capacity as the president of the assembly, read it to us!"

Buneaud put on his spectacles, opened the envelope, and read:

"My dear brother.

"You must believe me to be dead, since you have not had news of me for thirty years, and in tracing these

belated lines, I fear that I might not receive any response to them. If one arrives, I know in advance what cruel losses it will announce to me. Our parents are doubtless no more and I feel a veritable remorse in thinking that I have not even softened their last moments by correspondence. If, however, they are still alive, and if this letter reaches you, be my interpreter in their regard, my dear François; obtain their pardon for a son who has not dishonored them and who has only one desire, which is to repair the wrong he has done. My friend, it is necessary not to believe that one has a forgetful and desiccated heart because one has not written, when one is tempting fortune, like me, in distant lands, and a thousand interests drag you away from your better thoughts. In the end, thank God, I have succeeded. I have made a fortune, as they say, and now, I only ask to share my wellbeing with my relatives. I am very rich, François; so rich that, even in France, my fortune would appear exorbitant. Nevertheless, I do not want to confide an excessive sum to my letter, which might be lost if this letter fails to arrive. I am therefore only enclosing a draft for ten... thousand... francs...”

Buneaud interrupted himself, his voice cut off by astonishment, and let the letter fall on to the tray.

Then a piece of paper, part-manuscript and partly engraved in italic characters, with a stamp in the margin and a horizontally-lined spaced in the middle covered in writing slid slowly between the two pages of the letter.

Naigeot seized the blessed mandate, to the victorious cries of the students, and tore the letter from Buneaud's hands in order to finish reading it himself.

“It's not, my dear brother,” he continued, *“that I believe you to be in need, for I remember your economy and your assiduity in work. You must, for your part, at*

least have acquired a certain ease, and if our parents still exist, they are certainly not unhappy with you. But in France ten thousand francs is a tidy sum and if, against all expectation, you have not been favored by fortune, I would be happy if this money can come to your aid. If, on the contrary, you're rich, it will pay for a whim of your wife or extend the dowry of one of your daughters, for I suppose that you're married and the father of a family...

"Good brother! Excellent brother!" murmured Naigeot, wiping his eyes. "Ten thousand francs for me! Ten thousand francs...

"In the case that none of my dreams have been realized and you are still an old bachelor devoid of a fortune, would you care to undertake the voyage and come to aid me in my vast commerce, so that I can give you a share of it? You're fifty years old, if my count is accurate; at that age one is still young, and a few thousand leagues of sea ought not to be intimidating. Here, you'll find good relatives and friends, since I have them. My wife, who is an educated and intelligent American, very experienced in commerce, will rapidly acquaint you with our business dealings. My daughter—a child of eighteen, my dear François, pretty, gracious and bright—will love you and treat you as an uncle. America is a fine country and the climate of New Orleans is not as mortal as people like to say. In sum, in my warehouses, through which, produce from all the countries in the world passes, you'll make a fortune in five or six years. Think about it, if you're not as fortunate in France as you would wish, if you have a desire to travel, and if, finally, you want to see the brother again who quit you as a young man, almost a child, and whom you'll find as an old graybeard; who departed like a soldier of fortune with

two shirts and the malediction of his creditors, and who has become one of the most considerable people in the commerce of the New World.

"Adieu or au revoir. Write to me as soon as you receive this letter and its contents. With what pleasure I'll receive your response! With what pleasure I'll find you, like an echo of the world I left behind, and a blessing from my first family!

"Dominique Naigeot
*"New Orleans, March 18**"*

"Bravo, bravo, bravissimo!" cried the students, in chorus. "That's a brother! A brother who could well be my uncle! Naigeot, depart quickly for America, and take us all along as your children!"

"Well, my dear monsieur," said Buneaud, phlegmatically, who foresaw at the end of the general enthusiasm the loss of a boarder, "how strewn with ups and downs life is. It's all nothing but good and bad luck! You're rich now and you have no more need to do double-entry bookkeeping in order to pay for your monthly accommodation..."

"Monsieur will doubtless have no more months to pay you." observed an old woman who had kept apart until then, as if perfectly indifferent to the discussion. "It's probable that from now on, he'll cease to be our commensal..."

"Why do you suppose that our friend Naigeot is so miserly that he'll dispense with allowing us to share a little in his good fortune?" said someone in the camp of the students. "On the contrary, he'll have pleasure in inviting us all to dinner..."

"And in paying us the thirty francs he owes us!"

"So much the better if he cares to take his time and give us sixty francs tomorrow, ninety the day after tomorrow, a hundred and twenty in three days..."

Stupefied, flabbergasted by reading his brother's letter, not knowing yet whether he ought to believe his eyes and ears, François Naigeot held the draft for ten thousand francs in his hand, turning it over repeatedly—sniffing it, so to speak—and staring at it, without yet being able to take account of its existence.

Certainly, he would not have been more astonished if he had suddenly found himself the master of the golden fleece or the Garden of the Hesperides; so the acclamations and the compliments of his commensals only reached him at first as a confused buzz. But when the general reflections gave way to particular applications, when he understood that the three francs were being claimed, with the fabulous interest of a thousand per cent a day, in accordance with the previous day's joke, the bookkeeper raised his head instinctively in a sign of revolt against that extortionate usury.

There was no unexpected fortune that could make him comprehend so quickly that one could, in a day of folly, pay thirty francs of interest on three francs lent for twenty-four hours.

"Ah! Is Naigeot going to renege on his debt? Will he refuse to pay it?" asked one of the students, in a quasi-menacing tone.

Everyone stood up. The old boarders brutalized by the bourgeois boarding-house instantly rediscovered the energy to join the young men, and Buneaud sketched a sign of indignation.

"One moment, Messieurs et Mesdames," stammered the rich Naigeot, who saw that he was on the point of being overwhelmed by a general outcry. "It's agreed that I'll pay a supplement for this evening's dinner...provided that this draft is presentable today," he added, by way of correction.

"That's good!" said Buneaud. "I'll put on a goose to roast, then, order a chocolate cream, Bordeaux wine..."

"Let's see whether the draft is sound, then?" cried one of the young men. "Give me your piece of paper, Naigeot."

He did not hand it over, but he allowed it to be taken as he fell back, pale and weak, almost in a faint, on the back of his chair. Suddenly, a horrible dread had just bitten his heart,

What if the draft were false? What if the stamps were counterfeit...if the letter, and everything., were nothing but an infamous joke of those students...?

That sensation only lasted for a minute...a minute of poignant anguish, during which Naigeot, remaining suspended over the abyss that separates misery from fortune, suddenly understood with an extraordinary lucidity the difference between the two terms: to be or not to be!

The mandate, suspended above his head by a pitiless hand descended again, fluttering, to his knees.

"Perfectly in order!" cried ten voices at the same time.

Left alone in confrontation with his treasure, Naigeot took his head in both hands, as if to contain the incoherent ideas that were seething in his brain.

Immediately, as if by a thrust of a magic wand, that letter had reawakened the atrophied intelligence of the bookkeeper. He sensed life agitating within him, that being without a past, that old man who had not had a youth, in whom, at a stroke, a thousand unknown emotions were born...

Naigeot did not take account of the strange travail that was going on within him, but his mind was already opening to new desires. He reread his brother's letter, and exaggerated further the fortune that had come to him.

So, he said go himself, *I'm rich! I'm truly rich! For, in sum, I have ten thousand francs, with which I can satisfy all my desires...and when they're spent, if I want to depart for America, I'll find another fortune out there, ready made! if, on the contrary, I prefer to remain here, I can buy an annuity... I can easily get an income of six or eight hundred francs... all my expenses would be covered... I could live well. without worrying about anything, and if I worked, I'd still have a superfluity.*

That would be a nice little existence, ready made... yes, but it wouldn't be being rich!

But also, I wouldn't be obliged to embark...

Bah! I have time to reflect. For today, I'm rich...ten thousand francs! Ten thousand francs to oneself! That's a pretty penny, and I can spend without counting!

"Buneaud!"

The master of the boarding-house did not reply, doubtless because he had not heard.

Certainly, I'll give them dinner... and I have no need to pay attention to a few bottles of wine more or less, or to be stingy about the roast. I want to pay for a meal like rich folk, and my word, for today, it's necessary that these good folk have their share!

"Buneaud!"

What can they eat that's delicate, in sum, and rare, rich people?

"Buneaud! Buneaud!" he shouted, this time with all the force of his lungs.

Buneaud arrived, astonished to be disturbed at an hour that was not that of any meal, and ready to take offense at the authoritarian tone in which he had been summoned; but when he recognized the newly enriched man, his discontentment changed into an obsequious smile.

"What is it, Monsieur Naigeot?" he asked.

"What are you making for dinner?" said Naigeot, in an imperious tone. "That's three times I've called you!"

"Oh, how stiffly we're talking… I'm *having made*, as I told you, a roast goose, a chocolate cream… and then there'll be the soup, a salad…"

"Pooh!"

"What! Pooh?"

"Yes. All that's common, my dear…I've eaten it before."

"Oh!" said Buneaud, stupefied. "Order what you like, then."

"Expensive things… extraordinary things."

"Fried soles? Floating islands?" the master of the boarding-house hazarded, timidly.

"Better than that."

"Good. Duck with olives? Punch? Soup of Italian pâtés?"

"That's better... but it's necessary not to fear giving me all that there is of the best. I can pay!"

"Damn! Unless I order your dinner from Chevet's..."

"From Chevet's? But why not, in fact? Do rich people order their dinner from Chevet's?"

"Very rich people... but I don't think that you..."

"Yes, precisely, my friend. In truth, what you offer me isn't suitable! It's vulgar! There's no need to have ten thousand francs in one's pocket to eat that! On due

101

reflection, I'll go to Chevet's on my way back from collecting my money. At least have the table set properly in your hovel!"

And Naigeot went out, without saluting, slamming the doors.

"Wouldn't one think that he's a millionaire, with his ten thousand francs?" murmured the furious Buneaud.

When the bookkeeper had crossed the threshold of the bourgeois boarding-house and found himself on the pavement of the Rue Copeau, with a draft for ten thousand francs in his pocket, he breathed in the air with a hitherto-unknown satisfaction. The sunlight seemed to him to be fluid gold, the horizon broadened. Paris seemed to him to have been transfigured.

Never before had he wondered about the meaning and the usage of a thousand things that poverty had placed beyond his reach. He had never even enjoyed those that were offered to everyone. That was because the appreciation of all those good things implied a relative idleness, or at least a certain freedom, and the unfortunate Naigeot had spent his life in ingrate and continual toil. Whatever the weather, he went to his daily work with his head bowed and his gaze vague, carrying his bag and dragging his halter, under the incessant lash of the whip of necessity, like a cab-horse under that of a pitiless coachman. So he had not even admired the magnificent foliage of the Jardin des Plantes and the rich collections that Europe envies us. For him, Paris was contained within four points: the wine-market, the Boulevard Saint-Denis, the Rue Saint-Honoré, where he went to keep his books, and the Rue Copeau, which contained the Buneaud boarding-house.

But today, he thought he had conquered the world, and felt the need to know all its riches. That is why he went along the Rue Saint-Victor with his nose in the air, his hands in his pockets and his face beaming, looking at the shops, bumping into passers-by here and there, and swerving at random like a drunken man,

As he was about to turn the corner of the street that goes down to the quay after the wine-market, he wondered, for the first time, where he was going, and took his brother's draft out of his pocket in order to look at the banker's address. He read the name of Rothschild, and, lower down: 17 Rue Laffitte.

Good, he thought, *but Rue Laffitte is a long way from here; it's in the direction of the Boulevard Italiens, I think. After all, what prevents me from taking a cab?* he added, mentally, summoning a passing coupé for hire with a gesture.

"Coachman! Rothschild's!"

"By the hour or the distance, bourgeois?"

"Good God, by the hour; I'm not in a hurry."

"So much the better, bourgeois. I have eleven twenty on my watch."

Never in his life had Naigeot climbed into such a vehicle. He had occasionally taken an omnibus, but only for extraordinary journeys, and he had only ridden in a fiacre two or three times, on the occasion of important ceremonies, such as marriages, baptisms or burials. As chance would have it, the coupé was clean, and even elegant. The interior was lined with green velvet and garnished with assorted trimmings; the windows were bright and the banquettes comfortable. Naigeot settled down as best he could, sunk in a corner, and stretched out his legs in the long silky fur that served as a carpet.

Then he let his overexcited imagination wander through his new dreams, and while he crossed Paris, without having to be careful to avoid dirt or being elbowed by passers-by, he looked back over the years gone by and perceived that he had been horribly unlucky. He saw himself passing by the day before, with his bleak expression and his threadbare coat, his umbrella under his arm, and all his meager accoutrement of an old paper-scratcher; and for the first time, he perceived its hideousness. His entire life appeared to his memory like a despairing mirage. He demanded a reckoning from eternal justice for that constant misery and that brutalizing labor, which had made him the old pedant of yesterday, whom the rich man of today took pleasure in splashing with mud in his imagination. Then he passed through his head whimsical thoughts revolt and vengeance, and then a mad rage to know all the human joys that had been dead letters for him, to catch up in a few days with the youth that had passed unperceived between the four grilled panes of his bookkeeper's cage.

The coupé stopped in the Rue Laffitte outside the offices of the celebrated banker. Naigeot woke up in the middle of his dreams and waited for the coachman to open the door to descend. When he was on the sidewalk he looked at him uncertainly, as if to ask him whether he ought to pay, but the other, who had understood better than his client the convention of being kept for the hour, climbed back on to his seat, letting a scornful gaze fall upon the unaccustomed bourgeois.

"I'll wait for you, then," he said, settling down.

The bookkeeper was amazed. *Good! He knows that I'm rich, no doubt. So much the better! I can travel in a vehicle, in fact!*

He went into the temple of fortune and asked the people he encountered where the cashier was and if, in verity, he could obtain ten thousand francs.

As he approached, he felt his breast burned by the warm effluvia of hope and dread. As he reached the realization of his dream, a secret terror of seeing it vanish nailed Naigeot to the spot on the threshold on the door where the seven capital letters forming the word CASHIER appeared to be flamboyant.

He put his hand to his heart to compress its tumultuous beating, and before turning the handle he had time to realize, with amazement, that he had never felt such a volente emotion.

Finally, he opened the door, approached the grille and passed the draft through the wicket.

The clerk examined it in order to assure himself of its validity and the signature, and without even raising his eyes toward the person presenting it, he silently counted out ten thousand-franc bills.

During that count, Naigeot experienced something akin to vertigo. *Has the world turned upside down?* he asked himself, mentally. *What! It isn't me who's paying, it's me who's being paid! It's no longer me who's behind the grille, it's me who's proudly presenting my entitlements at the door!*

The clerk handed over the banknotes indifferently. Naigeot seized them, counted them again, and remained planted on his legs before the wicket, gazing at his twin with wide eyes.

"Well," exclaimed the other. "Haven't you finished? Leave the place to others now."

Naigeot perceived then that newcomers were pushing him, and stepped back in order to attach the banknotes to his gusset solidly with a pin. Then he headed for the door again, not without having darted a last glance at the desks and the crowd that was pressing at the cashier's station, and not without having lent an ear one last time to the clink of the gold ringing in the bowls.

He rejoined his carriage, wondering whether he was acting in real life or in a temporary phantasmagoria that some stroke of a bell was about to cause to vanish.

"Where to, bourgeois?" asked the coachman.

"Home," said Naigeot, mechanically, "...or, rather, no... yes... wait... do you know where Monsieur Chevet resides?"

"Monsieur Chevet? Well... is that the merchant of comestibles?"

"Yes."

"Good—known! Off we go!"

The coachman whipped his horse and set off in the direction of the Palais-Royal.

During the journey, Naigeot had time to return to recalling his memories.

He entered deliberately into the establishment of the celebrated furnisher of the best tables in the world and asked if a dinner could be brought to him.

"Of course," replied the manager. "For how many people?"

"Twenty."

"Good. What price did you have in mind? Is it the fixed tariff?"

"As you wish. I'll pay the price that's necessary. I want good things."

"Would Monsieur like to make his list?"

"What list?"

"The menu. Would you like a truffled turkey for the roast?"

"Yes, that's it!" cried Naigeot, enthusiastically, for he remembered having heard mention of truffled turkey as an exquisite dish reserved for rich people. "Yes that's it—a truffled turkey!"

"And with it a turbot in lobster sauce, a bisque, quail in pastry, a pheasant salmi…," said the merchant of comestibles volubly, who realized immediately what he was dealing with.

"Yes…yes…yes…that's it," Naigeot repeated, overjoyed at hearing so many good things proposed, of which he had never heard mention.

"With suitable hors-d'oeuvres, entremets, dessert and wines?"

Yes, yes…here's my address: Rue Copeau, Pension Buneaud. Ask for Monsieur François Naigeot, the brother of Monsieur Dominique Naigeot, who…"

"That's all right; that's sufficient, Monsieur. At what time?"

"Six o'clock."

I believe I'm going to dine well, Naigeot thought, as he climbed back into his coupé, *and those poor devils too! The fact is that it isn't good, Papa Buneaud's cuisine. Pooh!*

"Where to now, bourgeois?" asked the coachman.

"Take me wherever you wish. Where do the rich people go?"

"The Champs-Élysées? The Bois?"

"Yes,"

Naigeot allowed himself to be conducted, abandoning himself to his dreams, well ensconced in his coupé, like a cat in its fur when it makes its "wheel," as housewives say.

After two hours of traveling, however, he began to examine the carriages that were passing his coupé in all directions and comparing the outfits of the riders who were making their horses prance on the road with his own. Only then did he perceive that the fortune had not yet changed his dull appearance, and his garments, worn at the elbows and shiny at the knees.

"Coachman," he said, "I want to go to a tailor. Take me back to the Palais-Royal! There must be tailors at the Palais-Royal!"

When the coachman, setting him down in the Cour des Fontaines, asked him for eight francs for fur hour, the bookkeeper's first movement was a start of astonishment; but he paid promptly.

Am I not rich? he said to himself. "Here, my good man."

"And my tip?"

Naigeot rummaged in his pocket and pulled out five sous, majestically. *It appears that rich people give tips,* he thought.

And he drew away without hearing the maledictions of the coachman, who was calling him a thief.

He went under the arcades in the middle of the crowd, bumping into passers-by, marching at random--- or, rather, in accordance with the fantasies of the intoxication of Paris that was beginning to seize him. Each boutique attracted the dazzled gaze of the enriched bookkeeper in its turn. He had traversed the Palais-Royal a thousand times in every direction, but he had never paid any attention to the displays that offered strollers all the creations of luxury. Like the monk interrogated regarding the beauty of a famous courtesan, he was able to respond, speaking of Paris: *I saw it, but I didn't look!*

This time, on the contrary, he devoured, all eyes, the rich fabrics, the golden fruits, the diamonds with a thousand facets and the women who were admiring them. Here, he ordered a waistcoat whose silky palms had seduced him; there he bought a gold watch, a chain with charm, to avenge himself for having aspired to those things all his life without having been able to obtain them; further on an incrusted tortoiseshell snuff-box, a cravat-pin, a lorgnon and an elegant collar.

Gradually, he reached the passages of the Rue Vivienne, still walking through Paris as if in the realm of the fays. It was four o'clock, but it was foggy and the gas was illuminated everywhere, mingling its ruddy light though the mist with the dying daylight. Naigeot was still going straight ahead, naively astonished by the splendors of the great city, where he had lived for fifty years, as if he were a beardless student arrived from his province the day before, wandering in the midst of animated groups discussing rises and falls in the Place de la Bourse and throwing money without counting it at all his fantasies.

When he reached the boulevard he had already ordered a complete outfit, which he augmented continually with new garments. Finally, he stopped, weary of seeing gold shine and velvet sparkle, his pockets full and his hands charged with rings. He wanted to see the rich people, after having savored the joys of wealth. He mingled with the idle strollers, the elegant women, remarking, on the one hand, the gracious costumes and the proud gait of those who accosted those queens of the world; and on the other, seizing in passage "frozen" words, as Rabelais put it.

"Can you lend me ten louis?" one young man asked another. "I've come out without any money; I'm dining with Lucie and we're going to the theater afterwards."

"What a mantlet you have there, my dear, and what lace!" two women further on, surrounded by admirers, were saying.

"Oh, nothing! Simply Chantilly, and not dear, of course—fifty francs a meter."

"I lost five hundred francs at lansquenet yesterday."

"Damn!"

"Bah! I won two thousand last month."

Naigeot, dazed by the noise of carriages, the lights and the buzz of the crowd, collected these scraps of phrases avidly, and, in spite of his confusion, gathered all of his bookkeeping faculties in order to construct fantastic fortunes with those figures dropped at hazard. He calculated fearfully how many thousand livres of income it required to dine with Lucie, to give a woman lace worth at least fifty francs a meter, to gamble, to have carriages, etc., etc. A veil tore in the torpid intelligence of the unfortunate cashier; the abysms of luxury opened their infinite depths before him, vertigo seized him and he was perhaps about to fall when he was recalled to himself by the impact of a carriage-pole.

He perceived that darkness had fallen completely and that the restaurants were filled with customers.

Good God! he thought. *Am I going to be late?*

The idea that rich people could lack exactitude had not yet entered the head of the bookkeeper.

He hailed a cab precipitately, climbed aboard and shouted "Rue Copeau!" to the coachman as six o'clock chimed.

Rue Copeau!

How far it was from that filthy back street to the Boulevard de Gand, from illuminated clubs to the smoky refectory of Père Buneaud, from the dirty Naigeot who went along the Rue Saint-Martin yesterday to add up other people's receipts and outgoings to the Naigeot who was traversing Paris in a coupé in order to do honor to a dinner served by Chevet!

Once, he had envisaged the figure of an annual income of six hundred livres as the paradise of his dreams; now, his needs and desires were progressing by the hour; he was dreaming of millions; he experienced in inextinguishable thirst for riches and pleasures.

When he arrived at the bourgeois boarding-house he found the house, ordinarily so sad, full of noise and merriment. The soup had been served, the delicate hors-d'oeuvres were arranged around the table, and unaccustomed dishes were arriving from the kitchen, where a cooking-pot arrived from the Maison Chevet was simmering. Buneaud was running like a madman from the kitchen to the cellar and from the cellar to the dining room. The old folk seemed to be having a ball, and the young ones gave their benefactor the noisiest of ovations. A few students, seeing such fine fare, had gone to fetch their mistresses in order to enable them to participate in that feast, on various pretexts, and those ladies surrounded the aged bookkeeper with their most seductive coquetries.

Naigeot blossomed with happiness and gave himself entirely to the delights of the table, the noisy communicative joy and the caresses of the crazy children of pleasure who were finally making him forget the majestic graces of Madame Gobain. He was living as he had never lived. His blood was running hot in his veins and beating in his arteries at a hundred pulsations a minute. One might have thought that his body was participating in the rejuvenation of his mind, so much younger and stronger did he seem; what a fount of youth, hope and happiness are!

He was the last to quit the table and go up to bed, intoxicated by all intoxications, fascinated, stuffed and crazy, but still demanding luxury and pleasure.

Finally, slumber put an end to all the revolts of youth, thirty years late; Naigeot went to sleep and dreamed of the feasts of Sardanapalus and the houris of Mahomet.

The next morning, when he woke up in his bedroom, so bare, so cold and so scantly propitious to illusion, he thought at first that he had returned to reality after a deceptive dream. Gradually, however, he recovered his senses and rediscovered his memories in the form of a host of new objects scattered here and there. He leapt out of bed, seized his waistcoat, forgotten on a chair in the abandon of drunkenness and detached the blessed banknotes feverishly in order to count them again at his ease. But it was in vain that he recommenced the count twice; he only found nine; the dinner, the purchases and the rest had taken one of them...

Hum! thought the bookkeeper, returning to himself. *At that rate, I'll only have enough for nine days...which is to say, eight, given that I'll have to pay for my orders...*

Naigeot remained thoughtful for a moment. Then, suddenly, he shook off his preoccupations.

Eh! What does it matter, after all? he said to himself. *Do I not have a fortune ready made in America?*

By virtue of a singular phenomenon, his passions, contained by fifty years of poverty, had awakened with an extraordinary violence. He felt gripped by the follies and vertiginous aspirations of youth. He was dreaming of amour, luxury, horses, and the thousand pleasures that fortune gives when one is twenty years old. Perhaps none of that was clearly formulated in his mind, but he saw the whole of the previous day passing before his imagination like a phantasmagoria; he recapitulated all the enjoyments that he had glimpsed and would have liked to have them all.

Oh, yes, yes! he said to himself, *to live no matter what it costs, to savor all joys, to drink from all cups of pleasure, to seize again at whatever price, a few days of lost youth...and then depart!*

Are the rich not happy everywhere? And anyway, I'll hasten to make a fortune, and I'll come back...to Paris!

"After all, I'm not old yet!" he exclaimed, raising himself up on one foot, the poor bookkeeper who, twenty-four hours before, had not had the courage to wager three francs on his future!

II

Three months have gone by. We are in New Orleans. The port is in uproar, for a French ship has just arrived. Americans are agitating all over the dock, awaiting merchandise or voyagers. The harbor-pilots are hastening around the ship with their launches to disembark the passengers.

The heat is torrid. The deep blue sky is cloudless. The sea is equally blue. The sun is drying its rays vertically upon the crowd, cutting out the shadows neatly in curt black silhouettes. Meanwhile, the Americans, in straw hats and white jackets, surround the new arrivals, in order to be the first to know what news old Europe is sending them. People are shouting, coming and going, shoving one another. Luggage is being unloaded on to the dock; sailors, negroes, men of all colors are piling into carriages to transport them in haste. There is a general hubbub, noise and movement, of which only those familiar with the prodigious activity of great mercantile cities can have any idea.

In the midst of the disembarking passengers, a stout bald man is agitating frantically, seemingly arguing with the ship's accountant and giving orders loudly to the sailors, with a self-important attitude.

That is François Naigeot, who is settling his account and handing over, for the price of his passage, the last écus that remain to him. After having spent the ten thousand francs sent to him by his brother, he has sold his annuity at a rock-bottom price in order to pay for the expenses of his journey. He is arriving with empty pockets but with a heart full of hope, and it is in a assured voice that he gives the order to take his luggage to the establishment of Dominique Naigeot and Company.

"Oh, Monsieur, that's not my affair," replied the sailor, drawing away from the ship with a vigorous thrust of the oars. "I'll put you down on the shore with your trunks, and you can make arrangements to be taken into the city with the colored men you see over there on the dock."

François had scarcely set foot on land than he shouted to a mulatto: "I'm the brother of Monsieur Dominique Naigeot, friend, Take me to his house with my luggage, and quickly!"

The laborer raised his eyes to his interlocutor with an expression of astonishment and uncertainty.

"Don't you know the Maison Naigeot, one of the richest in New Orleans?" said François, in a tone of self-important disdain that chilled the mulatto.

"The Mason Naigeot! Oh, yes, Monsieur," he babbled, in a patois half-French and half-English. "I've carried enough bales of sugar and cotton for the Maison Naigeot in my lifetime...but..."

"Well, what? What *but* can there be?"

"Oh, nothing, Monsieur, nothing," murmured the unhappy mulatto, evidently troubled, pulling his cart more forcefully in order not to continue the conversation.

They don't know me here; I'll evidently cause a sensation, the bookkeeper said to himself, following his luggage with great difficulty. *The name of Naigeot has an effect, eh! I must get accustomed to this land, where one gets rich rapidly. And my word, people will be saying before long: the Maison Naigeot frères...*

After all, it seems that one might well live here for a few years. If my sister-in-law is amiable and if my niece is as charming as the worthy Dominique says, it will truly be a pleasure to make a fortune in their company... During the day one can occupy oneself with affairs, the evening will be all pleasure: visits given or returned, assemblies, balls, concerts, spectacles, excursions at sea. I wasn't a bad swimmer once... I went up the Seine from the Pont de Bercy to the Pont-Royal. I believe that I was even stronger than dear Dominique...

"It's here, Monsieur" said the mulatto, stopping his vehicle.

François Naigeot shuddered like a man waking up with a start, raised his head, and perceived vast warehouses cluttered with bales, and busy people coming and going.

His heart was beating rapidly as he made his entrance into that new family and that new life. He pushed the lattice door, fitted with a bell, that separated the rather poorly-paved site of the warehouses from the street, resolutely, and he advanced between two rows of tarred crates.

"Monsieur Dominique Naigeot, if you please?" he asked, in a loud voice, approaching a group of people who were discussing the price of colonial commodities.

At that name, all the interlocutors fell silent and looked at the newcomer in amazement. A tall blonde woman entirely dressed in black, who was taking an active part in the discussion, turned toward him swiftly.

"We have had the misfortune of losing Monsieur Naigeot, Monsieur," she said, in a curt voice, affected by an unusual emotion, "but I'm continuing my husband's business, and you can address yourself to me for anything regarding commerce: orders or recovery, claims, brokerage or anything else. Would you like to go to the back of the warehouse, and, in the meantime, explain yourself to those messieurs who are writing over there in the glazed office? I'll come to join you shortly."

Assuredly, a lightning bolt falling at François Naigeot's feet could not have felled him like that news, with overturned at a stroke all his projects, all his hopes, and his entire future. He gazed at the woman with the energetic face, prompt gestures and precise speech, who had become the arbiter of his fate, without seeing her, and he spun around, as if stunned by his fall.

At his sister-in-law's words, so simple and so natural, he had felt the ground tremble under his feet, and all his castles in Spain collapse simultaneously. The Naigeot who had trod the soil of America so proudly a little while ago suddenly gave way to the former boarder of the Buneaud house. He trembled, and paraded an uncertain gaze around him.

"My brother... is dead? You're... my sister?" the unfortunate stammered, leaning on the heaped-up bales.

116

"Your brother?" repeated the widow, with astonishment.

"What! Mad... my dear sister, have you not heard mention of me? Did he not announce my arrival to you? Oh, Dominique, Dominique... my dear Dominique, my good brother!" cried François, finally able to weep.

The widow looked at him attentively, and doubtless found in that unfamiliar face a few of her husband's features, for she approached and held out her hand to him.

"I confess that I didn't expect you, my brother," she said, "and that my husband only spoke about you vaguely, but be welcome nevertheless. Ménard!" she shouted to one of the employees whom she had designated to François at the back of the warehouse. "Ménard, would you be good enough to take Monsieur to my daughter."

François Naigeot got ready to follow the employee, His sister-in-law had already resumed the commercial conversation that his arrival had interrupted. However, on seeing him draw away she added: "We'll get acquainted later; my good Ménard, give the order to have the luggage that's by the door brought in, won't you?"

Naigeot followed the clerk through warehouses, corridors and staircases, without being conscious of himself, as if drawn along fatally. He could no longer see, and from time to time he bumped into walls or furniture. The precariousness of his situation, the uncertainty of his fate and the coldness of his sister-in-law's reception were crushing him, so he gave little thought to the niece that he was about to see, and of whom his brother had spoken so eulogistically.

He scarcely noticed the change of aspect of the establishment when he had quit the warehouses to go into the apartments. However, nothing contrasted more with the simplicity of the hangars and offices than the elegance and comfort of the upper floors.

If he had observed that difference immediately, he would have understood that a young and charming woman, amorous of all delicacies, must live there and must take pleasure in arranging garden flowers and the songs of rare birds, but he had not seen anything or looked at anything, and when the employee, opening a door, put him in the presence of a young woman of striking beauty and exquisite grace, he uttered an exclamation of astonishment, as if he had suddenly found himself transported into another world.

"Mademoiselle," said Ménard, "This is the Monsieur that Madame your mother has sent to you—and who is, I believe, one of your relatives?" he added, interrogating François with his gaze.

"My dear niece!" exclaimed the ex-bookkeeper, genuinely moved, in the midst of his dolors, by the ravishing apparition.

The young woman raised large astonished eyes upon Francis, and bowed. Then she searched in vain to decide what reception she ought to give the unexpected relative. Fortunately, her mother arrived to extract her from embarrassment.

"Louise, Monsieur is your uncle, your father's brother," she said. "He has arrived from France aboard the *Vulcain*, whose captain I've just seen. Give him a good welcome, for you know that I can't occupy myself with him for now. After dinner, we'll talk, my brother!"

"Sit down near me, so that I can see you and recognize you, Uncle—for truly, your features remind me so much of cherished features that I ought to have thrown my arms around you at first sight..."

"Dear child!"

"But it's necessary to pardon my astonishment and surprise, and also," she added, with a hint of sadness, "the shock that the resemblance causes me..."

"Dominique had written to me that you were beautiful, and that you would receive me well, dear niece," said Naigeot, moved by hearing such sympathetic words, "but..."

"But what, Uncle? Dud he deceive you?"

"You're even more beautiful than I thought," the bookkeeper replied, naively.

She was, in fact, a delightful creature, Louise Naigeot: one of those exceptional beauties who seduce at first sight because they are complete, and draw an indefinable charm from the general harmony of the figure, the gestures and the voice, which no dissonance disrupts. Louise might have been eighteen years old at the most. She was blonde, but of a warm shade, like the blondes that Venetian artists have painted for us. She had the supple figure and the delicately pretty extremities of creoles, their soft and rounded movements without their languid idleness. On the contrary, she allied with that grace a vivacity of allure and repartee that added one attraction more to her whole person.

Never had Madame Gobain's ex-cashier, the sad boarder of the Buneaud house, seen anything that resembled, even distantly, that adorable young woman. He remained bewildered before her as before an ideal figure glimpsed in a dream, and he forgot all the events that put in question his present and his future.

Louise, who had not quit her father during the final months of his life, was not unaware of his regrets on the subject of the family in France too long forgotten. So, now that her mother had introduced her uncle to her, she tried, by the cordiality of her welcome, to repay the paternal debt. She was especially gracious and seductive for the bookkeeper. She sat down beside him, embraced him, and said a host of kind and affectionate things. Then she took him to visit the house, where François Naigeot admired for the first time the combination of luxury and wellbeing that cannot be improvised, but which comes slowly with years of habitude and fortune. She told him the names of her favorite birds and those of her mother's clerks: two old men whom she remembered always having seen in the same place, with the same faces, since she had come into the world. She talked to him about the city, American customs, her young friends and, in sum, everything that she thought capable of interesting him.

François Naigeot listened as if to celestial music to all that still-childish babble; gradually, he yielded to the charm of the conversation and the caresses, wondering if his life of the last three months had been a dream or a reality—if fortune really had come to seek him out in the Buneaud house in order to render him his lost youth and all the happiness that he had neglected to obtain at its time; and he inclined toward hope, toward calm, toward happy ideas. He told himself that, after all, the death of his brother did not destroy his future; that the two women left to govern such an important establishment alone would need help, and that he was their natural support. He smiled at the idea of living with such a charming niece, of being her only friend, and he was already recommencing the series of his castles in Spain already seeing himself, rich and fortunate, taking Louise back to France, to make her shine like the pole star in the midst of the Parisian constellations, when the dinner bell rang.

That was the moment when he was about to find himself in the presence of his sister-in-law again and make the acquaintance of the other residents of the house. Meanwhile, he followed his niece into the dining room almost reassured, almost happy.

Madame Dominique Naigeot had announced him as her brother-in-law. When he appeared, she introduced him, one after another, to the two clerks who had been part of the family for many years, and a young man who was the last to enter and came to make his compliments to Louise with great urgency.

"Monsieur Ménard," she said first, "whom you have already seen, my brother—not an employee but an old friend of the house.

"Monsieur Naudin, a great commercial intelligence and my best adviser.

"Monsieur Charles Montessier, the son of Monsieur Guillaume Montessier of Boston, and my future son-on-law."

Why, at that final introduction, did François experience a shock to the heart that suddenly put a stop to his happy thoughts? No one, perhaps, any more than him, could have said, but he felt a surge of hatred against the young man who sat down beside Louise, and who spoke to her with the ease of permitted happiness. It was rapid, like a thought that is born and dies in a fraction of a second, but enough trace of it remained for the uncle to be unable to salute his future nephew amicably.

The dinner was cheerful, however, for Louise, who was the queen of the dwelling for everyone, animated the conversation with joyous bursts of good humor. It was already nearly six months since Dominique Naigeot had died, and in young minds nature, full of sap, soon expels sad memories. Between her fiancé, who loved her, and her uncle, of whom she was making a fuss, she found it easy to be charming. The old clerks, whose idol she was, provided echoes of her joy, and Naigeot could not help listening to her and looking at her with delight.

Only Madame Naigeot seemed preoccupied. At dessert she engaged her daughter to go for a walk on the jetty with the clerks and Charles. After half an hour of general conversation everyone left, and she remained alone with her brother-in-law.

"Well," she said to him, "you must have experienced a cruel disappointment on arriving here? You've come to find sad news."

"That's true, my sister. When one makes such a long voyage in order to see a brother again, it's terrible to arrive too late... but you and your daughter have both given me such a good welcome that I dare not...and then..."

Naigeot stopped, not knowing how to finish his sentence. He sensed that the moment for explanations had come, and he was trembling.

"My husband did not say much to me about his family," the widow went on. "It's necessary for you not to be astonished if your arrival has surprised me. I will even admit to you that if the captain of the *Vulcain*, who is one of my friends, had not assured me of your identity, I would have hesitated to receive you in my house, in spite of a certain resemblance to your brother. What do you expect? I have a great responsibility, and...."

"But my sister, here is a letter that I received from Dominique. He engages me to come; he talks about you and my niece, about his affairs, and so on. I'm astonished that you have no knowledge of it."

"My God, it's now nine months since that letter was written. There was vague mention of it at the time, but I didn't pay any great attention to the idea of a sick man, and I admit that... I was no longer thinking about it."

"Read it, my sister," said Naigeot, opening his brother's letter himself in order finally to place the thorny questions squarely.

While his sister-in-law was reading, the poor brother trembled, anguish in his heart, and followed with his eyes the clouds that passed over her forehead, and her energetic and decided expression.

He experienced both impatience and anger on seeing his fate, by virtue of a caprice of destiny, entirely in the hands of that woman, who had scarcely suspected his existence the day before, and whom no bond any longer attached to him.

When she had finished reading, she turned the letter in her hands several times, with a visible embarrassment. Finally, she broke the silence.

"So, my brother," she said, "you've come here with the intention of entering into the commerce?"

"Yes... my sister," Francois stammered, his voice cut by emotion.

"But do you know commerce?"

"Undoubtedly, since I've been a cashier and bookkeeper for thirty years."

"Ah! Well, that might serve you. Evidently, before long you'll find a suitable position."

"I'll find!" he cried, bounding in his seat as if he had suffered an electric shock. "I'll find! What do you mean by that? On coming to my brother's house, at his invitation, I believed that I would be established there."

"Of course; and as long as I remain at the head of the house myself, you'll have an assured place here, but I'm marrying my daughter at the expiration of her mourning and I'm retiring from the business. On my recommendation, however, it's probable that my successor will keep you on. I can even make it a condition if you desire.

"And," said Naigeot, hardly able to believe his ears, "it's a place as an employee that you're offering me?"

"But what do you expect, then, my brother?"

"So," he said, beside himself and almost choked by anger, "Dominique has left an immense fortune; I arrive in France after having sold my last piece of bread in order to come, and I find here the ledger and the meager salary that I quit in Paris! And when you've departed, taking away your millions and my niece, I'll have an uncertain shelter in a strange house...far from France! Oh, no, Madame! No, it can't happen like that!"

"And how will it happen, then, Monsieur?" demanded the widow, staring him in the face,

"After all, Madame, I am François Naigeot, Dominique Naigeot's legitimate brother, and I ought not to be thus frustrated of his succession."

"Frustrated! Get away, my brother," she said, calmly. "You're mad. Reflect, and dot get carried away so quickly. Let's not commence our relations with a quarrel and let's look at the situation together. You'll understand that I'm doing for you all that I can."

"Ah!"

"Undoubtedly. My husband, in dying, naturally left his fortune to his daughter, did he not? By what right do you demand a share of it? To what law are you appealing? So long as he was alive he was perfectly free to give you whatever he wished. He could have sent you a hundred thousand francs instead of ten thousand, and we would have had nothing to say about it. Believe that we would even have seen him giving you wealth with pleasure. He might also, as you suppose, on a fictitious basis, have associated you with his affairs. But today, can I take away from my daughter a portion of her father's fortune in order to give it to you? She is marrying, and bringing her inheritance as a dowry. I count on abandoning a part of my own wealth to her. You see, the position is quite clear, and, unfortunately, I can neither alter it or modify it."

Naigeot, dumbfounded by that logic, which fell upon his dreams of fortune like a cascade of icy water, wept with rage on recognizing his total impotence. If he had abandoned himself to the fury of his unleashed passions he would have strangled that woman, who, with her tranquil words, had just annihilated all his hopes, placed an insurmountable barrier before all his aspirations and imprisoned him forever behind the grille of the back room of a shop, where he had lived: a paperscratcher still, as before, but without his indifference and his regrets in addition.

He tried to protest again, in a halting voice, for, until the last moment, he refused to accept his misfortune, but the widow stood up in order not to continue a painful discussion any longer.

"You'll reflect, my brother," she said, as she went out, "and you'll understand that I'm right. In any case, I'll make you a very supportable life here and you'll find yourself, even after our departure, better off than in France."

When the poor bookkeeper was alone, he uttered cries to exhale his dolor. He writhed, he rolled on the floor, he cursed Heaven and implored Hell. All the enjoyments glimpsed and dreamed of, all the intoxications he had brushed, like the preludes to more entire intoxications, suddenly reappeared before his imagination like a troop of phantoms, which surrounded him like a magic circle, dancing madly around him and appealing to him by turns with their most seductive smiles. Then, thirsty for pleasure, when he tried to launch himself toward them, they drew away from his efforts, laughing, or vanished into smoke, leaving before his a large open ledger, an inkwell, a worn leather lectern and a black desk.

Certainly, if Satan had appeared to him at that moment, as he used to appear, in a tangible form, and had asked him for his soul, Naigeot would have sold it without hesitation and without regret, in order to seize the fortune with which evil spirits had lured him, in order to annihilate forever the clerical apparatus that had enveloped his youth in a shroud of blackened paper...

"My uncle, what are you doing here all alone?" a harmonious voice suddenly asked him, while two small cool hands were placed over his eyes. "Are you asleep?"

Naigeot raised his head, seized the pert little hands in his, and looked at Louise, who was laughing, agitating her blonde curls around his head.

Then he made her sit down next to him, played with the flaps of her white dress, with her slender pink fingers, with the pearls of her necklace, kissed her forehead, her eyes and her cheeks, and fled like a madman.

Alas, necessity is a fatal law, which no one can resist. It was therefore in vain that Naigeot revolted against his sister-in-law's propositions, that he agitated in all directions, and that he formulated the most extreme projects in succession. A short time after his arrival he had once again taken up the pen, the ink, the black desk, the worn lectern and the great ledger of parchment with coppery green corners, the blue and gold sand, the penknife, the scraper and the sandarac; he had been given half the employment of Naudin, who only kept the cashbox. From eight o'clock in the morning until six o'clock in the evening he made flourishes, drew lines of ink and counted the receipts and outgoings of the Maison Dominique Naigeot.

Destiny, after having transported him momentarily into superior regions, had thrown him back pitilessly behind the grille that he had fled. Only, it had come in search of a poor, brutalized being, forgotten by others and forgetful of himself, inoffensive and resigned; and it rendered him a man enraged at having lost his life, cursing his past, blaming God and the entire world for his misfortune: a man avid for enjoyments that he divined but could not know, envious of the wealth of others, incessantly devoured by insensate desires, constantly tempted …and devoid of hope!

Yes, that bald and withered man, that quasi-dotard, is dreaming of a thousand impossible or criminal things, sharpening his pens between his brother's two aged clerks. He says very little, but his silence is replete with stormy thoughts. While he is believed to be occupied in some regulation of accountancy, he is calculating the chances of death, or other events by means of which he might attain a part of the immense fortune that is passing by him without stopping; while he is making up the balance of the day, or the monthly account, his rebellious heart is beating with hatred against Charles Montessier, that unknown, that stranger who will soon be the possessor of the fortune inscribed in the great ledger of human prosperities under the name of Naigeot, and of the adorable creature who has awakened a twenty-year-old heart in a fifty-year-old body.

Foe, it is necessary to say that since Naigeot has seen Louise, so radiant and beautiful, a new revolution has taken place within him. All his disappointed aspirations have come together in a single passion, as violent, insensate and inexorable as only the passions of old men can be who want to avenge themselves, by means of one last joy, for their squandered youth. He is madly in love with his niece. In vain he represents to himself, in his lucid moments, that no plausible event will arrive to change his life; that his fate is fixed forever; that he has for a future solitude and misery; and that the young woman, finally, treats him as an uncle and a friend, but keeps her amour for her fiancé; he senses invincible desires seething within him; he feels a hot blood flowing in his veins that rises to his head and intoxicates him.

His nights are full of tempting and deceptive dreams. Sometimes, he sees gold streaming like a river that opens space to him and overturns all the obstacles on its banks; sometimes, Louise appears to him, more beautiful than ever, and appeals to him with amorous words.

And yet, he says to himself on awakening, *that fortune and Louise might be mine! An uncle can marry his niece... What prevents me from seizing both happinesses at once? Monsieur Charles Montessier! A stranger to me...an insignificant, futile individual who could disappear tomorrow without... But no! I'm mistaken! If I were to put paid to that Montessier, the mother would still be there, watching over her daughter incessantly, defending her fortune, organizing the future with her infernal activity and her inflexible will; it's the mother that forbids all hope!*

And the pensive Naigeot allows his inactive pen to fall upon the big book. He does not hear his sister-in-law's voice announcing a debit or an entry to him. One of the clerks whispers in the other's ear, "The poor fellow isn't strong; it will be necessary to pay attention to his accounts!"

At other times, on the contrary, he plunges feverishly into infinite calculations, in order to estimate approximately the fortune that he envies with an ever-increasing rage, and he deploys a singular intelligence.

But what does not vary is his hatred against everything that surrounds Louise; against his brother's widow, against Charles Montessier, against Ménard and Naudin, who second their employer with all their strength, make a fuss over Charles, and talk incessantly about Louise's marriage.

In addition, those clerks, interested in the house for more than twenty years, are going to retire with a tidy fortune at the same time as Madame Dominique Naigeot; and the bookkeeper shudders with anger in thinking that he alone, who bears the opulent name of Naigeot, will remain in the business of his brother's successor, attached to the toil of his odious métier of scribbling clerk!

But if she loved me, he said to himself, *what would all that matter? If I could take possession of that heart, capture that naïve mind which knows nothing of life as yet...! And after all, why shouldn't she love me? The ardor of my passion might warm her dormant heart! She might sense, beneath my words, the beating of my heart! That Montessier doesn't love her like that!*

And he tried to steal, by surprise, his niece's heart, in order to enable him to glimpse another life than the one that awaited him in America with his future.

"Wouldn't you love," he said to her, to come to Paris, where your beauty and your millions would make you a queen? Where you'd see fêtes of which you can't even conceive the idea, a luxury that has no parallel in the world? Where you'd live incessantly in the midst of splendors, where your carriages would eclipse those of princesses?"

"Yes!" cried Louise, kissing her uncle's jaundiced forehead joyfully. "Yes, certainly, I desire to be beautiful, to amuse myself, to go to balls, to live in Paris! But Charles will take me there!"

Struck in the heart, Naigeot cursed yet again that man who had stolen Louise and Dominique's millions from him, and he tried to steal a few feverish kisses from the ignorant young woman.

"To be loved well is also a joy, child! What if, every day, at every hour, you sensed an infinite love beside you... an intoxicating, mad passion... which would make your husband your slave... who would surround you with all pleasures..."

"Charles loves me well!" she said.

While the bookkeeper, devoured by his increasing passion, abandoned himself to the craziest dreams, to the most absurd projects, time went by. Every day, the dreaded epoch of Louise's marriage drew nearer. Already, the preparations for the celebration were occupying the whole household. One might have thought that the mother had an intuition of the evil passions that were agitating her brother-in-law, and that she desired to hasten the marriage.

Naigeot suffered martyrdom. He would have like to prevent time from flowing, the future from arriving, events from being accomplished. But if he clung in vain to shreds of hope, his reason incessantly showed him his impotence, as if to crush him. He sensed that all resistance was futile, and yet...

And yet, at the price of his life, at the price of his soul, he wanted to triumph!

Suddenly, a sinister rumor spreads through the city; the promenades are deserted, the houses closed. It is announced that, with the advent of the dog days, yellow fever has arrived to claim its annual harvest. Coffins circulate; mourning-dress appears on all sides; everyone fears for his family, for himself. The scourge, it is said, is more redoubtable than ever. There is not one house without a funereal exhibition, not one family that is not weeping for one of its members.

What if they were to die! Naigeot said to himself, while writing an account under the dictation of his sister-in-law. *If three biers were to deliver me of the mother and the two clerks!*

And surges of warm blood rose to his brain rose into his brain. He experienced a sort of daze.

How quickly I would liquidate! How soon I would take her away, as her natural guardian! How cheaply I would get rid of the Montessiers! How quickly I would marry Louise… willingly or by force, damn it!

"Are you afraid, Monsieur Naudin?" he asked his neighbor to the left, his voice strangled by emotion.

"Oh, my God no! First of all, since it's necessary to die, what does it matter which disease will carry me away? I'm sixty years old and, in truth, death can take me whenever it wishes. I've lived!"

"You're very happy, then?" exclaimed the bookkeeper.

"And then, you see, we're old soldiers, the two of us; we've already fought the beast and vanquished it. Now, there are few examples of the yellow fever returning to its victims twice."

"It carries them away or it shows them mercy," said Ménard,

"Personally, I haven't had it, my friends, and I want to safeguard my responsibilities," said the widow, gravely. "So, I ought to arrange my affairs for any eventuality. We'll meet this evening. I'll alert my sister; Montessier will come and I'll make him party to my dispositions."

"My dear Madame, don't alarm yourself thus; you're habituated to the climate, you're strong; besides which, at the slightest symptom all the physicians in the city would be here."

"My sister!"

"Oh be tranquil, my friends. You know that my mind doesn't alarm easily. I have every hope of not getting the fever, but I have my duty as a businesswoman and my duty as a mother, that's all! Come on, my brother, quit that sinister expression and don't be afraid!"

"Yes, Monsieur François, it's necessary not to believe that the yellow fever carries away anyone who isn't American by birth!"

François Naigeot had, in fact, gone horribly pale.

The idea that the epidemic might, in a single day, remove all the obstacles to his happiness, and that the mother looming up between him and Louise like an inflexible barrier might suddenly disappear, had been succeeded by another, horrible, poignant and infernal.

But what if I were to die? If the yellow fever took me, a foreigner? If I fell here, poor and unknown, without having possessed either a fortune nor amour, without having emerged from my back room, without having savored any of the joys of life...oh, no, that's impossible! And yet...

That evening there was a family council of sorts. Madame Naigeot's sister came, with her husband. She too was an intelligent and strong woman who had once conducted important affairs and willingly associated her-self with courageous measures. Montessier was grave, and affectionate toward everyone. Louise was sad on seeing that almost funereal solemnity, for the two clerks brought a notary go the house.

"My friends," said the widow, "I'm going to make my testament; but please don't be convinced that you're at my interment. I've never been healthier than I am to-day, but during an epidemic it's necessary to anticipate anything. If something bad happens to me, I want my affairs to be in order. Thank God," she added, laughing, "testaments have never killed anyone!"

Those people, habituated to take life seriously, to manage their fortune and that of others, promptly put themselves in unison with Madame Naigeot. All painful sentiment vanished; they simply talked about the liqui-dation of the Maison Dominique Naigeot and the manner of transferring all of her mother and father's fortune to Louise. Naudin, Ménard and Charles Montessier agreed on the means of execution, as a matter that only con-cerned them. Then they passed on to family arrange-ments. Madame Naigeot expressed the wish that her daughter marry Charles Montessier immediately if she should die. She asked her sister to serve as mother to the orphan in that instance and to receive her in her home until the marriage ceremony. "My brother," she added, "Monsieur François Naigeot, will naturally replace my husband as his niece's legal guardian."

That was the first time there had been mention of the bookkeeper in all the affairs to be regulated, Perhaps he had never felt as foreign to his brother's family as at that moment.

Madame Naigeot doubtless remarked a painful con-traction of his features, for she went on in an amicable tone, turning toward the clerk: "These Messieurs know, my brother, that in ceding the house to Stephenson & Son of London, I have imposed as a condition that you keep your present position. I will not mention the small annual income that I am recommending my heirs to give you when you retire from commerce. That goes without saying."

Naigeot nodded his head, unable to articulate a word. It was necessary for him to express gratitude, and anger choked him. He would have liked to kill with a look all the people who had just carved him a slice of that fortune in his repose, that future from which he alone was excluded.

So, he thought, *this is my fate! The odious work that I've been doing for thirty years, as long as I have hands with which to write, eyes to distinguish figures and a head free enough to count... and after that, the bread of an invalid. I'm a pawn in a game of chess, or a zero that has no other function than to give a value to the number that precedes it. All these people are going to take away a fortune; Montessier is stealing Louise from me... I'll be left in a corner... and if, by chance, they have need of me some day, they'll come to fetch me, like a piece of furniture, like an old family portrait, only to send me away thereafter.* "Oh, but I'll avenge myself," he murmured between clenched teeth, his gaze fixed.

And he thought that, six months before, that life would have seemed like paradise!

When the notary had written down all that had been dictated to him, refreshments were served. The conversation continued, but it took on a less serious tone.

Louise came to offer a sorbet to her uncle, making him a thousand caresses. She understood that, of all those in attendance, he had the smallest share of good fortune, and as she could not expel from his visage the somber reflection of his thoughts, she added in a low voice: "We love you, my good uncle. If you're bored here, you can come to Boston with us. Isn't that right Charles?"

The young man hastened to join in with his fiancée in expressing his affection to the disinherited uncle; but Naigeot stood up, still in no state to respond, and suffocated by the most violent passions. After having paced back and forth in the drawing room he went out. All of Hell was passing through his heart.

As they separated, the family agreed that Charles ought to choose the moment of the epidemic to make a final journey to Boston before the marriage. Madame Naigeot's sister offered to take Louise to her country house on one of the islands in the Mississippi delta— where, she said, yellow fever was less to be feared that in the city.

In spite of the pleas of Charles Montessier, the latter matter was not settled immediately. The mother hesitated to quit her daughter, even momentarily, and Louise did not want to absent herself at a moment when the epidemic, being at the height of its violence, might render a separation of a few days eternal. The decision was postponed until the next day, and the family members dispersed.

Naigeot had shut himself in his room, where he was agitating, pursued by furies. The idea that such struggles might tear apart the human heart had never occurred to him. He felt, by turns, the most dissimilar resolutions succeeding one another in his mind and disintegrating one after another. It seemed to him that a hurricane, as violent as those of the tropics, was uprooting all the innate principles that coexisted with his own life.

For the first time, Naigeot, the brutalized bookkeeper or frantic *viveur*, wondered what his conscience was, the unknown power that stood up within him to combat his unchained passions. Who had given it to him? From what importunate tyrant did it come? Was it necessary to obey it and vanquish himself, at the price of his very life? Or, on the contrary, was it necessary to chase away those unworthy scruples and seize happiness, even if it were necessary to traverse crime in order to do so?

It was midnight; everyone in the house was asleep—everyone except the bookkeeper, who could not find repose.

He emerged from his room, where he was stifling, and wandered like a soul in torment along the corridors.

The padded doors opened and closed soundlessly; footsteps were muffled by the carpets; Naigeot could only hear his heavy and rapid respiration, but even that respiration frightened him; he would have liked to retain it and try to penetrate his soul with the calm that reigned around him.

It was in vain; on the contrary, the more his thoughts approached real life, arresting on Louise or her mother, on the clerks or Charles Montessier, the stormier they became. There was a moment when he almost lost self-control; without taking account of what he was doing, he lifted a door-curtain that hid the entrance to his niece's apartment. Through a glazed door fitted with a muslin curtain he could see the gleam of the night-light, like an opaline reflection in mist.

Insensibly his gaze fixed on that light. Gradually, he distinguished objects in the penumbra: first the table that supported the lamp, then the bed where Louise was asleep, and the ebony crucifix that stood out blackly against the white curtains, and then the girl, calm and smiling, like a little child.

How long did he stay there, motionless, his feet nailed to the carpet? What mad ideas, what infamous temptations, succeeded one another within him? No one can say, for time cannot be evaluated at such moments by the banal measurement of clocks.

Suddenly, a hand fell on his shoulder,

"What's the matter my brother?" the mother asked him, looking him in the face.

He went pale, tottered and recoiled, his eyes as haggard as in confrontation with a specter.

"I... I... was watching her sleep," he stammered.

"You have insomnia, then, my brother?"

The unfortunate man thought he was the victim of a nightmare. He leaned on the wall to sustain himself, and only responded in monosyllables.

Madame Naigeot rang. Two domestics can down.

"Take Monsieur back to his bed," she said, "and go fetch a doctor. He has the fever."

The next morning, Madame Naigeot took Louise to her aunt's house.

The doctor's potions doubtless stopped the progress of the disease, for the bookkeeper went down to his desk at the customary time. Naudin and Ménard even re-marked that his mind had never seemed to be so frankly occupied with his work.

That was because Naigeot finally wanted to take account of the state of affairs and to know where the liq-uidation was. For several days he carried our research in old ledgers, checked accounts, calculated balances and reports with a strange fervor. No one worried about that, and his brother's widow did not seem changed in his regard.

Meanwhile, time passed. The epidemic had decimated the city, but no one had been attained in the Maison Naigeot; the widow, the two clerks and bookkeeper had lived in peace, making up their accounts and placing their orders during the day and spending the evening walking in the harbor. No interior had ever been calmer in appearance, but never had more violent passions menaced the future as much.

Seeing, on the one hand, Madame Naigeot coming and going in the warehouses, giving orders and deciding everything with her usual calm and surety, and coming to sit down in her large leather armchair with the clerks, and, on the other, the bookkeeper curbed over his desk, leafing through his notebooks, checking his additions or sharpening his pens, no eye could surely have divined which of the two individuals would have liked to suppress the other at the price of his eternity.

Finally, the epoch fixed for Louie's marriage arrived.

Two days before the one when Charles was to return from Boston with his entire family, Madame Naigeot announced that the same evening, Louise would be brought back from her aunt's house.

The weather was fine; it was a true excursion to go by canoe to the isle of ***. As soon as the warehouses were shut, Madame Naigeot, her brother-in-law and the clerks went down to the harbor.

There was no lack of boats and sailors. They chose a long and elegant pirogue, which had a little green and pink dinghy attached to the poop by way of a lifeboat, but they refused the oarsmen who offered themselves, Naudin and Ménard were accustomed to handling oars, and Naigeot protested that he would gladly resume that exercise of his youth—of the happy days, he said, when he was still a child and Dominique had taught him to swim along the banks of the Seine.

They set forth.

"Well, at least you know how to swim, Monsieur Naigeot," said Naudin, taking the oars first.

"One always swims as best one can."

"Personally, I don't know what's wrong with me, but I've never been able to learn. Can you imagine that water causes me an unhealthy terror? As long as I'm in a boat, with an oar in my hand, I'm all right, but once it's necessary for me to agitate my arms and legs to follow the métier of fish, the force is lacking. I find myself as awkward as a child."

"That's singular, especially for an inhabitant of a seaport, for you must have had opportunities to learn to overcome that weakness."

"Everything has been done to correct me; my parents and my friends made fun of me, but it was no use— and for sure, it's too late to apply myself to it now!" he added, smiling.

"Why? Better late than never."

"Because he no longer has movements agile enough for that!" Ménard exclaimed. "Do you believe that after spending forty years writing behind a counter, when one has rheumatism in one's belly, one can jump into the water like a petty clerk?"

"It does you good!"

"Thank you! Well, I could swim like a fish, and I once made bets that I could stay at sea for two hours, always swimming, but I believe that I'd cut a sad figure in the water now that I have gout!

"Get away! I suppose that if we capsize," said Naigeot, with a strange smile, "it will be necessary to count on my sister and me to fish both of you out?"

"I even believe, my brother, that you might well have three people to get out of trouble, for I've only ever tried my strength under the surveillance of my swimming teacher and seeing a pole held out four brasses in front of me."

"Fortunately, there's no fear of any mishap," said Naudin, pointing at the deep blue sky, where stars were shining like a sprinkle of diamonds.

"What an evening! You don't have spectacles like this in Paris, my brother?" queried the widow. "Look over there at the harbor, which is illuminating, and the beacon on the jetty, which is shining like a sun, and the vessels bobbing, and the waves beating the dike with their phosphorescent foam."

"You talk about the Seine," added Ménard, who was French, "but it's a muddy gutter for Americans. Can one return to live in that old Europe when one has become accustomed to our immense, spacious, linear cities? Can one believe in rivers like the Seine when one has seen the Mississippi and its eight mouths?"

Naigeot was not listening. Suddenly, he had fallen into a strange absorption; his brow was furrowed, as if under the effort of a fatal thought, and his eyes were plunging their fixed state into the river.

"What are you thinking about, my brother?" asked the widow, astonished by that silence.

"Nothing… which is to say, about our excursion, my sister."

"Are you regretting Paris?"

"Paris!" he exclaimed, vehemently. "Oh, yes! Paris is a city unique in the world! It's the port where it's necessary to land with a cargo of gold, the center where it's necessary to pour out the wealth that one brings back from all the lands of the Earth!"

"You want to give me a desire to go there—but no, I'm no longer young enough for that."

The conversation lapsed. Ménard took the oars from Naudin's hands and each of them followed a personal reverie. The rower was absorbed by the attention he was paying to his task. Naudin was reposing, parading his gaze over the starry sky, where the moon was beginning to sketch a thin crescent, over the distant boats shat resembled errant shadows and over the lights shining in the port, along the quays and on the buoy. The widow was prey to a visible preoccupation. She was astonished by her brother-in-law's agitation, his passionate language and his extraordinary disturbance.

As for Naigeot, he was trembling in the grip of a fever more violent than ever. The blood was throbbing in his temples and making red clouds pass before his troubled gaze. He was no longer master of his thoughts, which were passing incoherently through his brain. One might have thought that an alien spirit had entered into him and was shaking him like the possessed of the Middle Ages.

Visions succeeded one another rapidly and madly in his imagination. Sometimes there was Paris, which unfurled in a vast panorama its luxuries, its pleasures, its intoxications and its debaucheries, which the aged bookkeeper had known for a week; sometimes the humble desk, on which his great ledger and awkward pens lay; sometimes Louise in a wedding dress; sometimes, finally, Louise again, still dressed in white, but emerging with him from a church in Paris.

All that spun, mingled and disappeared, only to reappear again in more vivid colors.

And the pirogue cleaved through the water and advanced toward the buoy, swaying gently on the waves that were going upriver; and the sky was still blue and limpid, and in the air impregnated with marine odors, the sounds of the port were dying away like a distant harmony.

Naigeot paraded his wild gaze over his sister-in-law and the two clerks

In sum, the tempting spirit said to him, *you have them! They're here, in your power. You can annihilate at a single stroke all the living obstacles that hold the key to fortune and happiness... another hour... another moment...and your fate will be decided... and you'll be riveted forever to your miserable life. You're going to see Louise again and you're going to bring her back for another—you stupid individual devoid of courage!*

Well, what are you going to do? cried a rebellious voice inside him. *Do you want to kill them, then? Will you dare to be a murderer?*

Conscience! Conscience! A terrible power that lurks in the depths of the human soul, like an echo of eternal justice! Conscience, God's bailiff, which summons the guilty to pay his debt! A pitiless avenger, an inflexible Nemesis, the archangel with a flaming sword who separates virtue from crime. Conscience! Conscience!

"It's your turn to row, Monsieur Naigeot," exclaimed Ménard, throwing the oars across the boat with a sigh. "Oof! It's tiring, at length!"

The bookkeeper went mechanically to take his place in the prow and dipped the oars into the water again. Then, still prey to the fever of his thoughts, he maneuvered the pirogue without method, with jerky movements.

The boat advanced in fits and starts, sometimes lifted by the waves, sometimes almost overturned by an imprudent thrust of the oars.

"How badly you row, my brother!" said the widow. "We're not on one of your tranquil rivers fifteen brasses wide! There are reefs and sand-bars—be careful"

"The most skilful pilots fear the Mississippi delta in bad weather," added Ménard, "especially in the vicinity of the buoy. Steer to the left, to the left—there's a whirlpool near here."

Naigeot agitated the ors, shivering. *A whirlpool… sandbars… reefs… What it we were to capsize?* he thought. *I can swim, me… me… I can swim!*

"Oh, I'm going to take back the oars, my dear Monsieur!" exclaimed Naudin, leaping from his bench. "One stroke more to the right and we'll capsize! Pass me the oa..."

The end of the sentence was lost in a cry uttered by four different voices. Suddenly, the pirogue disappeared, swallowed by a whirlpool, and the echo repeated the sinister sound of several bodies falling into the water.

There was an instant of bleak silence. The river, violently opened, closed up again, seething. An overturned boat and oars reappeared on the surface, like the wreckage of a disaster.

Then a man found himself alone in the little dinghy. He seized an oar and headed for land,

This time he did not allow his boat to wander at random; he rowed straight and firmly, as if he feared being pursued.

He had scarcely covered a few lengths when he was violently arrested in his course. A cry of distress had traversed the air, and two clenched hands clung on to the edge of his dinghy.

He shivered, as if he had been seized bodily by the executioner himself.

"My brother…my brother…help!" cried the widow, struggling against the current.

Naigeot stared at her with bloodshot eyes, and hesitated momentarily…for one second! Then he lifted his oar and brought it down violently on her head, shoved the body into the depths of the river and resumed his flight, even more rapidly.

When he was near the shore he searched with his eyes for a deserted beach, in order to land there without being seen. Then he rowed gently in order not to attract the attention of the coastguards. He almost lay down in the bottom of his dinghy, because it seemed to him that his silhouette would appear against the sky like the shadow of Cain; and as soon as he set foot on land, he shoved the boat and the oar that had brought him out to sea again.

He slipped along the quays, avoiding gazes; he went through the most solitary streets and devoured space, as if to put a greater distance between his victims and himself.

When he had traversed the city and the outlying districts he sat down at the foot of a tree and took his head in his hands, to try to gather his thoughts.

Since he had committed his crime they were no longer the same. He did not feel an immense joy in being rid of all the obstacles that forbade him Louise and her fortune, but a glacial astonishment; he experienced neither a mad rage to profit from the moment to abduct his niece, to take possession of bonds and titles and flee, nor the energy of a bandit who calculates his chances of defeat or triumph. No, he was gripped by a vague but acute terror. He darted fearful gazes around him, as if he dreaded seeing the agents of God's justice appear.

However, what remained of his reason cried out to him to assess his situation more rapidly, to choose the path that he wanted to follow and to embrace it without delay. Every minute brought a new danger, every hesitation pushed him closer to the abyss.

When the reality became clear, it seemed to him that his resolution was made, that he was going to go back to the Naigeot house alone with his wet clothing in disorder and run to the magistrates to announce the shipwreck, weeping and protesting his efforts to save the victims; but soon he saw himself pursued by furies that denounced his crime and gathered against him all the fanatics of human justice. Sometimes, on the contrary, he thought he had had a horrible dream while he was lying in his bed with the fever, and that his sister-in-law was asleep in the next room. At times, he even dared to hope that the nightmare had lasted for a long time and that he would wake up in the meager bed of his bourgeois boarding-house to the ringing of the breakfast bell.

But in the meantime, he heard the flutter of the wings of nocturnal birds above his head, and, in the distance, the dying echo of the sounds of the city.

What to do? What to decide? he wondered, in the anguish of not knowing whether he was in his right mind. *If it's a dream, let it end! If it's a reality, may I finally have the courage to grasp fortune and happiness!*

And he sought to reawaken his passions, which had been extinguished in his terror, to see Louise again, to remember Paris and his joys—but his memory was impotent and his imagination remained cold.

Suddenly, through the silence of the night, he heard a clock chime. He recalled his senses and counted eleven strokes.

I'm doomed, he thought, *if I don't run this instant to report the disaster and take over the government of my niece's house in the capacity of guardian. Another hour of absence and I'll become a criminal tracked like a wild beast and killed by the hand of the executioner.*

He got up, and marched precipitately toward the city.

By a supreme effort, he had gathered all his courage for that final step. So, he marched with a feverish rapidity through the streets, now deserted. At about half past eleven he reached the magistrate's house.

His blood was hammering in his arteries; his teeth were chattering. Finally, he raised his hand to seize the door-knocker.

"You're mad to think that Louise would ever marry her uncle!" exclaimed a familiar voice beside him, with a burst of laughter.

Suddenly, his hand stopped and remained suspended; his pulse ceased to beat; he was nailed to the ground, his mouth open and his eyes fixed.

"Above the calculations of men, there is the justice of God!" added a second voice.

This time Naigeot was able to turn his head and look behind him. By the gaslight, he distinctly saw Ménard and Naudin crossing the street, arm in arm. They were chatting as they walked. When they turned the street corner, Naigeot recovered the use of his limbs in order to run after them.

Am I mad? he said to himself. *Are they alive? Have I seen ghosts?*

But when he arrived at the corner around which the two clerks had gone, he could no longer see anything except the shadows of the street-lamps on the roadway.

Midnight chimed.

"It's a hallucination! It's vertigo!" exclaimed the unfortunate, who collapsed on a boundary-marker without daring to return to the magistrate's house.

Is it really them? Have I not killed them? he suddenly thought, with a surge of joy. *But no; I heard their bodies fall into the water... they cried out... I struck my brother's wife, who swam after me...*

A night patrol made the road resonate under its measured tread. Naigeot fled at random without looking back.

When he stopped, he found himself, to his amazement, at the door of his brother's house. The most profound silence reigned. All the shutters were closed and no light was shining through the cracks. Was that the livery of mourning or that of slumber?

For a moment, he had the idea of knocking in order to wake the domestics; but as he was about to conquer his fear, he felt his garments brushed, as if someone had passed beside him.

"Why the devil don't you go in, Ménard?" said Naudin's voice, impatiently. "Are you going to let us sleep outside?"

"The keys are still back there in my coat pocket," Ménard replied. "It's very cold!"

"Where's Madame Naigeot?"

"Still out there; she'll arrive last, her head is hurting so badly!"

Naigeot fell backwards and lost consciousness.

When he opened his eyes again it was daybreak. The noise of the city was already beginning; doors were opening and closing, carts were rolling and matinal industries were agitating; life was reborn, and around the house the shutters of the warehouses were being raised.

Ideas commenced to arrive one by one; then memories reappeared like menacing phantoms. He got to his feet abruptly, in order to flee, spurred on by terror.

"Good God, what are you doing there, my dear Monsieur Naigeot!" exclaimed Ménard, in his frank and joyful voice, appearing on the threshold of the door.

The bookkeeper looked at him with dazed eyes.

"Do you like to sleep under the stars? At our age, it's no longer the season. Go and have your cup of tea, which is waiting for you, still hot, in the dining room!"

Ménard was there, such as Naigeot had always seen him with his beaming face. his nankeen trousers and the charms on his watch chain, which clinked every time he moved.

Naigeot got up, but could only succeed in maintaining himself on his unsteady legs with great difficulty.

"I slept here, then?" he asked, in a trembling voice. So…I was also dreaming, then?"

"Naudin!" shouted Ménard, turning toward the interior of the warehouses. "Naudin!"

The second clerk advanced, his hands in his pockets and a quill behind his ear.

"Well?" he said

"What do you think of the conduct of Monsieur Naigeot, who slept in the moonlight last night?"

"Oh, really? But if you were late, why didn't you knock to have the door opened? Did you renew your acquaintance with French wine yesterday evening?"

"Where is my sister?" asked Naigeot, who felt his reason escaping him, in wondering whether he had dreamed the night or whether he was dreaming now,

"Madame Naigeot will come down; come in, then!"

"How is she this morning?" Naudin asked is colleague.

"Her headache is very bad," Ménard replied.

Naigeot shivered. He remained immobile before the clerks, not daring to advance or to flee.

Naudin took a step forward and took the bookkeeper by the arm in a familiar fashion. "Come on!" he said. "Have you become a statue, my dear Monsieur? Quickly! Have your tea and come to the office."

This time, Naigeot went in with the clerks, for Naudin's hand drew him with an irresistible force. It seemed to the unhappy bookkeeper that the plump and ruddy hand was digging into his flesh and leaving its imprint there like a steel claw.

Everything in the warehouses had its customary appearance. The doors that were slamming on all sides made them resemble a hall opened to the air currents; natives were sweeping and organizing the scattered bales of cotton. A mulatto was dusting the furniture in the glazed office where the clerks, Naigeot and his sister-in-law each had an armchair.

All those people coming and going were moving with a slavish indifference, without even remarking their masters.

Naigeot went mechanically to the dining room, where he found his breakfast prepared; he drank his hot tea, ate a few slices of buttered toast and walked back and forth, palpating the furniture in order to assure himself that he was in the real world.

Evidently, I had vertigo! he said to himself.

When he went back to the warehouses he found his sister-in-law sitting in her armchair and chatting with the clerks. Nothing had changed, either in her manner or in her person, but she had a large blue-tinted bruise on her left temple.

"Bonjour, my brother," she said to him. "It's necessary to balance the Marcoud account today; don't fail to do so!"

Naigeot sat down, opened his ledger and set to work without saying anything. While he sensed his mind dissolving under the effort of contrary terrors, the bookkeeper's quasi-mechanical faculty of bookkeeping did his ordinary work, like a wound-up clock.

From time to time, he was woken up with a start by the voices of strangers who came to place orders. Then he responded as best he could, astonished that they were not addressing themselves to the widow and the clerks, as usual.

Then the negroes and the mulattos asked him for instructions regarding a host of details that Madame Naigeot had the habit of supervising herself. The captain of a merchant ship came to negotiate a cargo of sugar, and it was to him that he was referred. A planter proposed the acquisition of his cotton, and it was necessary again for the bookkeeper to conclude the bargain.

Madame Naigeot and the clerks seemed, meanwhile, to be very busy around him—but one might have thought that the strangers did not see them.

"My sister," Naigeot asked, unable to understand English and not knowing how to respond to many of the people, "what ought I to say to this monsieur who has been speaking to me for a quarter of an hour?"

"Tell him that the hundred bales of cotton will be expedited to Valparaiso on the thirteenth of the month," she replied.

"But my sister, why aren't you dealing with this matter yourself?"

"My head is making me suffer, my brother..."

At midday the lunch bell rang. Naigeot followed his sister and Naudin, who were sustaining an argument against Ménard, into the dining room.

As he sat down he was astonished that the dishes were placed before him, who never carved.

"Why isn't it you who are doing the honors, Monsieur Naudin?" he asked.

"The cold has reawakened my rheumatism, Monsieur Naigeot.

"When will Louise be returning?" ventured the bookkeeper, tremulously.

"We would have brought her back yesterday if I hadn't received this blow on the head," said the mother. "Eat, then, my brother!"

But Naigeot had dropped his fork; an icy chill ran through his body from head to foot. *Am I in the company of three specters?* he asked himself.

He bounded from his seat in order to run away, but Naudin retained him with the terrible hand that had already seized him that morning.

"I believe that you're also ill, my brother," said the widow. "If you aren't hungry, do as we do and don't eat!"

They returned to the warehouse. Madame Naigeot and the clerks went through the hangars and circulated in all the parts of the establishment. The bookkeeper accompanied them with a distracted gaze, and remarked that no one paid any attention to them and that they did not speak to any of the slaves, any more than to the people who came in and out of the vast commercial depot on various pretexts.

When they came back to sit down beside him, he experienced a violent sensation of fear.

However, nothing had changed in their appearance, and the voices he heard resonating in his ears had their familiar accents. Naudin opened drawers and counted the money in his cash-box. Ménard wrote down orders and took note of acquisitions.

Around him, he recognized the cries of carters, the imprecations of slaves, the rumble of laden carts, and the muted grumbling of the mulatto who was commanding the blacks—in sum, the din that the everyday labor made.

The day went by, however. Gradually, the noise ceased, the comings and goings disappeared, and night fell.

The black men refitted the shutters that they had removed in the morning and replaced them in their grooves, singing. Soon, nothing could any longer be heard except the hasty footsteps of pedestrians crossing the road and the hammer-blows of the workers fitting the last seals.

When nothing remained open any longer but the access door, a lighted lamp was brought to the bookkeeper's desk. Then all the slaves went out through that door and dispersed.

Naigeot got up, madly possessed by the desire to follow them, but Naudin quit his armchair first, and before the bookkeeper had time to traverse the office, he had locked the door, of which he took away the key.

Fear chilled Naigeot's blood when he found himself alone with the widow and the clerks. He returned to sit in his armchair without being able to speak and without daring to look at his companions.

He heard Naudin come back into the office and rustle the banknotes that he was counting. Then, gradually, all the sounds of life died away around him.

Fear held him immobile for a long time. Finally, he turned his armchair slowly, in order to get out of that place at any price, where he sensed that he was going mad. But suddenly, his hand collided with something cold and wet, which left him a strange sensation. He dared to look around, and uttered a scream.

His sister and the two clerks were still there, but livid and icy.

Their eyes were fixed and covered by the dull cloud of death; their limbs were inert and rigid. Instead of the blue bruise that the widow had on her forehead he recognized a horrible wound.

At that sight, the bookkeeper leapt up like a madman, shouting for help.

Naudin was in his armchair, across the entrance to the office. In one hand he was still holding a wad of banknotes; in the other, he was clutching the key of the house with all the energy of a final grip.

Naigeot circled that glass cage, the eternal prison of his life, as if in a circle of the Inferno, He shouted for help with all his might, but the house was deserted and his voice died away in a deathly silence. He was there, in the midst of his victims, as if the center of an enemy army. The immobility of the cadavers was an ineradicable barrier that he could not cross. He pleaded, he wept, he tore his hair, he consecrated himself to eternal expiations, but nothing came to interrupt his horrible vision.

From time to time, he only felt drops of fetid water streaming over him.

In order to get out, it would have been necessary for him to take the key from the cashier's rigid hand, seize the arm of his cadaver and shove him out of the exit that he was blocking.

Naigeot stiffened all his will-power and advanced with a supreme resolution; but as soon as he felt the shock of that inert body and the chill of the water, every drop of which, in sinking into his flesh, seemed to be drilling a hole all the way to his bones, he stopped, as if repelled by an invincible force, and clung to the grille in order not to fall over. Hours, as long as hours of agony, and as horrible as centuries in Hell, went by thus.

Finally, in the midst of the silence of the night, Naigeot heard a rumor, distant at first, then closer, which was spreading from street to street within the city.

That manifestation of life gave him a last surge of courage; he launched himself forward, pushed the cadaver away violently, tore the banknotes and the key away from him and ran to the door of the warehouses.

He tried to make out the lock, but his eyes were troubled; he searched for it, groping, but his hands were trembling.

The rumor was still getting closer. One might have thought it a growing crowd that was amassing before the house and uttering cries.

Naigeot agitated the key with a feverish haste, but did not succeed in opening the lock. Then he shook the door and struck it with blows whose force was multiplied tenfold by fear. Finally, the lock yielded.

At the moment when he was about to cross the threshold he found his passage barred by a living wall. The crowd he had heard coming was there, breathless, urgently demanding vengeance.

Before he had distinguished a cry or a face, he was tied up by vigorous hands.

"In the name of the law!" cried the solemn voice of an officer of justice.

The stunned bookkeeper allowed himself to be taken away, without making any effort. People stood aside from his passage; the two battens of the door were opened and three stretchers draped in black appeared in the middle of the crowd.

On recognizing the body of his sister-in-law and those of the clerks, Naigeot uttered one last cry, strident and shrill: the cry of triumphant madness.

"Yes!" cried the furious people. "He's the guilty party! He's the murderer!"

"He was seen coming back alone and hiding in the shadows, like murderers!"

"He had forgotten that the tide would denounce his crime by bringing back the cadavers!"

"His lifeboat was found, and the oar, still bloody, with which he struck his sister!"

"Here are the banknotes that he was carrying away, fleeing like a thief...!"

The three cadavers were deposited in the mortuary and Naigeot was taken away, bound, on one of the stretchers. He passed before the court. All the evidence was united against him, and but for his evident and declared madness, he would inevitably have been condemned to capital punishment.

After three months of examination, the tribunal had him transferred from his cell to a room in the insane asylum.

He died ten years later.

On the register of deaths, the chief physician of the hospital wrote under the date of 18 July 1850 the following note:

No. 72 died today during a fit, having been placed in the house in 1841 after a judgment of the criminal court. Since that epoch he had not ceased to be prey to intermittent fits of fury and imbecility. No glimmer of reason ever returned to him. Nevertheless, in his moments of calm, he amused himself making interminable commercial accounts in a large ledger, very neatly kept. On examining those accounts, I recognized that they were always accurate, that the arithmetic never contained any error, and that the balances were perfectly exact.

Monsieur and Madame Montessier, who are Catholics, have erected a chapel at Notre-Dame-du-Secours.

Isobel the Resuscitated

A Legend of the Banks of the Rhine

It was already late, for vespers had been sung and the benediction was commencing in the little church in Cologne that contains the bones of the eleven thousand virgins. It was All Saints' Day 1538, and for the Vigil for the Dead, one of the most celebrated preachers in Germany had come to remind the faithful of the virtues, the courage and the martyrdom of Saint Ursula and her companions.

So there was a crowd at the sermon and at vespers, although the church was one of the smallest in Cologne. Not only had the burgers and the manual laborers of the city come running, filling the nave and the aisles, but the nobles and important people from the surrounding area had also come, with their entire households, to take possession of the lateral chapels and the work-benches.

Among the splendid and touching festivals that Catholicism celebrates, the feast of the dead is perhaps one of those that make the most profound impression on the heart. The universal mourning that suddenly envelops Christendom, and the thought of the dead that looms up, terrible and menacing, in the depths of all consciences, have something so solemn about them that no one can then resist the pull of religion and the need for prayer.

When All Saints, the last beautiful festival of the year, has thrown the joyful sound of its bells rung at full tilt to the wind, when it has scattered the petals of its pale chrysanthemums over the steps of the altar and

157

gilded with a ray of sunlight the rare leaves that still festoon the treetops, one does not hear the funereal knell of the first vespers for the dead without a strange emotion. Suddenly, cheerful thoughts are extinguished in the depths of the heart, and the crepes of the dead that veil the sanctuary seem to envelop the soul of the Christian.

That is why, at the moment when this story begins, the meditation was profound among the faithful of Cologne. The preacher had just descended from the pulpit and the officiating priest was giving the blessing to the Holy Sacrament. All heads were bowed. A religious silence reigned in the church, and only the little bell that the deacon agitated from time to time awakened echoes under the low and massive vaults.

The church of Saint Ursula was perhaps, on that day and at that hour, the blessed enclosure most appropriate to evoke thoughts of eternity in pensive and poetic souls. The declining daylight filtered through the stained-glass windows, colored with pale light, which harmonized with the flickering light of the candles to envelop the entire scene with a kind of dubious clarity, fugitive and phosphorescent. Certain parts of the church, plunged momentarily into thick darkness, seemed suddenly to light up and surge forth from obscurity to show the astonished eye of the observer unexpected and almost fantastic silhouettes. The shadows of individuals hidden in the depths of the lateral chapels or leaning against the pillars, suddenly seemed to elongate or shrink immeasurably, or make strange grimaces on the wall. Sometimes, one could have believed that one saw hideous gnomes agitating, impatient and teasing, in the corners of the basilica, like damned souls pursued by Satan; sometimes, angels extended their wings in order to launch forth toward the heavens like blessed spirits summoned to their last abode; sometimes, finally, there were capricious and changing phantoms, as those of souls in pain ought to be, who are condemned to an eternal expiation.

The human bones that cluttered the church of the eleven thousand virgins and rendered it one of the most curious in Christendom added further to the fantastic aspect of that vigil for the dead. The opening contrived in the thick walls allowed the sight of piles of heaped-up relics, which seemed to be the veritable pillars of those massive catacombs. There were entire generations thrown pell-mell into the dust, whose souls, suddenly evoked by the festival of the dead, seemed to be fluttering under the somber vaults with strange noises. On the panels of the walls and before the stone altars, the stripped skulls, hands, feet and torsos of skeletons formed capricious figures and mosaics, which the play of light and shadow caused to change form and aspect continually, and whose ridges, brightened on one side by the pale daylight filtered through the colored stained-glass windows, and on the other by that of the candles, seemed to be bordered by fire-follets.

At the moment when the priest, at the last tinkle of the choirboy's bell, gave the blessing to the crowd of Christians, a man enveloped in a large black cloak came out from behind one of the pillars of the porch and went up silently toward the middle of the church under the left-hand aisle.

Having reached, at some distance, one of the lateral chapels most charged with relics, he stopped and moved aside the folds of his cloak slightly, which hid a part of his face.

He was a man still young, if the vivacity of his dark eyes could be believed, which shone with a strange fire beneath thick eyebrows, but already worn by passions or by study, for his forehead, deprived of hair, had become immeasurably high, and profound wrinkles furrowed it with inflexible lines. His bony and hooked nose resembled the beak of a bird of prey, and his thin, taut lips seemed to be barely holding back a skeptical and mocking smile.

At the present moment, he was backed up against a pillar and draped picturesquely in his cloak, the folds of which his left arm was holding at waist-level. His head, tilted forwards, was leaning on his right hand, which was playing capriciously with the gilded hairs of his russet moustache. He seemed to be completely absorbed by the observation of the nearby chapel, where one of the magnificent reliquaries of the eleven thousand virgins of Cologne—which Monsieur Strauss,[15] our skillful orchestra-leader, who is also one of our most distinguished antiquaries, possessed four years ago—was still shining in all its richness.

It was not, however, the reliquary that attracted our observer's interest so keenly, but a ravishing and ideal creature whose figure was by no means the most remarkable in the church of Saint Ursula on All Saints' Day 1538. Behind the carefully-closed grille that sealed the chapel, a young woman accompanied by a single page seemed to be praying fervently.

That was Madame Isobel, the chatelaine of Linkenberg, one of the highest and most solitary keeps bordering the Rhine. For long years, the death of her first husband, Baron Ulrich von Saul, had left her the lady

---

[15] The reference is slightly enigmatic, although the intended reference might be to Johann Strauss I (1804-1849), assuming that the story was written some while before 1853.

160

and mistress of the manor of Linkenberg. To count the number of All Saints' Days when the powerful Baroness had come to say her paternosters in the church of the eleven thousand virgins, and the anniversary masses that she had had said for Sire Ulrich and the two other husbands she had had since his death, one might perhaps have thought that the days of her youth were long past, but a single glance was sufficient to convince that the years had not marked her with their seal. She was still a young woman; she was at least fifty, but did not appear more than twenty.

Rich, powerful, noble enough in her own right to ennoble a whole family of commoners, Madame Isobel ought to have been sought in marriage by the greatest lords in the land. There were none, however. Never, in long years, had a joyous cavalcade of hunters intoned the halloo to have the drawbridge of Linkenberg lowered, nor had knights and ladies come to visit her lofty keep. She lived alone, enclosed in Linkenberg, without seeing any other face than that of an old steward attached to the family for sixty years, and that of a page, a poor, sad and sickly child who seemed scarcely to have the strength to carry her missal when he accompanied her to the church.

Isobel von Saul was, moreover, a very exceptional creature. She was so thin, so frail and so pale that she did not seem to belong to the earth or to owe life to other human beings. At the moment when we just caught sight of her she seemed rather to be the queen of the fantastic and invisible beings who populated the comber chapels of the church of the eleven thousand virgins than a real and living woman. A long black velvet dress enveloped her entirely, only allowing her slender hands to be perceived, as white as porcelain, and her face, as white as her hands, in which two dark eyes could be seen, which seemed to illuminate the chapel with their luminous effluvia. Her back velvet head-dress was impotent to contain her pale golden hair, which escaped in wisps as light as clouds, sometimes reflected in shiny spangles and sometimes in soft and vaporous shadows, a multiple play of light that seemed to envelop her head with an aureole.

While the crowd of devotees began to flow out slowly through the main door, Isobel exhaled a final prayer; her page got up first and opened the grille of the chapel gently.

At the faint grating of the hinges, a young man whose costume enabled him to be recognized as a student, and who had remained near the grille until then, in the shadow cast by the tomb of Saint Ursula, raised his head precipitately and darted a rapid glance at Isobel. Then, seeing her still kneeling, and taking advantage of the position of the page, who could not see him, he slid toward the door, which stood ajar. Having reached it, he crouched down, and tried to contain a visible emotion, for Isobel had given her missal to her page and was advancing toward the door.

It was impossible that in passing by she would not brush the student's forehead with her long, dangling sleeve. At that contact, he could not retain a convulsive shudder. And when, after having followed the noble chatelaine with his gaze all the way to the exit from the church, he finally saw her disappear, he remained motionless momentarily, his gaze fixed on the door, as if lost in infinite thoughts.

Neither the great lady nor her page appeared to have noticed the poor student's maneuver. However, Isobel had not missed any of her timid lover's movements. While, with her eyelids lowered, she appeared to be isolating herself from the external world in order to enclose herself in prayer as in an immaculate sanctuary, she let a long gaze slip through her half-closed lashes, simultaneously caressant and avid. And when she emerged from the chapel it was certainly not a pure effect of chance that her velvet sleeve passed a long, intoxicating caress over the forehead of the young man.

Only the man in the cloak had observed that mute scene. While the most scrupulous devotees went to the door and the sacristans began to extinguish the candles, he advanced with a light tread and tapped the student on the shoulder.

The young man turned round swiftly, allowing the sight of a charming face full of melancholy and mildness, framed with a fortunate harmony by curls of ash-bond hair.

"What do you want, Master Sturff?" he exclaimed, brusquely, like a man woken up with a start by real life in the midst of a poetic dream.

"Your wellbeing, my dear Franz," the stranger replied, "but by God, what were you doing there since the beginning of the service?"

The student seemed greatly annoyed by that unexpected encounter, and got up go leave. "But Master Sturff," he replied, in a hostile tone, "what do you expect me to be doing here, except what so many worthy people are doing... including yourself?"

"My dear Franz, you're in love with the chatelaine of Linkenberg..."

The student turned round, in a movement more rapid than thought, and looked at Master Sturff with an expression charged with anger. "What does that matter to you?" he snapped,

"Don't get annoyed, you young fool. What, indeed, does it matter to me?" My God, do you think that if you were as indifferent to me as the crowd of your fellow students I would worry about knowing where you place the affections of your heart? But, poor child, I've remarked in you all the sublime follies that reveal so clearly the amorousness of a twenty-year-old, and I wanted to know who had inspired it; I wanted to know at whose feet you had placed the delightful flowers of amour and candor that emit their perfume before a first love..."

"Well?" said Franz, with a slight tremor in his voice. And the student raised his eyes to look at his companion with an expression of imperious prayer. His anger had faded before Sturff's sympathetic words, but it had been replaced by a curiosity full of anguish.

"Well, my friend, I see you with a profound sorrow attaching your footsteps to following Isobel. I shiver to find you always at the corner of Saint Ursula's tomb, because the solitary chatelaine who never lowers her drawbridge and never emerges from Linkenberg except when festival bells are rung, who comes six times a year to say her prayers in that grilled chapel..."

"I love her!" cried the student, in an emotional voice, in a tone that did not admit objections or advice. Then he hastened toward the door, as if to put an end to an awkward conversation; and in the inflexibility of his silence, in the fire of his gaze, there was a complete revelation of that profound and hopeless passion.

"You evoke my pity, like the poor moths that I see fluttering around the flame of a lamp, until they burn their wings," said Sturff when, after they had both crossed themselves with holy water, they lifted the heavy tapestry curtain than closed the interior of the church. "I'd rather see you in love with the Loreley," he added.

"But why, Master?" asked the student, in a tone in which impatience and anguish were mingled.

"Because she can never be yours."

"I don't see why not!" cried Franz, with a movement of rage. "And after all, Master Sturff, by what right are you spying on the movements of my heart? By what right are you asking me to account for a secret that I wanted to keep to myself? You're neither my father nor my confessor. Do I owe you anything?"

Master Sturff said nothing, and frowned.

"My God!" the poor student went on, sighing. "Be sure that I have never nourished the mad hope of being loved by her! Do I not know that between the chatelaine of Linkenberg and a poor fellow like me there are abysms that nothing could fill in? Oh, don't worry, Master; if Franz the student, kneeling at the corner of Saint Ursula's tomb, lives in amour, dreams and poetry, at least he does not forge unrealizable chimeras for the life of this world. I have neither ambition nor pride enough to aspire to the chatelaine of Linkenberg. I know full well that when she passes close to me, while I shiver and tremble, she does not even see me...and I'm not unaware that one day, perhaps imminently, some noble and powerful lord will marry her and take her away to his manor..."

Stifled sobs cut off the student's voice; for a moment he let himself fall, in tears, on to his friend's shudder; then, as if ashamed of his weakness, he suddenly straightened up and made a movement to escape definitively.

"My friend," said Sturff, gravely, retaining him with his hand, "you haven't understood; in saying that Isobel cannot be yours, I had no intention of reminding you of the social distance that separates you and making you sense more cruelly obstacles that you know as well as I do. No; if I've delved into the coverts of your heart to surprise the secret, it's because I thought it necessary to disabuse you. There is a barrier between you stronger and more invincible than all social prejudices...for one can sometimes overcome those...

"Isobel can no more belong to a noble and powerful lord than to you. Isobel is not an ordinary woman; she does not belong to the earth. In fact, you must be new to the country and incurious regarding popular legends to be unaware of the strange story that surrounds her mysterious life... Oh, have no fear; no one will take her away from you. No lord would be bold enough to marry Isobel the Resuscitated..."

"What does that mean?" exclaimed Franz, in a tremulous voice. The young man's heart was beating with a strange violence, with simultaneous terror and joy, for he said to himself that although a redoubtable secret covered the existence of his beloved, at least he had no rival.

"Come with me; I'll tell you the story, which would be incredible if all my contemporaries had not been witnesses to it."

Master Sturff too Franz's arm and drew him through the somber, narrow and deserted streets of Cologne, It was dark, and only a few rare belated townspeople were still lighting the route with their flickering lanterns, Master Sturff undoubtedly lived some distance away from the church of the eleven thousand virgins, for they walked for a long time before arriving at his dwelling.

It was a solitary house built in large stone blocks, pierced in the exterior façade by irregular and narrow windows, which almost gave it the aspect of a fortress.

That house inspired in the vulgar a kind of respect mingled with terror, for it had been inhabited a few years previously by Cornelius Agrippa.[16]

Sturff had been a friend of the celebrated magician for a long time and had inherited his house and his furniture when, shortly before his death, the illustrious sorcerer had quit Cologne, his homeland, for the last time, in order to liberate himself imprudently from the wrath of Madame Louise de Savoie, the dowager queen of France. The adventurous Agrippa had known Sturff when he was still a student, and since his benefactor's death, the former student passed in the minds of the vulgar as the inheritor of his master's science and power, as well as his laboratory and his instruments.

Thus far, no one had ever been able to cite the slightest evidence—neither any action nor any speech—

---

[16] Heinrich Cornelius Agrippa von Nettesheim (1486-1535) was an important polymathic scholar who studied at the University of Cologne and returned there in later life after extensive travels, including a stint as private physician to the mother of the French king François I, Louise of Savoy. He is primarily remembered for *De occulta philosphia libri tres* [The Three Books of Occult Philosophy] (1531-33) a comprehensive study of occult science which attempted to employ a syncretic amalgam of neoplatonist metaphysics and ideas from the Cabala to oppose skepticism, while avoiding heresy. In the latter aim he did not succeed, and his work attracted the attention and disfavor of the Inquisition. Inevitably, he obtained a popular reputation as a magician, which was cemented in 1559 when an unknown writer published a fanciful book on ceremonial magic in the guise of a fourth volume of *De occulta philosophia.* He was incorporated into the "Hermetic tradition" promoted and popularized by the promoters of the French Occult Revival, including "Éliphas Lévi."

capable of giving any certainty to the conjectures, but there was no inhabitant of Cologne who did not salute Master Sturff politely or who had no fear of counting him among his enemies.

At any rate, the heir of Madame Louis de Savoie's astrologer apparently led a very tranquil life. His studies had finished a long time ago, but he still conserved his title of student and often attended courses in order that no one had the right to contest it. In his quality as a doyen of the university he obtained both the respect and the homage of his companions, who, more audacious than the townspeople, willingly accepted his society, but not one of whom would probably have dared to admit publicly a close friendship with him.

Among the young recruits to the university, Franz Mullingen, the son of a merchant newly established in Cologne, was distinguished by a precocious and active intelligence, a generous and noble soul and a courage proof against anything. Delivered since the early years of his youth to philosophical and mystical reveries that had drawn him into regions of dream, and preoccupied with the scientific questions that were then the order of the day, he had soon drawn close to Cornelius Agrippa's pupil.

It was not that the cold and sardonic visage of Master Sturff had attracted his sympathy keenly, nor that he sensed the slightest inclination, to begin with, to have any recourse to the occult sciences, but in his eyes, Sturff was a representative of a series of fine minds too passionately contested not to have a right to a serious observation.

The student's research had had flattered Master Sturff, who could not help giving him a large part in his affections. He followed the progress of that young intelligence with a secret joy, and felt moved by the first explosions of a veritably passionate soul. Soon, he longer had any other desire than to attach himself to the young student permanently, or any other thought than to associate him with his research and his endeavors.

"Come on, a little courage, my dear Franz," Sturff exclaimed, on seeing the kind of convulsive tremor that had seized the poor lover since his last remark. "you'll know before long the strange lineage of which the beautiful Isobel von Saul is the last scion. We'll see thereafter whether you, a poor son of a commoner, want to belong to such a nobility!"

While speaking, Master Sturff lifted the knocker of the low door of the house. He struck a single blow, curt and imperative. The rap had scarcely resounded than the door was already tuning on its hinges, and a valet appeared, lamp in hand.

Franz went in first and Sturff closed the door again.

The student had never been into to the mysterious house, little frequented even by the strong minds of the school. In spite of his preoccupation, he darted a rapid and curious glance over the apartments that he traversed.

On the ground floor there were low-ceilinged rooms, somber and smoky, cluttered with flasks, furnaces, alembics and instruments of every kind, which were scarcely appropriate to give a cheerful aspect to the dwelling. On the first floor, however, spacious and comfortable apartments extended, which Agrippa's well-known sybaritism seemed to have furnished with all that the luxury and comfort of the epoch had invented of the most agreeable and the most useful. High windows overlooking a magnificent garden distributed daylight there prodigally, and permitted the perception of boscage that a prince of the royal blood would have envied.

It was in those magnificent apartments that Master Sturff had established all the comforts of his residence.

After having traversed a large reception room hung with Cordovan leather and an oak-paneled library filled from top to bottom with the rarest and most curious books, the wonderstruck Franz arrived in his friend's bedroom. It was a vast room hung with ornately-woven tapestries and decorated with gilded sculptures around the cornices and the beams of the ceiling. The alcove plunged to the left into a mysterious gloom, scarcely allowing the sparkling silken embroideries of its curtains to be glimpsed. The parquet, arranged in mosaics, designed the most capricious figures, and in the configuration of all the furniture the sculpture assumed the most bizarre and fantastic forms, appropriate to the stimulation of the imagination.

Master Sturff sank into a large tapestried armchair before a bright crackling fire that illuminated the room on its own, invited his guest to take passion of a similar seat facing him, and ordered his valet to bring them a few bottles of a generous French wine. The valet obeyed, with the miraculous dexterity that had already surprised the student. In less time than it takes to write it, he had placed between the two friends an occasional table of sculpted wood sustained by a chimera with extended wings, and on that table three bottles of the best French wines, two sculpted goblets and a large silver bowl, into which the wine was poured in order to warm, with various spices.

When everything was ready, the first draught had been drunk, and the penetrating warmth of the flames and the liquor had warmed up their limbs, numbed by the cold north wind, the two companions looked at one another momentarily in silence, and Master Sturff commenced his story.

"If you know a little about the science of heraldry, and the history of the origins of the noblest families in Europe," he said, "you must be aware, my dear Franz. That the very noble and very powerful family of the Jagellons[17] descends in a direct female line from fays. That origin, which might seem at first to be somewhat mythological, is nevertheless established by tradition and popularized by legend. The Jagellons are very proud of that nobility and do not suffer gladly that anyone speaks ill of the land of Elfland, where their first lady reigned, nor that anyone attack too closely Messire Satanas, for you know that mesdames the fays are distant cousins of the devil. That is why the noble Jagellons bear his escutcheon on their arms, as allied by the female line, and every worthy knight of that respected family carries in the time and place, the banner of Hell.

"Now, among the numerous legends that the chroniclers have collected regarding that great family there is one that asserts that almost all the branches of its genealogical tree finishes with women, and that those women, the last of their line, are especially close to the common origin whose roots are planted in the land of the fays.

"That legend was scarcely present any longer except in the memory of old servants of the house of Verghten when young Isobel found herself, by virtue of the death of her uncle, the unique heir of that branch of the immense genealogical tree of the Jagellons. Isobel von Verghten was not rich, but as she was very beautiful

---

[17] The Jagellon, or Jagiellonian, dynasty originated in Lithuania in the fourteenth century and included kings of Poland, Hungary and Bohemia

and the barons von Saul had already been allied once with the house of Verghten, Sire Ulrich asked for and obtained her hand.

"Ulrich was then, thirty years ago, a noble and bold paladin. He seemed the living type of the knights of olden times, who lifted effortlessly the enormous masses of weapons that we can no longer see without alarm suspended above the hearth of old feudal castles, and who drink the stirrup cup from immense tankards too heavy for our feeble arms and too copious for our degenerate stomachs.

"His unique pleasure was indulging in all the violent exercises of the body that rendered our ancient heroes so strong and so valiant. He loved to manipulate, with agile movements, the heavy two-handed swords that other lords feared, and showing them, in all the tourneys and hunts, all the superiority of his physical strength.

"That rude life had imprinted a sort of brutal savagery on his manners. Isobel, a timid and gentle creature, could scarcely accustom herself, in spite of all her respect for her redoubtable husband, to that coarse and discourteous behavior. She shuddered when she heard him curse, and the noble sire did not hesitate in his frequent fits of wrath to abuse Heaven and Hell. She was afraid of his caresses, fled the noisy expression of his vulgar joy and wept in the silence of her oratory.

"She eventually languished and became etiolated under the domination of her terrible spouse, like a delicate flower in the climes of the North under the burning rays of the African sun.

"For his part, the sire of Linkenberg, who exhausted himself in feats of strength, magnificent gifts and protestations of amour, could not understand that melancholy at all. That was because Isobel only experienced terror for all the din of human joys; she seemed to belong to another world and to be spending the time of her exile down here. You see her very frail, very pale and quite seraphic; well, in those days she was like the shadow of what she is today, and the more Ulrich surrounded her with amour, the more she weakened visibly, as if so much strength had crushed her weakness, as if the powerful life of her husband had absorbed her fragile life.

"She became a mother, however. After a year of marriage she put a son into the world, strong and healthy, who promised, on growing up, to resemble his robust father.

"The baron, transported by joy, celebrated the birth of his heir with warrior fêtes, and testified even more amour for the spouse who had given him to him, but the labors of maternity had exhausted Isobel and Ulrich's noisy explosions of gratitude ended up conducting her to the grave. She faded away in a matter of months, without apparent suffering, in her husband's arms, amid his vassals...

"'What! She fell ill, you mean?' exclaimed Franz, lifting his head, with astonishment and terror painted on his features.

"Madame Isobel was dead," replied Sturff, calmly.

Franz shivered.

"Come on, my boy, another goblet of good Côtes-du-Rhône wine to cut the vigil and reheat your courage!"

"Thank you," said Franz, "I'm not thirsty. Finish the story of the chatelaine of Linkenberg for me. Isobel wasn't dead!"

"So utterly dead, my boy, that the baron, who was in despair, prepared the most magnificent funeral for her, and wanted her to be exhibited for seven days and seven nights on a bed of State.

"The bed was set up in the great hall of the castle ad Isobel was laid upon it, dressed in her richest garment. The entire country came to pray at her bedside. To begin with, the noble chatelaine had been good and charitable while alive, and the poor folk remembered that; then too, there was rumor for ten leagues around of the splendors deployed on that occasion by the Baron von Saul.

"Although I was very young then, I remember having been taken by my mother to Linkenberg and taken into the noble Isobel's mortuary chamber

"The impressions of childhood are the most vivid and the only ones that never fade away. I've seen many strange things since then, and my soul has been stirred by many emotions, but I can assure you, my dear Franz, that nothing has ever struck me as forcefully as that visit to the castle of Linkenberg. It was the first time that I saw death face to face, for you will believe without difficulty that I did not want to remain by the door and that it was necessary for me to look at the dead woman at close range.

"In spite of the ravages of death, I recognized that pale and regular face, which I had sometimes remarked in the church of Saint Ursula. The chatelaine was still beautiful, but her emaciated and drawn features, her blue-tinted lips and her eyes—her eyes above all, which they had not been able to close and whose dull and immobile pupils seemed to be staring into infinity—offered the most gripping image of death capable of striking a young imagination…I can still see it!

"The baron made the funeral ceremonies last as long as he could, for they occupied his dolor; but in the end, when all the prayers of the church had been said, the coffin had been sealed and lowered into the grave before the entire population of Cologne and the surrounding area, it was necessary for him to return to his castle and resume his ordinary life.

"He devoted the greater part of his time to supervising the first steps and the primary education of his dear child; but, either because he reproached himself for having involuntarily abridged the life of his dear Isobel, in sacrificing her to the vulgar habits that caused her to suffer, or, contrary to common usage, because the memory of the dead woman become more vivid as time went by, his dolor increased further every day. He ended up falling into a black melancholy, from which even the joyful frolics of young Conrad could not distract him. His people began to fear for his life, for his health soon deteriorated visibly...but for God's sake have a glass of wine, my dear Franz, for you have a fever!" cried Sturff, interrupting his story.

"I'm only thirsty for the end of your story...or your tale," Franz replied, with a tremor in his voice."

"Say history, my dear boy! It was nearly a year after Isobel had died when the baron fell ill. His prodigious strength diminished gradually; his vivacity was extinguished; an ennui, vague but immense and irremediable, had taken possession of his soul.

"The long corridors of the castle no longer resounded with hunting calls or battle cries. His weapons remained suspended in the low rooms and but for the cares of the valets, his coats of mail, his breastplates and his gauntlets would have rusted.

"Devoured by a slow but inexorable fever, Ulrich no longer even had the strength to go up to walk on the terraces of Linkenberg. He no longer left the apartments in which Isobel had resided. He sought out her traces incessantly. That terrible man was weaker than a child in the grip of passion.

"One day, his most trusted valet found him unconscious in the room where Madame Isobel had died. On his knees before the bed of that adored spouse he had been weeping for a long time, his forehead buried in the silk hangings; then the physical and mental dolors had exhausted him and he had lost consciousness.

"He was laid in that bed, abandoned since the death of the chatelaine, and he remained there, for the illness augmented instead of diminishing.

"Sometimes, however, chagrin was replaced by anger in that soul once habituated to see everything yield to his command. It seemed to him that by stiffening his distended will he could extract Isobel from the very depths of her tomb; or, rather, without rationalizing or formulating his desires, the savage baron adjured Heaven and Hell to return his wife to him, like a mutinous child who would like to resuscitate by screaming a sparrow that he has killed.

"At that time, many people came to the castle, summoned by the baron. In addition to habitual visitors, good priests were seen who were reputed to perform miracles, and also a few other equally powerful persons of less good renown. My excellent master, Cornelius Agrippa von Nettesheim—God preserve his soul!—went there, it's said, but I'm not entirely sure about that and I wouldn't like to charge his memory with what has happened since at the manor of Linkenberg.

"Kraupt, the old domestic who is now Isobel's factotum was then the baron's valet of confidence. He was the one who watched over his master, spending the night by his bedside and presenting him with the calming potions that ought to have ameliorated his malady. He had a sad responsibility, for Sire Ulrich, in the final stage of consumption, had been abandoned by all the physicians in the locale and his death seemed imminent. While awaiting his end, the baron only emerged from his tears to enter into terrible fits of anger, always demanding Isobel, whom he could not obtain.

"One night, Kraupt, sadly sitting in a large armchair by the fireside, was listening to the hours chiming slowly. He was thinking about the future of the house of Saul, now reduced to a single scion still in swaddling clothes. He remembered that the family was once numerous and powerful, and thought that in a matter of hours, the last castellan would probably have died.

"Suddenly, he was extracted from his reverie by the baron, who called to him in a faint voice. He got up, opened the curtains of the alcove, and found his master very agitated. "Kraupt,' he said, 'did you see her, as I did?'

"'Who, Monsieur?"

"'Madame Isobel, who has finally returned.'

"Kraupt shivered. He thought that the last hour had sounded, and that he had just heard the first divagations of delirium. 'God preserve Madame Isobel in his paradise,' he said, signing himself.

"'God! God! Leave God tranquil and rather welcome my cousin, the prince of Hell, who has rendered her to me!'

"'God preserve us, my lord,' the valet continued, imperturbably. 'Madame the baroness is dead and buried.'

"Kraupt headed for the door in order to go and wake the chaplain and have the death knell rung, but he had scarcely let the curtains of the bed fall back than he

177

heard them running along their tringles and saw them agitating in the gap to the left.

Who can be there? he wondered. *My lord doesn't have the strength to draw the curtains himself.*

"By an effort of will he shook off a commencement of terror, and summoned all his presence of mind in order to look around.

"The vast, high-ceilinged chamber that the chatelaines of Linkenberg had inhabited for centuries was still the same, except that a door that gave access to the late chatelaine's oratory was ajar, and the objects on the dressers had changed places, as if a strange hand had come to reestablish order among the goblets and ewers.

"Kraupt retraced his steps, went into the alcove on the right side, lifted the curtain, and could not repress a cry of terror. A woman enveloped in her night-clothes was standing facing him, holding Sire Ulrich's feverish hand in her own pale white hands, as if to feel the pulse of the blood in the artery.

"That woman was, without any possible error, Madame Isobel: Madame Isobel, such as the old servant had seen her many times before.

"Kraupt, terrified, wanted to flee, but his legs would not obey him. All that he was able to do was to seize a branch of box-wood at his master's bedside and dip it in the holy water, in order to sprinkle the alcove and the curtains.

"One drop fell on Isobel's forehead. She shivered, and wiped it away, with a movement so natural and so alive that the poor valet took his head in his hands and asked himself whether he was not mad, and whether he was dreaming now or had been dreaming in the past when he had seemed to see his mistress die.

"She was there! She released the baron's hand and picked it up again by turns... she looked at him... she acted like a living creature...

"But she was even paler than in the past; the fire in her dark eyes contrasted more strangely with her ardent hair, which the reflections of the light doubtless sowed with jets of flame; and her lips, her bright red lips, caused the whiteness of her sharp teeth to stand out even more.

"'You can go to sleep, my poor Kraupt,' she said, in a clear and soft voice like that of old, 'I'll watch for you tonight.'

"The domestic ran out of the room and closed the doors behind him, as if he feared that he might be pursued. When he was lying in his bed in his own room, having shot all the bolts, he did as children do, hid his head under his sheets and invoked God and the angels, while a convulsive tremor agitated his limbs...

"Come on, for God's sake!" cried Master Sturff, interrupting his story with a burst of laughter. "Quit that sinister expression, Franz, my good friend. How is it possible that you're hearing the history of Isobel for the first time in a land where it's told during every late night?"

"I haven't stayed up late often enough with the burgers of Cologne, my master, to have heard all their fantastic tales. But thanks to you, I've lost nothing, for I doubt that any of them knows how to terrify or torture a heart thus .You've chosen your moment well, damn it, and you've made me pass a vigil of the dead that I'll remember! Don't touch too forcefully one that I'm capable of defending, though, for I love Isobel with all the force of my soul, you know!"

"I've told you, Franz, that I'm your friend; and as for the history of Isobel, others than me will tell it to you. We were, I believe, at the moment of her resurrection....

"Kraupt only woke up in broad daylight. When he saw the sunlight filling his room with golden light he shook off his memories like a bad dream. Brought back by everything that surrounded him to a sentiment of reality, he gradually convinced himself that he had been the victim of a hallucination and that the late chatelaine had appeared to him in a dream.

"The more he woke up, the more the petty events of daily life displaced the memories of the night and blurred the excessively vivid colors of the vision. However, he was astonished to have slept in his own room that day, instead of watching over his dying master....

"I order to try to vanquish his last preoccupations and to dominate his weakness, he walked on the terraces of the castle in the fresh morning air; then he chatted to the men-at-arms and woke up the old steward, Thomas Münt, whom he succeeded a few years later. After much hesitation, as he could not resolve to return to the baron's room alone, he told him about his nocturnal illusions.

"The old man recited his paternosters, admitting to Kraupt that for some time, the baron and the people he had summoned had delivered themselves to damnable practices. Then he got up and accompanied Kraupt to the sire of Linkenberg's room.

"They both went anxiously and fearfully, Kraupt because his mind was still floating in uncertainty in spite of the reassuring sunlight and his companion's exhortations, the old steward because the coincidence of

Kraupt's vision with the baron's despair made him fear an accident both anticipated and dreaded.

"Having arrived at the chamber inhabited by their master, they opened the door quietly in order not to wake him if he was asleep. At the moment when Kraupt was about to lift the tapestry that formed a second door, he felt something creak beneath his feet. He bent down mechanically, and picked up the object in which he had stepped.

"It was the branch of blessed box with which he had sprinkled the specter of the chatelaine.

"Seized by an invincible terror, he stopped Thomas Münt with a gesture and remained nailed to the spot, without daring to make a movement forwards or backwards, In vain he invoked all his reason and all his courage; in vain he signed himself and recommended his soul to Our Lady and all the saints; nothing could any longer make him believe that the previous night's apparition had been a dream.

"Immobilized by terror, uncertain of what they ought to do, both men remained between the door and the tapestry, listening.

"Then, they heard light footsteps in the chamber; then, a shower of sparks, as if someone had struck the log on the fire with the tongs; and then the clink of spoons stirring tisanes and options in goblets.

"Extreme terror produces extreme courage. They stepped forward, parting the tapestry,

"Madame Isobel was sitting in her large armchair, carefully mixing honey and syrup with her husband's refreshing beverages.

"Furthermore, everything was in order, to the extent that is possible in a sickroom; the fire was crackling in the hearth, the night-light was dying in its crystal lamp, and medicaments were scattered here and there, on the dressers and the tables.

"Those details, so simple and so astonishing, that vision in broad daylight, so completely deprived of the supernatural, the hideousness and the horror with which the imagination ordinarily accompanies apparitions of the dead, chilled the two men with a cold, sharp and intense terror, which changed them momentarily into stone statues.

"At the sound of their footsteps the chatelaine had turned round and was looking at them with bright and profound eyes.

"Then she got up and advanced toward them.

"She was so calm, so beautiful, and so similar to herself, that the two domestics bowed.

"'My good friends,' she said to them, 'the weather is fine today in spite of the advanced season, and although the yellow leaves are falling on the ramparts, the sun still retains its heat in the middle of the day. Have a table set up on the terrace of the castle, then. The baron, my noble husband, has recovered a little courage. After such a long illness he will be happy to see the sky again in my company, and he will be glad to take one last meal in the sunlight before the frosts...'

"What can I say? At one o'clock the table was served on the platform of the castle, in the shade of an arbor half-deprived of its foliage, from which one could see, though a gap, a magnificent view of the banks of the Rhine, bathed in mist and sunlight.

"The baron, sitting in his large armchair of Cordovan leather, cut up a quarter of venison. The baroness, slightly pale and languid, stretched her delicate limbs in the sunlight. Around them, the entire personnel of the castle contemplated that spectacle with an amazement in which surprise was more powerful than fear.

"It was also the most delightful day that one could see! The sun shone with the radiant glare that illuminates certain autumn days with such a splendid light that the face of the world seems transfigured. The air was warm and charged with balsamic and intoxicating exhalations; the birds were singing to celebrate the renewal of their amours; and the last leaves, carried away by the wind, came to flutter one by one over the terraces of the manor, causing the warm reflections of their yellow and red glints to shine in the sunlight.

"A piquant little breeze, which arrived from the Rhine, reawakened Sire Ulrich's appetite. As for Madame Isobel, she was more beautiful than ever. Her beauty had even taken on a strangely vivacious character. Urgent and indolent by turns, she sometimes surrounded the baron with her cares and attracted his interest to multitudinous points; sometime slack and listless she remained lying in the depths of her armchair, like a snake in its nest.

At dessert, a beautiful and strong nurse brought Ulrich de Saul's young heir. The child went to play on his father's knees, with a spontaneity that indicated an acquired habit, but when the baron, after complaisantly allowing his hair and beard to be tugged, tried to place him on Isobel's knees, either because the child did not recognize his mother or because he had an invincible antipathy toward her, he started to cry like a little devil and hold out his arms to his nurse. One strange thing that was clearly remarked is that the aversion—or terror, if you wish—was not temporary, and since then, young Conrad never wanted to receive any caress from his mother…which did not prevent him, poor innocent, from soon dying in that company!"

"Since then?" Franz put in, impatiently throwing on to the blazing firebrands the remains of a glass of warm wine that Master Sturff had obliged him to sip. "Are you mad, my master, and do you believe everything you've just told me? Since then? But really! Can that apparition, that phantasmagoria have lasted as long as this?"

"The following Sunday," Sturff went on, tranquilly, without paying any heed to his guest's interruption, the entire city of Cologne was able to see Madame Isobel in the church of the eleven thousand virgins, behind the tomb of Saint Ursula, in the lateral chapel with which you're familiar, who was following the office in her book of hours beside her husband/"

Franz started. "Master!" he exclaimed, seizing Struff's velvet doublet, "Don't toy with me, for God's sake..."

"I've told the truth," the pupil of Agrippa replied, calmly, freeing himself from the student's grip.

Poor Franz fell back inertly in his seat, as if thunderstruck. Sturff picked up the tongs and brought the disjointed firebrands together, causing a rain of sparks to spring forth; then he placed his silver ewer on the ashes and slowly poured a bottle of French wine into it.

When everything was disposed to his liking he sank his head into the back of his large winged armchair, folded his arms in his long sleeves and blinked his eyes in the direction of the window.

"The nights are long by All Saints' Day," he said.

Franz did not reply.

After a full half hour of silence, Sturff raised his eyes to his guest. Two large tears were rolling down the poor student's inflamed cheeks, and the pulsations of his heart were almost audible in the calm of the night.

"Come on, come on—courage, my child, my friend," said Agrippa's heir, squeezing his hand. "If I hadn't had the prudence to tell you all that, others would have done so one day… perhaps too late…"

"And afterwards?" asked the student, mechanically, without emerging from his torpor.

"After what?"

"Finish the story of Isobel for me!"

"Well, Isobel and Ulrich lived as husband and wife, castellan and chatelaine. The people of the region were astonished at first by that resurrection, and but for the religious disputes that were commencing to occupy all minds then,[18] messieurs the doctors would have got mixed up in the matter; but the noble lady gave generous alms, and sent beautiful reliquaries to the convents, with the consequence that she was tolerated, partly out of dread, partly out of gratitude.

"Gradually, in any case, people became accustomed to seeing her, and sought to explain her reappearance by natural means.

"Some—those who had not seen Madame Isobel's body exposed in the mortuary chamber—said that she had not really died, but that she had absented herself for some time after a quarrel with the sire of Linkenberg. Others sustained that she really had died, but that the baron had married for a second time a twin sister that she had, and who resembled her.

---

[18] Martin Luther's ninety-five theses were published in 1517, and the condemnation of his ideas by the Edict of Worms in 1521 provoked religious controversy throughout the Holy Roman Empire.

"Notwithstanding those explanations, nobles and commoners all fled the manor of Linkenberg. No one cared to enter into relations with the chatelaine. Ulrich deployed a regal luxury in vain, bringing cooks from France and wines from all the countries in the world; only a few adventurous young lords dared to cross the drawbridge of the castle to see Isobel the resuscitated.

"Madame Isobel was, however, very beautiful! Certainly, there was not a woman in the entire land, among the aristocracy or the commoners, worthy of being compared with her. And she knew how to make her castle a magical palace! She arranged her braided hair with pearls from Golconda and diamonds from Visapour! And how her robes shone with the richest colors, and golden spangles played in hr veils!

"When a guest arrived, the entire castle was decorated with flowers by day and illuminated by night! Everywhere, on the crenellations and the towers, on the terraces and the arched doorways, red and blue flames ran, or iridescent garlands. From as far away as the eye could see, one could distinguish the high keep on its sheer rock, like a carbuncle in the night. As far away as the ear could hear, trailing music invited people to waltz. The joyous notes awoke the echoes and the lights cast a thousand reflections in the Rhine. From the height of her balcony, Madame Isobel distributed largesse to the poor.

"In the vast halls of the manor, tables were extended for feasting, and the guests danced in long sarabands, That was because, once one had seen Madame Isobel in the midst of her fêtes, one wanted to see her again. Gradually, the number of her knights augmented. Each of them brought his companions in arms, and they all formed a court around her. They loved her beauty, so powerful in a body so frail; her supreme grace made her a queen everywhere and always. People loved to see her commanding the dance, her arms rounded and her hair loose, or pouring wine with her white hands into sculpted tankards, and foolish intoxication into young hearts with her gaze.

"German dreamers came from far and wide, ever more numerous, coming up or down the Rhine to arrive at the manor of Linkenberg. And Madame Isobel made her fêtes more brilliant every day. Unknown women sometimes arrived with the knights, but more often, the Resuscitated constrained her vassals to come and dance with the lords; for prudish women or chatelaines avoided Linkenberg, and even signed themselves when they saw its crenellations bordered by fire in the distance.

"They danced and they danced; and the young fools, ever more intoxicated, returned incessantly to burn their hearts near Isobel, like moths to a flame. Sometimes there were races, sometimes carrousels, sometimes brilliant fêtes. The entire country resounded with fanfares and joyful cries.

"Meanwhile, the sire von Linkenberg, reanimated at first by Isobel's return, so proud and so happy to preside over the feasts and dances, grew older. The terrible castellan, more amorous than ever of the seductive fay who made him lead such a grand life, no longer touched a sword or a suit of armor except in play. Always at Isobel's feet, he kissed her long white hands a hundred times a day. He lay down on the reels of wool and silk with which she wove marvelous tapestries and went to sleep in the delights of that soft existence.

"Scarcely two years had made of that man, so strong and so renowned, a debilitated dotard. To see him riding, his back stooped and his face inclined over the pommel of his saddle, one would have thought him the father of that lively and brisk lady in bright garments, with the noisy cortege, who devoured space on her spirited mount.

"Soon he could not even follow the cavalcades in the country, among the rocks and through the forests; but he would have died on the road rather than leave Isobel for an hour, rather than renounce the pleasures of her young court. In vain he heard in his passage the laments of his vassals, who saw him perishing. In vain the physicians ordered him to rest. More avid every day for enjoyments that seemed to flee him, he demanded fêtes himself when Isobel did not give one. When the young knights were drunk, he still held out his empty glass. When they collapsed wearily after hectic dances, Ulrich, surrounding Isobel with his thin arms, demanded a night of amour.

"But, the day after one orgy, the castle was draped with black. The flowers, torn from the turrets and the windows, were thrown into the current of the Rhine, which was traversed by a boat of mourning. The guests fled at top speed on their horses, and the knell sounded in all the surrounding churches. It was the funeral procession of the sire of Linkenberg, having died decrepit, in middle age, while Isobel the Resuscitated, younger and more beautiful than ever, recited psalms and led the mourning."

Master Sturff paused momentarily to look at Franz, who, his respiration halting and his eyes staring, no longer seemed to be listening to his story. He was worried by the student's strange ecstasy.

"Well, Franz," he said, "have you understood me? Ulrich von Saul had died under the devouring kisses of that daughter of Hell..."

"Because she was beautiful!" exclaimed the young man, his lips quivering and his eyes humid. "What intoxication and what joy! Oh, my master, I want to follow the cavalcades and the noisy hunts and the mad dances! I want to love her too, to run after her, to drink the wine poured by her white hands and hold her silks while she embroiders, and, mad with happiness, to waltz with her, eye to eye!"

"Insensate! A thousand times insensate! Have you not understood that that creature is a devouring willi,[19] a daughter of death and of Satan, who would drink your youth and your life? Franz, my son, wake up!"

"What does death matter to me? What doe Hell matter to me? I love her recklessly..."

"Franz, my son, Ulrich is dead."

"I want her amour; I'm avid for the joys she gives!"

"Listen again, wretch! It's twenty years since Ulrich died, and since then..."

"Since…!"

"My dear child, there are no more fêtes at the manor of Linkenberg. No lords or ladies go near it any longer, as you well know. The turrets are black; yellow wallflowers are growing in the walls. Madame Isobel is alone, always alone! That is because her beauty is decep-

---

[19] Alphonse Karr's oft-reprinted story "Les Willis" was reprinted in his *Contes et nouvelles* (1856) in the same year as the publication of *Minuit!!* but must have appeared previously in a periodical. Nadiot probably knew Karr, a close friend of Théophile Gautier, whose libretto of the ballet *Giselle, ou Les Willis* (1841) was similarly based on the German legend on which Victor Hugo had based his poem "Les Fântomes" (1829).

tive bait, which hides a mortal poison, and two more coffins have already followed the baron's.

"When she was widowed, fear took hold of the urgent troop of her knights, and then doctors in black robes came to say masses at the castle. In addition, muted anger agitated the region. There was talk of infernal possession and exorcisms. Half voluntarily and half by obligation, Madame Isobel shut herself away for the duration of her mourning.

"A year after Ulrich's death, when all the noise had died down, she gradually emerged from her retreat—no longer with a entourage, this time, for her din and her orgies would not have been tolerated in the region now that the Sire von Saul was no longer there to protect the Resuscitated; but she mounted her ardent horse again and rode around the country like a woman possessed; or she set out on the Rhine in a long and narrow boat, singing night and day.

"Then, she was no longer the reckless willi made for pleasure, who intoxicated her followers with wine and amour without respite or repose. She was a fay of eccentric allure. She was seen passing, like the spirits of ballads, over the mountain ridges and through somber woods, or guiding her boat along the reefs.

"Still beautiful, as no one else was beautiful; still as seductive as the ideal of youthful dreams, she seemed to float above abysms, or skim the mountains in sublime flight. When she was seen to appear behind ivy-clad keeps in her white dress, like a spirit of olden times, or traversing roads with her veils blowing in the wind, people accompanied her with their eyes with the regret of being unable to follow her, and the dreaming mind ran after her.

"There was a young count at the castle of Irrenfels, a great hunter, who descended the Rhine more often than any other in order to see Madame Isobel drifting on the river at the whim of the current. He soon fell in love with her—like you, poor child, like all the others…madly.

"He even wanted to marry her, in spite of the advice of all his relatives; but Madame Isobel refused for a long time to accept his hand. She took pleasure in rendering him madly amorous by means of her damnable coquetries, incessantly drawing him in her wake, amusing herself intoxicating him with her tricks, always to disappoint his ardent desires.

"Sometimes, she fled under the dense oaks of the Niederwald or met up with all the fantastic spirits of Germany; and Count Heinrich encountered teasing sylphs in tortuous paths, which amused themselves by throwing branches in his face; in the middle of clearings, deceitful fays that agitated their sky-blue scarves made him believe that he had reached the edge of the forest.

"Sometimes, she launched her boat on the Rhine at the hour when the sun pierces the clouds and embroiders them with golden reflections, while the river, covered in mist, does not yet allow its banks to be distinguished; and when her lover was ready to join her, she gained two or three lengths and disappeared into the fog, throwing jets of water into the air, which fell back, scattered by the breeze into a thousand pearly droplets.

"That's the Loreley," said the boatmen, signing themselves. "She chats in the evening with the King of the Alders and sings by night in the Tower of Rats. Flee, sire!"

"But Count Heinrich did not listen to anyone., and Madame Isobel celebrated her second marriage. Six months later, Franz, after only six months, the bells of the region sent forth a funeral knell again. Count Heinrich had died, like Baron Ulrich."

"Poor woman!" murmured Franz, his eyes full of tears.

"Poor woman, you say? Rather a vampire thirsty for blood...a leech that drinks human life in order to sustain her infernal reign..."

"How I would love to follow her through spaces...to forget the vulgar world by her side...to live in the midst of the spirits that populate the land of dreams. Isobel! Isobel! Flower of poetry, queen of pleasure, ideal of amour!"

"Yes, that is what Conrad von Hütten, the savant doctor, thought. He came to Linkenberg after the death of Count Heinrich in order to clarify the history of Isobel the Resuscitated, and he stayed here, at first because he wanted to inform himself thoroughly and then because the chatelaine knew so many things and talked so well...and then because he loved her, as Ulrich and Heinrich had loved her...to damn his soul!

"She was a bacchante, and a fay; he was a doctor...and that was all there was to it!

"This time, the marriage, celebrated without pomp in the chapel of Linkenberg, only preceded the funeral of Doctor Conrad by a few days. But few bells were rung, there was no display of splendor, and Madame Isobel no longer dared cross the drawbridge of her castle, for the peasants would have stoned her.

Several years went by before she reappeared. Some even thought that she had returned forever whence she had come, and people were beginning no longer to fear her, when, on a beautiful feast-day—it was two years ago, I believe—she was seen reciting her prayers in the church of Saint Ursula, as she had done before she had died and been resuscitated.

"Wise men trembled and drew away...young fools looked at her, and followed her at a distance. You, sad insensate, you love her!"

Franz made no response; he seemed scarcely to have heard the last part of the narration and remained absorbed in his dreams. But he suddenly raised his head at Master Sturff's final words and looked him in the face.

"Tell me, Master," he cried, "on your honor, is everything that you have told me true?"

"On my honor!"

"You aren't playing with me? You aren't taking pleasure in creating phantoms and terrors for me?"

"No,"

"Well, so much the better," said the student, bounding from his seat. "So much the better, for in that case, I can obtain a glance from her, a thought! Who knows? If, as you say, she is abandoned by everyone, if noble lords draw away from her fearfully, perhaps she might love a humble student who would give her his blood, his heart, and his life..."

"Franz, Franz my son, you're mad! Sit down and stay here."

"Adieu, Master, adieu," said the young man, launching himself toward the door without wanting to hear any more. "I'm running to Linkenberg to throw myself at her feet, t obtain her love and to die."

But before Franz was able to reach the door, Sturff had seized him with a powerful hand and forced him to sit down again.

"Shut up!" he said, energetically. "If it's necessary to use force to retain you, I'll use it, but I won't let you escape in order to run to a certain death. You're my favorite child; I've attached my heart and my mind to you, and I won't suffer that you throw yourself as pasture to that monster who lives on human blood!"

"If you keep me here I'll escape tomorrow, and if you retain me tomorrow as well, I'll escape the next day, or in three days—at any moment, in sum, as soon as I can."

"But my friend, can't you see that that creature isn't a woman—that she belongs to another race than yours? Don't you realize that you can't possess her without dying?"

"Who is talking about possessing her? You're only thinking about vulgar and carnal desires, and you can't conceive of the amour that intoxicates me. Let her only look at me, let her love me and tell me so—that's all I want from her, all that I need from that immaterial creature..."

"Poor fool," murmured the master affectionately. "Poor fool! You're all like that, young dreamers of twenty years. That pale woman with dark eyes and golden hair, whom you love and from whom you only want a glance or a word, isn't she an illusion that is devouring you and killing you, all of you? Oh, many have loved her, perhaps many more will love that fantastic beauty who has killed them or will kill them!

"And yet, there are chaste and charming young women in Germany made to render them happy and to be good wives for them! Young women like your sister, Franz...!"

"I love Isobel and I want her love, I tell you! Your remonstrations excite me, and that's all. My God—you, a magician, the pupil and friend of the great Cornelius

Agrippa, can't you save me by warding off the evil spell?"

"Alas, my friend, don't believe with the vulgar that we scholars can do the impossible. I know how to distil Arnaud de Villeneuve's ardent water, the clear liquid that ignites on contact with fire and gives, with its little blue flame, without light, a heat more intense the hottest braziers[20]; I know how, by means of the combination of unfamiliar acids, to melt, dissolve and transform metals; I know...but what does it matter? No human power can prevent Isobel's gaze from pouring poison into your soul, her caresses from devouring your life, and her kisses from killing you!"

"Oh, a truce on lies. Scholar or sorcerer, you can do something for me. If not, what will you do, then, you who have watched my movements and interrogated my heart, you who have just told me this horrible story, you who have taken pleasure, and are still taking pleasure, in filling my soul with terror and hope? Come on! You can give her to me...and you aren't doing it, and you don't want to do it?"

"Child! Poor child! Poor fool!"

"Oh, but do you know that I'm going to kill you?" cued Franz, seizing Sturff by the throat with the energy of anger. "You're going to die if you don't talk, this instant! Recite your magic words, my master; send your infernal messages quickly, or your hour has sounded!"

---

[20] Author's note: "It was Arnaud de Villeneuve who first made alcohol." The name is the French version of that of the reputed alchemist Arnaldus de Villa Nova (c.1240-1311), whom legend credits with being the first person in France to distil wine to make "eau-de-vie."

With a bound, Master Sturff escaped from the young man's grip, and with a single effort of his wrist, he sat him down on an oak stool.

"I'm much stronger than you, friend," he said. "To convince me, it's necessary to adopt other means than those of brute strength, for you're a prisoner here, and if it pleases me to keep you here for many hours or days, I'll succeed without difficulty, by God or the Devil!"

Then Franz burst into sobs and fell at the feet of his conqueror.

"Oh, I beg you," he said, in a suppliant voice, "only let me see her! Let her speak to me! Let her know my amour and spare me a glance!"

At that moment, a hammer-blow resounded at the exterior door of the house. It was broad daylight, but visitors were so rare in Master Sturff's house that his eyebrows frowned while he lent a ear.

The door opened, and the magician's valet came upstairs rapidly and arrived in his master's room greatly upset.

"My lord," he said, "it's Madame Isobel, the chatelaine of Linkenberg!"

For the first time, since hearing his host's story, Franz experienced a sensation of terror at the unexpected apparition. Who had summoned her? What had she come to do?

That was as rapid as thought, for scarcely had the valet announced her than Madame Isobel entered majestically, followed by her page, Her dark eyes launched devouring gleams, whose attraction was invincible. Her white and diaphanous hands seemed to promise intoxicating caresses. Her hair, which resembled luminous clouds, surrounded her forehead with a radiant aureole.

She paraded a fixed and omnipotent gaze around the room, which subjugated those who had once received it forever.

"Master Sturff," she said, "you are a savant pupil of Cornelius Agrippa von Nettesheim, the illustrious astrologer of Madame Louise de Savoie. You have the science of the future as well as the past. I, Isobel von Verghten, widow of the Sires von Saul and von Irrenfels, request that you research my destiny in the divine book whose characters are stars, and see there whether I ought to await a new spouse."

Sturff stared at the Resuscitated woman in his turn, as if to prove to her that he could withstand her fascination,

"I will do as the noble chatelaine asks, as soon as night returns," he replied; "but will she deign to promise me, in exchange that she will never welcome, as a lover or as a husband, my friend Franz Mullingen, who is here, and whom I love like a son; for then, all the energy and power I possess would be employed in defending him, by any means."

Isobel turned her gaze slowly toward Franz, who, trembling, blind and half-dead, had thrown himself at her feet.

"Are you mad enough to love me?" she said, covering him with an ardent gaze.

"Forgive me, Your Highness...and return it to me!" cried Franz, who thought he might die after so much audacity.

Isobel did not reply to her lover, but she said to Sturff: "Bring me your response to Linkenberg at nightfall. I shall expect you."

Then she went out, as if she were in haste to get away from the house of the mage now that she had heard the student's confession.

Franz, motionless with astonishment and no longer knowing whether he was the victim of a dream, did not even try to follow her. As soon as he had recovered his composure slightly he threw himself into Sturff's arms and wept with joy.

"Is it true, my master? Did she speak to me? Have I seen truly, then? Does she know that I love her?" he cried, in a halting voiced. "Oh, that's happiness! She might love me!"

"Franz, that monster has divined your amour, has followed you here, and has come to look for you this morning. You're my prisoner, and you won't go out of here without having sworn me an oath."

"No longer to love her, perhaps? My master, I won't make one that I can't keep."

Scarcely had Franz let that imprudent speech escape than he repented of his frankness on seeing the windows firmly closed and the doors strongly locked, separating him from the outside.

"No, Franz, not that oath, but another, which you can keep...an oath not to leave Cologne for twenty-four hours—in sum, not to see her again before I have spoken to her."

"Master..."

"Swear, or you shan't get out! At least give me time to defend you! Let me find a means to preserve you. Go to your dear mother's house, child, and give me your word that you won't leave it before tomorrow."

"Well, I swear... yes, until tomorrow!"

It was with a sensation of infinite wellbeing that the student felt the morning air refreshing his brow, and external influences gradually acted upon the effervescence of his mind.

At first he could not take account of his own condition. Was he emerging from a dream commenced the day before, or had he really spent the night awake in Sturff's house? Had he heard the strange things recounted that were now confused in his memory? And Isobel? Ws it true that he had seen her, that he had spoken to her?

Those multitudinous ideas cast him into a dolorous uncertainty. His temples were on fire. His heart was beating with frightening violence. He crossed the city like an insensate, bumping into walls and pedestrians, scarcely thinking either of his mother and sister, who were waiting for him, or the promise that he had made to Sturff not to quit Cologne for the whole day.

His over-stimulated passions were seething within him with a previously unknown ardor. He had glimpsed the possibility of attaining Isobel, who had become a hundred times even more desirable since Sturff's stories had surrounded her with mysteries, and for love of her he would have gone through Hell.

The day before, his amour, great as it was, had remained in a latent state, like everything that is without hope; but since then, infinite horizons had opened to his pride and his desires. Through the fantastic memories evoked by Agrippa's pupil, nothing remained to him but the perception of a sublime being, an ideal creation satisfying to all the aspirations of the dreamer, to all the appetites of the human monster known as a poet. And he felt at the same time an inextinguishable thirst for poetry and an imperious need for enjoyment. In a word, he needed infinity, and the infinity that was Isobel.

Suddenly, he felt his incoherent march stopped by an obstacle that blocked his path. He raised his head and recognized he chatelaine's page, who saluted him respectfully.

"My lord," said the page, "my noble and powerful mistress invites you to come and visit her this evening in her castle of Linkenberg..."

Franz's exaltation became delirium. He fled through the city and the countryside uttering cries of joy and dancing insensate jigs.

"Isobel! Isobel! Mistress of my soul, source of all joy! Isobel! Isobel!"

Bells launched at full tilt were ringing the mass of the dead.

"Eternity is absorbed in an hour of amour! Isobel! Isobel! Queen of space, queen of time, queen of pleasure!

"What are you doing, my brother? Our mother is anxious. Where did you spend the night? Today is the day of the dead. Come and pray with us for the souls in purgatory."

For the second time, Franz awoke with a start in the middle of his dreams, and looked before him.

His sister, a pious and gentle girl, barely sixteen, had taken him by the arm to attract his attention. She was wearing cornettes of mourning, and was carrying wreaths of immortelles and her rosary in her hand.

"Are you ill, my brother? You have a strange expression. Would you like to go back home before the prayer?" the candid German girl went on, raising her limpid gaze to the student's troubled face,

"Leave me alone, for God's sake! What have I to do with the dead?"

"Franz, our father and our mother are praying for them. Don't you remember our relatives and friends who are no longer in the world?"

"Eh! Let the dead alone, I tell you, and long live life! Long live happiness, long live intoxication! Go away!"

And Franz ran away, repelling his sister, who signed herself with moist eyes, and prayed for him: "God protect you, my brother!" she said.

Franz made a gesture of indifference. What did the opinion or the blessings of the child matter to him? When he had put some distance between her and him he turned round to see her draw away, weeping. How simple and vulgar she seemed then!

Isobel! Isobel!

All day long Franz wandered like a madman, and when evening came he left the city to draw gradually closer to the manor.

Then, in his crazed head a thousand fantastic images spun: Isobel, transformed into a deceptive shadow appeared to him in the clouds with a gaze to damn the angels, while an amorous voice murmured intoxicating words in his ear. And he did not listen either to the knell, which seemed to be making songs of amour to everyone as a funereal accompaniment, nor to the cries of the ospreys that were fluttering beneath the terraces of Linkenberg.

The time seemed long—very long!—to him. Through the colored windows he saw lights blazing, as if, within the shadow of the walls, the proud chatelaine were preparing one of her old fêtes. In the distance, he seemed to hear a delightful music.

When it was time, he presented himself at the postern of the castle. Immediately, an archer sounded a horn and the drawbridge was lowered.

On the threshold of the manor he found Isobel's page in ceremonial costume.

The page opened the doors, bowing down to the ground. Franz followed him and traversed rooms dazzling with light but all solitary.

Silent valets were stationed at intervals, and saluted him with quasi-automatic movements. Doors were opened wide before him, with both battens, as if he were the long-awaited master of the deserted castle, but no sound struck his ears, except for a soft music that passed through the air at certain moments, launching a volley of chords, while intoxicating perfumes saturated the atmosphere.

Finally, the page stopped, and showed Franz the chapel of the manor, resplendent with gold and flowers. The altar was decorated, as on days of grand fêtes, and the lamp in the sanctuary was emitting its largest flame. Two thrones had been set up at the foot of the altar. Two prie-dieux supported gilded missals and a nuptial ring.

"There," said the page, "are the preparations for my lord's marriage. A chaplain has come from far away, and Madame Isobel is waiting for Your Highness in the hall of honor to walk to the altar."

Franz, dazed, almost made with astonishment, terror and amour could neither gather any of his scattered impressions not proffer a word. Mechanically, prey to an unknown ecstasy, he followed the page through the multiple detours of the immense manor. Through the confused perceptions of his mind he tried to rediscover a glimmer of reason, in order to convince himself that he had fallen asleep the day before in the church of Saint

Ursula and that he was continuing to mingle with a terrible nightmare the crazy intoxications of a dream of amour. Then he allowed himself to be led, fascinated by the seductive images; and, driving away all the anxieties of reality, he no longer feared anything except waking up.

Far from disappearing at the supreme moment, however, the phantasmagoria continued, for suddenly, in a hall even more splendid than all the rest, Franz found himself before Isobel, dazzling in diamonds and gold.

The poor student had never dreamed her so beautiful even while listening to Sturff's narrations. His imagination, launched at full tilt, had never glimpsed such seductions in his most foolish visions. He fell at Isobel's feet as she came toward him, losing consciousness of himself.

"So it's you, my dear husband," she said to him. "You've finally arrived! Come and give me the nuptial ring, my beloved. Come quickly, for I've been waiting for you for long days! The candles are burning on the altar, the wine sparkling in the cups, and the nuptial bed is extended under velvet curtains."

Sustained by the page, Franz allowed himself to be conducted to the chapel, where the unknown priest was waiting in grandiose costume.

When the future spouses were placed on the thrones that awaited them, the priest commenced the office in a foreign language. The ceremony was full of pomp and magnificence, but the organ did not play the sacred music that Franz loved; it was still the same distant harmony, with strange chords. Only the voice of the priest resonated distinctly under the Gothic vaults, the illuminated beams of which appeared over the somber windows like the mesh of a lace of light.

Finally, the officiant quit the altar and, returning to the spouses, he pronounced a benediction that Franz did not hear. Then he gave him the ring, in order to put it on Madame Isobel's finger.

The student obeyed, still under the empire of an irresistible fascination; but scarcely had the ring reached the second phalange of the delicate and transparent hand than he felt his loins gripped as if by a steel spring.

"Come, my husband!" said the chatelaine, drawing her spouse toward the nuptial chamber. "Come with your beloved! Come with the Isobel who attracts your heart invincibly, who occupies all the thoughts in your mind and who wants to drink all the amour of your soul. Come, my Franz! Come, Sire Castellan! This is your manor; this is your domain, these are your vassals! This is your wife; this is your bedchamber with rich drapes! This is your bed with crimson curtains, crystal columns and soft cushions!"

But while Isobel was leading Franz along a line of mute servants, the sentinels at the drawbridge were heard sounding horns with all the might of their lungs, and the page hastened after the spouses.

"Excuse me, Your Highness," he said to Madame Isobel, "but the magician of Cologne is at the postern of the castle. It's in vain that the guards have told him to go away, as Your Highness commanded; he wants to be introduced."

"Let the sorcerer enter! Let Master Sturff of Cologne enter, and let him see my beautiful nuptials! Go fetch him, and bring him before this high window, solidly defended by a fine steel grille, which plunges all the way from the platform to our alcove. Let him be brought, and quickly, with four archers for an escort, to hold him and accompany him to my balcony."

And Sturff was brought, as the chatelaine had said. Four men-at-arms carried him as far as the balcony, the window of which opened on that bedchamber dazzling with light and gold. Through the grille he could see his friend, almost his son, drunk with amour in Isobel's arms.

He uttered a heart-rending cry and tried to launch himself forward to defend him and take him away from the Resuscitated; but the narrow steel mesh stiffened against his efforts and the archers surrounded him like a living wall.

Isobel watched the convulsions of her vanquished enemy scornfully as he exhausted his strength in a futile struggle, and she summoned her new husband in an intoxicated voice. "Come, my sweet friend," she said. "Place your head on my heart… listen to it loving you!"

And Isobel took the young man's head in her beautiful hands in order to place it on her breast.

Immediately, Franz's forehead wrinkled like a flower desiccated by the ardors of the sun, and his hair, his beautiful ash-blonde hair, turned white, like flax soaked by the dew.

"Plunge your gaze into mine, sweet friend!"

Isobel the Resuscitated fixed the flame of her eyes upon the limpid eyes of the student. And Franz's eyes sank into their orbits; his pupils arrested, fixed in the irises, and were covered by a cloud, like those of the dead.

"Let's exchange our first kiss, sweet friend!"

The pale woman, her eyes ablaze, her tresses brilliant with light, surrounded Franz with her arms and kissed him with avid lips...

And while Sturff escaped, by a supreme effort, the crazed student fell to the floor, exhaling his last sigh...

The next day, the Archbishop of Cologne came with his clergy to look for Madame Isobel, who was having her manor hung in mourning for the funeral of her fourth husband. Sturff had summoned all the doctors in Germany to do justice to the willi.

And they said Isobel was so maltreated by the doctors, says the legend, *that she was never seen again.*

However, for a long time since then, mystics have still searched, on the Rhine, in the dense woods, or behind the ruined walls of the castle…and elsewhere…and everywhere—everywhere, beyond what is real.

In vain, simple and pure young women like Franz's sister call to them; in vain wise men cry to them not to throw their hearts as pasture to the monster that devours them. They run, they always run, after the deceptive fay… after Isobel… after the IDEAL.

The Reflection of Conscience

"For, Monsieur Hannequin, that poor Manoquet is mad, quite mad... and in that case..."

"In that case, my dear Vanvré, what do you want to do about it?"

"What do I want to do about it? But in sum, it's a very disagreeable proximity!"

"Possibly; but as long as Manoquet doesn't deliver himself to acts of exterior and patent folly, there is only Madame Manoquet..."

"Madame Manoquet is already not so sure, and if she dared... After that, you can tell me what she thinks of her daughter... Ha ha! That's double six. Monsieur Hannequin; the six or the six, you have the choice!"

It was toward the end of August 1840, in the principal café of a little town in the south of France, that Messieurs Vanvré and Hannequin were exchanging that conversation while playing dominoes and consuming their cups of coffee.

Monsieur Hannequin was the deputy of the maire of A***.

Monsieur Vanvré was an advocate, and had acquired a certain importance in the département by virtue of his skill, his verbal fluency and his liberal opinions.

As for the café, which was illuminated by gas and lined with mirrors, like those in Paris, it was one of the most brilliant in the province and one of the municipal glories of A***. It was the Café de la Mairie.

At that moment, Vanvré undoubtedly desired to obtain the good graces of his partner, for he was calculating his play in order to let him win. Evidently, the deputy maire was turning a deaf ear, and did not seem at all disposed to hostility toward Manoquet, once his maire and presently the flower of qualified citizens and the pearl of electors. But it was only half past eight, and Vanvré could keep him in the café until ten. Then again, Hannequin lived within rifle shot of the Place de la Mairie and could walk home with him; that was another quarter of an hour.

It was, therefore, with a sage slowness that Vanvré was sipping his coffee after the first round of dominoes. After every mouthful he clicked his tongue with the mild satisfaction of a man digesting while caressing his favorite hobby-horse and sure of his effect,

The maire's deputy, no less absorbed in the enjoyments of gastronomy, darted a circular glance around him and contemplated the customers of the Café de la Mairie; they were all people well reputed in the district, having incomes or fine properties under the sun, as befitted the clients of that model establishment, the moderate opinions of which were well-known. He calculated, on the face of each habitué, the present and future of their fortune, thought about possible and probable alliances of families, the dowries of daughters, the heritages of sons, and drew up the account of the district for the hundredth time.

"A tidy fortune, in sum," Vanvré murmured, in a distracted tone.

That exclamation, in the midst of the silence of his thoughts, had the effect of a rocket on Hannequin.

"Eh? Whose?"

"Manoquet's."

"Ah! Yes…especially since he's bought Les Bar-bettes[21]…and an only daughter. That will be a nice match!"

"It'll be necessary to see… for if the father's head is becoming unhinged, as people say… my word… adieu the deputation, and then..."

"Bah! That's small town gossip... it isn't a crackpot who can govern his affairs so well."

"The fact is that he's spent a little…"

"Yes: twenty thousand francs, Madame Manoquet's dowry."

"But how the devil, with twenty thousand francs, has he been able to buy Naugeac, a noble terrain, a châ-teau, and then the three Marne farms and Les Barbettes, which are worth a hundred thousand?

"For a start, he's inherited from his uncle Patureau..."

"Good! Twenty thousand francs! That makes forty, in all,."

"And his savings? He trims his sous well, Père Manoquet, let it be said without reproach."

"Let's say that in the twenty years that he's been thrifty, Manoquet has saved two thirds of his income, that only makes another ten thousand francs."

"And his wines, his eaux-de-vie?"

"Yes, yes, he has profits. Oh far be it from me to claim that Manoquet doesn't sell his wines well; he makes me pay dearly enough for them; but in the end..."

---

[21] The most common meaning of the word "barbette," from the Middle Ages to the nineteenth century was a kind of head-dress, or, more narrowly, a chin-band securing a veil. The term was expanded metaphorically to take in other supportive structures or partial enclosures.

"Well, what? Hasn't he also been able to obtain interest on his capital for twenty years?"

"Not bad... not bad. It's known that gold coins can have children; well, by lending at fifteen or twenty per cent to cultivators in difficulties..."

"Get away! My dear Monsieur Vanvré, don't say such nasty things, damn it! And then," the deputy maire added, in a lower voice, looking around the room, "walls have ears, Monsieur Vanvré!"

"I didn't say thirty...

"Shh! Come on, I know that those damned Barbettes hold you by the heart... for if Père Mornaix had bought them, Manoquet wouldn't have been able to pay the property-qualification for the imminent elections and double his daughter's dowry. Then you'd be able to aspire to the crown. That's the nub of the matter, isn't it?"

"Oh, I have no ambition. Certainly, if I wanted to marry an heiress I could find others than Mademoiselle Manoquet, and if, later, I wanted to become a député, it wouldn't be that fellow who's hinder me. It's true that today, it isn't men of talent that are necessary, but men ready for anything... hirelings who'll be the humble valets of ministers on every occasion... Never mind! Forget it, Monsieur Hannequin," said the puritan candidate, observing a significant frown in the part of the maire's deputy. "A small glass of Chartreuse, no, before recommencing the game? You beat me just now."

"As you wish, Monsieur Vanvré...it's your turn to start!"

"You always beat me; that's because you're strong. Waiter!"

The small glass of liqueur was swallowed in silence and the game was recommenced, with the gravity in regard to the petty details of life that is the foundation of provincial mores.

All memory of previous conversations vanished, at least from the deputy's mind, between the emotions of winning or losing. His eyes reported anxiously to the zigzag formed by the dominoes laid out in the table, to the mysteries of the game, carefully dissimulated from his adversary's gaze.

"Five or blank..."

"Blank everywhere..."

"Three or blank... "You can't go? Domino!"

That victory cry, uttered again by the deputy maire, caused Vanvré to start, who remained plunged in profound reflections in his turn.

"There are lucky people, all the same," he murmured.

"How you say that in a tragic tone, with regard to the loss of a simple game of dominoes," said the deputy, disguising poorly the real satisfaction that his win caused him.

"Everything succeeds for them...even misfortunes...even crimes," articulated Vanvré, without responding.

"Good God, who do you mean?" exclaimed the municipal officer, beside himself, opening eyes as wide as lotto balls.

"Manoquet!"

"Manoquet! But in sum, what are you trying to tell me, Monsieur Vanvré? What have you got against my friend Manoquet, our former maire, and what are you trying to imply?

"Oh, nothing, poor man!"

Monsieur Hannequin threw the dominoes back into their box furiously and put his elbows on the table. In the attitude of a man determined, no matter what the cost, to listen to what he would not want to hear.

"Finally, what do you mean?"

"As you wish, Monsieur Hannequin. It's quite simple, however; I mean that, as we were saying a little while ago, Monsieur Manoquet has been lucky all his life in his affairs, and I'll even make the reflection that the murder of poor Père Mornaix the day before the adjudication of Les Barbettes has been a real stroke of luck for him. But now he's gone mad!"

"In truth, my dear Vanvré, it's you who are mad!"

"By the way, how is the affair going? Has the murderer finally been discovered? You ought to have received news from the prefecture? Is the gardener who was arrested guilty?"

"The order for his release was issued yesterday. The alibi is sound and clear. It's incomprehensible! But there's ten o'clock chiming; let's go,"

As they got up to leave, their attention was attracted by an exchange of invitations and refusals that had taken place outside the door of the café. They were about go past the two interlocutors when four simultaneous exclamations attested a reciprocal recognition.

"When one mentions the wolf… It's truly a case for citing the proverb, my dear Monsieur Manoquet," said Vanvré, extending his hand first to the newcomers, with the social grimace that enables so many cowardices to be committed in the name of politeness. "Bonjour, Monsieur Gaujac."

The deputy saluted Monsieur Gaujac, who was his present maire, first, and then addressed Manoquet.

"It's true," he said, "we were talking about you. How's it going? Come in, then."

"Thank you, Monsieur Hannequin," responded a short, stout bald man, volubly, while taking three step backwards, lifting his hat and exchanging handshakes with the two domino-players. "Thank you, but it's ten o'clock and Madame Manoquet doesn't like me to be late back. I've been ill recently. Bonsoir!"

"Oh, no! We'll bring you back!"

"You only live a few paces away."

"A simple game..."

"No, no...bonsoir!"

"Get away! Does the Café de la Mairie scare you?" asked Vanvré, laughing at Manoquet's sincere efforts to get away."

"Scare me?" retorted the little man, with a start that seemed strange in such a trivial circumstance. "Oh, nothing scares me, Monsieur Vanvré. I have no reason to be afraid."

And Manoquet entered with a firm tread, but with his eyes closed, like a man going into fire for the first time. He scarcely saluted the lady at the counter, without turning his head, and went to huddle in the darkest corner of the room. His three companions followed him and sat down at the table.

Vanvré threw the dominoes on the table; the maire ordered punch, and his deputy started the game. As for Manoquet, he gazed at the veins of the grey marble of the table with a sustained attention.

"That's no good, my dear neighbor," said Vanvré rejecting a domino. "Five's required everywhere and you're putting down a two. Are you ill? How red you are! Look in the mirror!"

"The mirror, the mirror... let the mirrors alone," said the landowner, his physiognomy all awry. "I'd rather play."

"Poor Manoquet! You know that his head has been topsy-turvy since Mornaix's murder," said Vanvré to the maire, in a low voice,

Hannequin frowned, for the remark had been made loudly enough for everyone to hear. In fact, Manoquet had raised his head abruptly and looked his neighbor in the face. Like the majority of southerners, he went straight toward danger, perhaps out of fear.

"Why would my head be topsy-turvy, Monsieur Vanvré?" he demanded.

"Oh, a topsy-turvy head… did I say that? You must have misheard. But sometimes, one can be struck by an event like that, and there'd be reason enough! It's a horrible thing to think about, Messieurs, that in our land, with the gendarmerie, the public ministry and all the guarantees of civilization, someone can murder a tranquil bourgeois in his own house, take his money and go home, or elsewhere, with his hands in his pockets without anyone seeing him, without anyone pointing him out, without all the justices in the realm finding anything to render to the injured society but a release with no charge to answer."

His gaze fixed, his lips trembling, red enough to make one believe that he was about to have an apoplectic fit, Manoquet murmured: "Well?"

"It's disappointing, in truth," said the maire, "but what do you want? All possible research has been carried out and nothing has been discovered. Do you know anything? No, you don't, do you? Well then, let's not talk about it anymore, for it isn't cheerful. For myself, I confess that I no longer go back home without a certain terror."

"That's natural. You see, one thing is certain, which is that the murderer is local, that he knew Père Mornaix and his habits, for to be able to unearth the money from behind the mirror in the drawing room, he must have been sure of his fact."

"Vanvré, my dear friend, your neighbor really is ill," exclaimed the deputy, indicating Manoquet with his gaze.

In fact the landowner's eyes were bulging from his head, his respiration had halted on his lips and his trembling hands were dropping the dominoes. The punch had just been brought. Hannequin offered him a glass, but the unfortunate man tried in vain to raise it as far as his lips; his arm refused its service. Suddenly, he threw the glass at the mirror that was facing him and saw it shatter.

The belated customers who were still in the café raised their heads with exclamations of astonishment; the lady at the counter ran to the four domino-players' table and the three partners launched themselves toward the furious Manoquet.

Before they could reach him, though, their glasses, seized by Manoquet, had broken three more mirrors.

In an instant, the tumult reached its peak. Passers-by came into the café; the waiters took away all projectiles: cups, carafes and billiard balls. The maire put on his sash, his deputy tried simultaneously to restrain the madman and to appease the crowd; the lady at the counter was weeping.

Through the chaos, Manoquet, beside himself, searched for an exit in order to flee, but the solicitude of Hannequin removed all possibility of escape. After the first emotion, four vigorous arms seized him and sat him down forcefully on a banquette. He was made to swallow a few glasses of sugared water with ether; cold compresses were placed on him, and his hands were slapped, but it was all futile. Every fragment of mirror reflecting his image caused a further fit of fury; he treated his friends as executioners and demanded the guillotine repeatedly in exchange for such a torture. Finally, his efforts exhausted, the three companions let him go.

He launched himself out of the café with one bound and started running in the direction of his abode.

Vanvré, the maire and the deputy came out a few minutes later and followed him at a distance.

As can be imagined, that strange fit gave rise to a thousand comments. Hannequin admitted that Monsieur Vanvré had been right, and that the mind of his respectable friend Manoquet was perhaps deranged. The maire contented himself with affirming the alienation and recognizing that he would doubtless soon find himself in the unfortunate necessity of having his most considerable adminstratee locked up. As for Vanvré, loyal to the principle that effects ought to be traced back to causes, he repeated once again that the mysterious murder of Père Mornaix was an unusual event quite capable of disturbing the brain of a honest man.

After twenty minutes of walking and conversation. The three actors in the strange incident in the Café de la Mairie stopped, a short distance away from Manoquet's house. It was a fine rectangular house situated at the extremity of the town, whose façade, preceded by a garden-courtyard planted with trees and surrounded by railings gave the whole property the majestic aspect in which one recognizes, in every town in France and the world, the habitation of a master.

Thus, before that building, so evidently above all its surroundings, the maire and the deputy stopped talking about the event in order to devote themselves to their private reflections.

The whiteness of those intact walls, the green lawn surrounded by flowers, which resembled a carpet in the middle of the courtyard, the tall poplars that stood sentinel to either side of the door, and finally the railings so envied throughout the district, said clearly to the two municipal officers: *Respect Manoquet! Manoquet, who possesses that beautiful building and seven or eight farms; Manoquet, who pays a thousand francs in taxes and who, in consequence, might one day become your député; Manoquet, who dines with the prefect of the département twice a year; Manoquet, who could, if he wished, cause a upheaval in the district to the point that Gaujac would cease to be maire and Hannequin to be his deputy!*

Meanwhile, that demigod, whose decline put in question such an important affair, arrived at the threshold of the gate. It opened before him as if by enchantment; and a stifled exclamation was heard.

Vanvré made the observation that doubtless Madame Manoquet, anxious about the absence and madness of her husband, had been awaiting his return in the garden. The door of the house was heard to open and close again, and it was all over; it was necessary to return to town.

The return was more silent than the advent. It was late, and everyone was beginning to think about his lodgings, where a housewife was waiting, all the more impatient because, in spite of the advanced hour, rumor of the affair of the café could not have failed to spread. In any case, the maire and his deputy had already thought that things had become serious enough to demand reserve.

They separated, but not before the pitiless Vanvré had had time to say to the maire: "All the same, if I were the examining magistrate, and such a strange crime were committed in my arrondissement, I wouldn't forget the axiom of Roman law that recommends, before anything else, to seek whoever profits from the crime!"

Manoquet, that bourgeois so respected in the little town of A***, was one of the most important landowners in the province, squarely placed on a thousand arpents. In certain départements of the Midi, no one is more unassailable than people who possess "fine property under the sun," as they say. People have the highest consideration for territorial wealth, and above all for a man who has been able to acquire it himself. Then again, those fortunes and those positions, which seem infamous to us in Paris, have an enormous value in the provinces, and if one looks hard one would be astonished to see the influence they exercise even outside their immediate circle.

About two months before the epoch in which our story begins, the département had been disturbed by one of those crimes of which three or four are committed every year in France. An old miser, suspected in the region of hiding a treasure, had been murdered, along with his maidservant, in an isolated house near A***.

A vulgar clasp-knife known to belong to the victim, a broken mirror, behind which a hole in the wall still contained two or three louis forgotten by the thief, two cadavers and an open window were all that the law could collect or observe when its representatives arrived at the scene of the crime. Since then, it was in vain that they had searched for the author by all possible means. The weather had been dry, and consequently, footprints had been unable to serve as clues. No bloodstained garment had been seen on anyone in the region.

An old deaf gardener who lived in a hut at the extremity of Monsieur Mornaix's garden had been arrested, for form's sake, but as we have seen above, for lack of any evidence whatsoever, he had been released.

Perhaps the reader will already have glimpsed the horrible drama that had left two cadavers in that solitary house; perhaps, through the obscurity of a moonless night, he will have recognized Manoquet escaping with a fever from his beautiful house and proud railings, wandering through the countryside with no fixed plan, approaching the Mornaix house by chance, listening one by one to his incoherent thoughts. Perhaps he will even have followed the march of those thoughts, from the first, which was the crazy and unhealthy desire to obtain Les Barbettes—the fine property that would make him the master of two communes—to the last, which arrived as rapid and as somber as a flock of crows:

The adjudication takes place tomorrow...for cash. Everyone in the locale believes that it's me who was going to buy it. I've already received more tips of the hat because I'm believed to be the future proprietor of Les Barbettes. I've dined with the sub-prefect, who introduced me to the député of a neighboring arrondissement, saying: "Monsieur Manoquet, one of the richest landowner in the region...perhaps soon to be your colleague..." What will people say, then, if I don't buy it? "Manoquet isn't as rich as he seemed...Manoquet is ruined... So why has he built a palace with railings? Why does Madame Manoquet have an Indian cashmere, and Mademoiselle Manoquet hundred-franc dresses?"

"My word," Vanvré will say, "I'm not sorry not to have become his son-in-law, Ha ha! The dowry will only pay for Madame's toilette... He must be short of money not to have bought Les Barbettes, a property adjacent to

all his properties...which will put him continually at odds at home, and which will earn him three or four lawsuits a year...

There are people who put on less show and are more solid...little Père Mornaix, for example...there's one who surely has enough in his hidey-hole to buy Les Barbettes...and pay for them in cash... in good gold....

Little Père Mornaix!

Once that name is lodged in Manoquet's brain, his ideas take a fatal direction, unique and fixed, which nothing can change.

What the devil does he do with his money? He must have more than a hundred thousand francs hidden, since he's a hoarder... If that money had been invested for twenty years...in good land...! As long as he doesn't have the idea of buying Les Barbettes! But no! Misers love gold for its own sake... That's life, though! Why is so much money in the hands of that fellow? He's seventy years old; he's going to die soon!

To die! What if Père Mornaix were to die, in fact? Who the devil would be worse off? He has no wife, no children, no fine house, which would be carved up after his death for litigation between majors and minors...

But where does he hide his treasure?

And gradually, moved by an indefinable attraction, Manoquet tightened his circle around the isolated house. No sound could be heard, the shutters being closed. A ray of light filtered through one of them. Manoquet drew nearer...mechanically...

In the room that served as a drawing room, Mornaix was pacing back and forth. He was alone, and seemed to be prey to a violent conflict. From time to time, he stopped in front of the mirror over the mantelpiece and stood still there. However, it was evident that he was not looking at himself. His gaze wandered anxiously around him; he seemed to fear being seen in front of that mirror, yearning to approach it.

The money is there, Manoquet said to himself. *However, what if someone other than me, Monsieur Manoquet, former maire and considered bourgeois of the town of A , if someone in poverty, saw that old Mornaix, so paltry, so frail and so jaundiced...and that mirror, which defends a treasure...?*

For there must be a lot of money in there...double louis! The old miser has never changed any gold!

After one last glance, more fearful than the others, Mornaix took from his pocket his old black-handled knife, well-known in the neighborhood for having undergone more metamorphoses than Jeannot; he slid the blade, worn and chipped by usage, into the grove of the mirror, and leaned on it. The mirror opened like the door of a cupboard and allowed Manoquet's feverish gaze to see a hole crudely excavated in the wall, and in that hole an ironbound casket.

Mornaix opened the casket and took out piles of gold, which he stacked in front of him.

Manoquet took a step back from the window.

Double louis! They're doubles!

And he returned to his observation-post, trembling.

The piles emerged one by one, felt and weighed by the miser, and were lined up in two rows.

Damn! I believe that he could buy Les Barbettes, pay on the nail, and still have two good bags of ready cash...

Les Barbettes...

As if that name, which had just crossed Manoquet's mind, had awakened an echo, the little old man stopped lining up the piles of gold and took from a nearby table a yellow scroll of paper, which he unrolled. On that paper Manoquet read, in two-inch letters that appeared to him to be flamboyant:

Tomorrow, 23 June 1840
DEFINITIVE ADJUDICATION OF THE PROPERTY
KNOWN AS LES BARBETTES
Canton of A***. Commune of A***.
Woods, meadows, laborable ground, pond,
buildings of habitation, two farms, etc.

At that sight, what demon, what vertigo, seized Manoquet in its sharp claws?

To arouse jealousy, to smash the window with a violent blow of the fist, to leap on the old man, and to squeeze his frail neck between two clenched hands, was the work of a second.

A dull gasp was the only plaint of the miser, who gathered his last vestiges of strength in order to close the mirror over his treasure. The mirror, too rudely impelled, struck the wall violently and shattered.

But before the maidservant woken up by the noise had had the time to get up, Mornaix, thrown to the ground, choked by two muscular hands and bruised by the redoubled blows of his murderer, whose knees dug into his chest, had rendered his last sigh, without uttering a cry.

Then Manoquet seized the knife lying beside his victim and launched himself into the shadows before the maidservant. A struggle of a few minutes, cries, soon expiring in the unfortunate servant's throat, pierced right through, and then stifled sighs and the fall of a heavy body on the tiles, announced that the first crime would have no witness.

The assassin returned to the drawing room, pierced the already-lifeless body of the unfortunate Mornaix with several thrusts of the knife, replaced the scattered stacks of gold precipitately in the casket, seized the treasure, knocked over the lamp and fled through the darkness.

Who could have had the idea of walking on the roads at that hour? Who could have seen Manoquet reenter his house silently by a concealed door?

On arriving stealthily in his bedroom, his first care was to hide the casket under the mattress of his bed; then he fell, exhausted, into an armchair.

He took his head in his bloody hands as if to contain his brain, ready to explode.

Then he leapt up, under the first afflictions of terror, and thought of examining his clothing, which must be stained with blood, and to make all traces of his crime disappear.

Every movement, however, was for him the occasion of a new fright; the quivering of the curtains of his alcove when he brushed them, the sound of his footsteps on the parquet, the rapid scrape of the chemical match on the glass-paper... slight as they were, all those small impacts that he made caused him to shiver.

It seemed to him that he had awakened lugubrious echoes and that his wife was about to get up and come into his room, perhaps even his daughter...

Then he hurried, and the noises became more frequent and more sonorous, and the matches went out one after another, emitting a blue-tinted light.

Finally, however, the candle was lit; its first light caused Manoquet a further emotion. Nevertheless, by an effort of will, he shook off those puerile anxieties and first looked at his hands, which were stained with blood, already dry.

His first concern was to undress in haste and put on his night-clothes; then he washed his bloody hands, wiped them carefully, and came to stand before the mirror in order to see whether he might have blood on his face.

Then he went pale, lurched, and turned round swiftly, stifling a cry of fright.

In that mirror, the mirror in his bedroom, on the mantelpiece, it was not himself that he encountered; it was old Mornaix, such as he had seen him two hours before, his eyes staring, standing before another mirror, which hid his treasure. First, he leapt backwards, looked everywhere: in the curtains, under the furniture, in the corners; then he recalled his memories...

Mornaix was dead, quite dead, strangled and pierced with knife-thrusts. It was, therefore, not him; he had not followed him. But perhaps it was his shade...

That idea rendered courage and bravado to Manoquet. To be afraid of a specter, him, Manoquet!

Get away! he said to himself. *Am I a child?*

And he approached the mirror again.

The little old man was still there, with his nankeen trousers, his worn jacket, its sails and pigeon-wings, and that gaze, that insupportable fixed gaze that seemed to plunge its two rays into Manoquet's eyes like two jets of flame.

This time, the murderer remained riveted to the parquet before that vision, which became horrible. He wanted to flee but could not; on the contrary, an inexorable power drew him even closer to the mirror and the reflection.

Meanwhile, he heard three o'clock chime, and the fear of human justice, which was about to awaken with the daylight, rendered him strength. He tore himself away from the mirror, seized the clothes that he had just taken off, and carried them into the most remote corner of the room in order to inspect them. But it was necessary to return to the fireplace in order to fetch the candle, and he could not resolve to do that. His teeth were chattering, and fear chilled him to the marrow of his bones.

He took his garments one by one and tried to see bloodstains in the dim light, but it was in vain that his fingers palpated the cloth and his eyes pierced the darkness; the garments were dark in color and he could not distinguish anything.

Daylight was about to arrive, however.

Then, by a supreme effort of will, he marched forward, closed his eyes, seized the candle and returned at a run.

By an extraordinary hazard, his clothes were not stained. He turned them precipitately in all directions, carefully washed away all spots of blood, wiped them, dried them, washed his face and hair, and by an excess of precaution, rubbed with paper, which he burned thereafter, the drops of red-tinted water that had fallen on the parquet. Then he blew out the candle.

The darkness gave him courage. He dared to traverse his room at a stealthy pace, open a window cautiously, go out enveloped in a dressing gown and shift the surface of the freshly-dug earth of a flower bed, in order to bury the bloody water of his ablutions.

Finally, he went to bed.

Four o'clock chimed, and day was beginning to break; Manoquet, rolled in his sheets, hid his head in his pillows and summoned sleep in vain. His imagination, launched at full tilt, went astray amid his memories and his terrors. He was lying on Père Mornaix's casket, and the place where he was lying, where the thickness of the box made a lump, seemed to be hot. How could he hide that denunciatory casket? Where should he put it? Under his bed? It would be found. In his cupboard? But what if his wife asked for the key? Bury it? The daylight was too bright.

Only in the evening... which is to say, the following night... could he bury it... it would be empty then, the Barbettes would be purchased...perhaps?

Perhaps! For between now and then, many events might emerge with the daylight. That daylight was pale as yet, but it was increasing by the minute; the crime might be discovered. The two cadavers would be found...and what if one of the two were still breathing? What if Mornaix were still alive? What if he were about to show up at the adjudication of Les Barbettes and say, pointing the finger: "There's my murderer!"

Them the phantom of his victim loomed up in Manoquet's memory, just as he had already seen it twice in the mirror, and he closed his eyes, hiding his head under his bedclothes, afraid of seeing it again.

Then a thousand contradictory fears competed in his mind: fear of human justice, which was perhaps about to follow, step by step, his actions during that fatal night; fear of the first faces that he was about to see after his awakening, of the gaze of his wife and his daughter's morning kiss; fear of the gossip of the servants, who would soon find out about the horrible event, and of the expression his face would take on as he listened to them; fear of being afraid, above all, if he approached a mirror.

In vain he tried to prove to himself that his vision had been born of a moment of fever; in vain he assured himself, by means of the most convincing reasoning, that only a hallucination could have shown him the shade of his victim in the place of his own reflection; in vain he palpated his bald cranium and his nascent morning beard to prove to himself that he was really himself, and that the mirror could only send back his own—Manoquet's—image. An irresistible nervous tremor agitated all his limbs. Every gradation of the light augmented his anguish instead of dispelling it, for he was afraid as those who do not believe in phantoms are afraid and who mock remorse.

Finally, the time to get up arrived; it was necessary to get out of bed and get dressed—which is to say that it was necessary to see his clothes again, bloody a few hours before, to confront his family and servants, to mingle with social life…and pass before mirrors.

It was necessary to shave, to remain for twenty minutes before a mirror!

And Manoquet plunged even deeper into his pillows. *What if I don't get up?* he said to himself.

Yes, but that would be an indication…people would say: Manoquet usually gets up at six o'clock… at seven he is dressed, shaved, groomed… Manoquet has got up late…he must therefore have slept badly!

Come on!

Am I mad, in any case, to fear in broad daylight a hallucination of darkness? The dead are dead… Am I no longer a man? After all, am I not Manoquet this morning, as I was yesterday, and will I not be the proprietor of Les Barbettes this evening? I'm buying it, I'm paying in good gold coin…my God, isn't that all that's necessary? Who would dare not to respect me…to suspect me? Me! What folly!

And with a leap, this time, Manoquet was out of bed. He got dressed in haste, darting one last glance of inspection, in daylight, over his garments, and traversed his room resolutely in order to go to the window and attend to his beard. He went past the chimney-breast without turning his head.

But what unknown force obliged his gaze to become oblique, in order to interrogate the mirror furtively? What magical painter sketched therein, in less than half a second, the hook-nosed profile of Père Mornaix and his white-powdered side-whiskers?

Was the vision real, then? Was it constant?

A horrible idea traversed Manoquet's mind and combined all his terrors into one alone, but sufficiently intense and poignant to make him forget all the rest, his future wealth and his present dreads alike; to make him search with his gaze for some nail or coat-peg from which he could hang himself by making a noose with his cravat.

He wondered whether that implacable apparition would be visible for him alone...whether others, in seeking Manoquet with their gaze. might not see Mornaix standing by his side, or behind him, or in his place—in sum, like him, seeing him in mirrors.

He heard the sounds of wakening in his house, footsteps in the corridors, doors opening and closing, the bell at the gate announcing suppliers; Minute by minute he felt the moment approaching when his domestics would bring his breakfast, when his wife would come into his room, when a first gaze was about to meet his own and see...what? Him, or an accusing specter? Him, or the phantom of that emaciated miser, paltry and old, lying in his own blood, facing the hidey-hole of his pillaged treasure?

That increasing anguish became unbearable; before that odious dread, all the punishments of human justice seemed go him to be child's play, and he scarcely remembered taking the stolen casket from beneath his mattress in order to hide it temporarily in a cupboard. What did that proof matter, if the shade of the owner were there, demanding his stolen property in front of everyone?

Finally, the key turned in the lock and the door opened. It only took a second, but it was one of those seconds during which hair turns white.

Madame Manoquet came in.

"Well, Manoquet," she said, "have you heard the news?"

"No," replied the unfortunate, in a stifled voice.

"They say that it's that old skinflint Mornaix who is going to buy Les Barbettes."

"Oh! But how do you expect me to know that? Why ask me that?" he stammered.

"Because you went out late yesterday evening, you could easily have seen people who would have told you; they even came to tell me!"

"I went out late? No, no…you're imagining things. Don't repeat that, at least!"

"What, that you went out late yesterday? All right, if it's a secret, I won't say it."

Manoquet breathed out; the crime was not yet known, and the specter was not visible to all eyes.

"Bah!" he said. "He doesn't have Les Barbettes yet, the old miser…and it'll be necessary for him to bid high to snatch then away from me!"

"You're buying them, then?" exclaimed Madame Manoquet, overjoyed, leaping on to her husband's knees. "But how have you found the money?"

"It's all right, don't worry; I can pay."

"You must have money hidden, then... what savings are you hiding from me? Come on, confess, confess!"

"Perhaps," replied Manoquet, whom the prospect of being the owner of that land, so much desired, intoxicated him to the point of making him forget everything else.

"What happiness! What joy! What a surprise! Instantly, we'll be the foremost everywhere. You'll be a député, Manoquet. I'll be able to go to Paris for six months in winter. And that Vanvré, that petty advocate without cases who's still paying court to Élisa—I'll show him the door. I want to marry our daughter in Paris and not in this provincial hole... What do you think?"

"Yes, truly."

"Manoquet, I want a carriage, to go to our country houses and to show myself in the city."

"We'll see, we'll see, Madame Manoquet," replied the bourgeois, flattered in the most secret inclinations of his départemental vanity. *I was mad*, he thought. *The specter has only ever existed in my brain. Let's chance it! Who the devil could suspect me?*

"Oh, you're hiding things from me? Where do you hide your money, then?" said Madame Manoquet, in a fashion common enough among women, which consists of circling a secret until they discover it, willingly or by virtue of lassitude.

"You're too curious."

"Yes, yes, that's why monsieur plays the werewolf all night..."

"Will you shut up!" cried Manoquet, bounding in his seat. "For a start, there's nothing true in all that. I don't have any money hidden anywhere other than my writing-desk; I've combined with my savings a few loans adroitly contracted outside the arrondissement, and I'm going to buy the property boldly. I still need ten thousand francs for the payment, but take my word, when the deal is done, your uncle Bajac will lend them to me... and it'll require a disaster for the whole sum not to be reimbursed within a year. That's my business, my dear!" said Manoquet, delighted with his improvisation. "Now, stop talking!"

Madame Manoquet was too sincerely delighted not to be content with that explanation. She stood up and released her husband's head, which she had not ceased to caress, pet, flatter and kiss.

"Come on, it's necessary to get dressed now, have breakfast and hurry to the adjudication as soon as possible. I'm going out this evening. Trim your beard!"

That proposition made Manoquet tremble from head to toe.

"Bah! It'll do until tomorrow," he said,

"Tomorrow! Are you mad? Since when do you no longer trim your beard every day?"

"For once!"

"Yes, and it'll be noticed? People will say: *Manoquet is so troubled today that he's forgotten to shave.* Get away! Courage!"

"Leave me alone."

"Look, here's your shaving soap, prepared; look how foamy it is! Here are your razors, here's your mirror. Hup! Let's go!" And with a rapid movement she daubed her husband's chin with soap.

The latter had summoned up all his courage for one last proof. He darted a glance into the mirror and fell back against the back of his armchair, vanquished.

It was still Mornaix that he had just seen in the mirror that his wife was holding out to him, but Mornaix in a shirt collar and a face daubed with soap.

"Oh!" he cried covering the mirror with his hands.

"Well, what's the matter? Are you afraid of your shadow now?"

"Of…my…shadow…?" stammered the unfortunate, with wild eyes. "That's not my shadow…"

"Come on, my friend, what's the matter with you?" demanded Madame Manoquet, frightened this time by her husband's distressed expression.

For a moment, Manoquet did not reply. He appeared to be making a difficult resolution, and was still pushing way the mirror with both hands. Finally, he looked at Madame Manoquet with an anguished and pleading expression...

"My wife," he said, "do I...have white hair?"

"You know very well that you're balding, and that the hair you still have is dark."

"So I'm not seventy years old? I'm not powdered, I'm not thin and jaundiced, like..."

"You're mad, my friend."

"But...I really have soap on my face?" said the unfortunate, hesitating between hope and terror.

"Of course."

"Let's see, then!" he cried, with a new energy, abruptly taking his hands away in order to look in the mirror. "Is that me…?"

He did not finish his sentence, because he had just found the same head facing him: the same head covered with soapy foam like his, and with the intent gaze that he must have, and behind that head, the astonished but calm face of Madame Manoquet.

His eyes bloodshot, he broke the mirror into a thousand pieces, and only just had time to open a window in order not to suffocate.

Madame Manoquet stood there, motionless and consternated, without understanding anything of that strange scene.

Suddenly, Manoquet, to whom the impression of the air had returned self-control, turned round and looked at his wife with a frown that announced a resolution forcefully made.

"My good friend," he said to her, "I can no longer see a mirror in my house, and that instantly, right away! Begin by covering the one over the mantelpiece for me with a napkin, your shawl, your apron—whatever you wish."

"But…?"

"Do it immediately, without delay!" he said, in a tone that did not suffer any reply.

Madame Manoquet set about obeying, very anxious about her husband's mental derangement, but without attempting any further observation.

When the mirror was covered, Manoquet breathed out and started striding back and forth in his bedroom like a prisoner accustoming himself to liberty. Then he finished getting dressed, after having wiped his face and brushed his hair.

"You've understood what I said, haven't you?" he asked his wife. "It's necessary that this evening, when I return, all the mirrors in the house have been removed; those employed by you and your daughter must be dissimulated by a curtain or, put in a cupboard as soon as you have concluded your toilette."

"Yes, my friend."

"From tomorrow on you'll make arrangements for a barber to come to shave me every morning."

"Very well."

"And above all, not a word to anyone about this…find a pretext… a story… take all that upon yourself. For me it's a matter of life or death, you understand?"

"Don't worry," replied the poor woman, trembling.

"Now leave me to my affair. Les Barbettes will be purchased this evening."

A few hours later, in fact. the town of A learned simultaneously about the acquisition of the envied property of Les Barbettes by Monsieur Manoquet, the former mayor and future député, and the horrible murder of old Mornaix and his maidservant. As can be imagined without difficulty, in spite of the exaggerated importance attached by the principal individuals of the town to the adjudication, a crime so audacious had the effect of a revolution. The anxiety and dread were unanimous.

No proof or indication put the police on the track of the guilty parties, and the more impenetrable the mystery that enveloped the bloody drama seemed, the more the terror increased. Some believed in a gang of murderers organized for theft and pillage; others, more clear-sighted, recognized the characteristics of a isolated crime, but were only more fearful of a murderer who was able to hide his tracks so well and escape all the investigations of the law.

The crime had been discovered at about midday by the gardener, who, not seeing his master come out at the usual hour, had entered the house to request his orders. At one o'clock, the entire male population who were not at the adjudication of Les Barbettes had been informed, and at four o'clock the examining magistrate, the sub-prefect and the king's prosecutor began their enquiries.

As can be imagined, there was a general agitation in the town square when, after dinner, everyone summoned transmitted his information, his impressions and the terms of the witness-statements. All suppositions and all the most improbable conjectures were put forward by turns. But in the midst of the concert of felicitations that Monsieur, Madame and Mademoiselle Manoquet received regarding the new acquisition, through the prestige that surrounded that fortune, henceforth ranked among the most considerable in the département, who would have dared, even in imagination, to make a connection between the purchase of Les Barbettes and the murder of Père Mornaix?

And yet, there was already in that square, so noisy and so animated, one person who did not let herself yield either to banal curiosity or to the pride of wealth. While the smoke of incense intoxicated, for an hour, the murderer himself, a gnawing worm had taken up residence in the heart of his wife. That presentiment, the dread that she did not dare to name, which she rejected and stifled under reasonings, hollowed out a furrow and left its black trace. She was afraid.

Thus, in spite of the fortune, life became dolorous in Manoquet's beautiful house. Bizarre incidents succeeded one another there, and were like the chimes of a bell that recalled dread to the heart of the poor woman as soon as she relaxed into facile life while chasing chimeras.

Manoquet became taciturn and somber; a host of trivial things displeased or offended him. After the irrevocably-proscribed mirrors, to the great astonishment of the servants and visitors, it was the turn of all brilliant surfaces: polished marbles, shiny furniture, crystals and glassware.

In vain Madame Manoquet searched for pretexts and excuses; in vain she deployed, in regard to everyone, the cleverness that is the genius of women, even the vulgar, when important interests of the heart are in danger. Nothing could hide completely from the eyes of her daughter, her domestics and her intimate friends the increasing eccentricities of her husband; nothing could chase anxiety and suspicion away from her own thoughts.

And then, Manoquet went out! He went to his affairs. As little as possible, he went to see people that he could not avoid without attracting attention. And everywhere, he found mirrors! And everywhere, in spite of his precautions, in less than an instant, he found himself in the presence of the accursed apparition. Then he went home prey to fever and delirium.

That life became horrible.

Sometimes, the unfortunate, losing all hope, made the resolution to put an end to that poisoned existence by suicide; sometimes, he reattached himself by ambition to the hope that abandoned him incessantly. For a moment, he thought he glimpsed the end of his torture; he convinced himself by force of will that he would vanquish the specter and subdue his remorse.

One day, a few weeks after the acquisition of Les Barbettes, Mademoiselle Élisa expressed the desire to see the beautiful property and to "hang up the cooking-pot" there. Manoquet welcomed that request with joy, which reattached him to life via his pride as a landowner, and his wife was glad of a project that seemed to promise the invalid a distraction that might be salutary.

They departed, therefore, as a family; and to begin with they admired the fine "cattle carpets," as country landowners say—the meadows—that surrounded the barns and farmhouses. They calculated the product of the harvest; "tasting," so to speak, the quality of the land; they admired the beauty of the trees, the wise distribution of the crops, with the enthusiasm of connoisseurs habituated to comparisons.

As they approached the house, everything became a new joy; the orchards were rich, the fruit-trees bearing well, the ponds seemed to be full of fish. Then there were flowers, fountains, grassy banks and verdant arbors—in sum, the multitudinous glories of a landowner, which make a country house the foremost in the arrondissement and its fortunate possessor the object of general envy.

First they went into an elegant vestibule preceded by a perron of several steps, then into a vast dining room where the farmers were preparing a meal furnished by the fish of the ponds, the birds of the poultry-yard and the fruits of the gardens; then Manoquet opened the door that communicated with the drawing room and took a few steps in the dark, for the shutters and curtains were closed because of the sun's heat.

Scarcely had his eyes pierced the darkness, however, than a hoarse cry escaped his breast and he fell stiffly on to the parquet.

Madame Manoquet and her daughter ran to help him. The farmers came running; the unfortunate was transported into the open air and the light; his face was violet-tinted, his mouth foaming, his teeth clenched.

Madame Manoquet cut her husband's cravat, threw water in his face and made him breathe salts, while the weeping young woman asked for a foot-bath and slapped the hands of the moribund,

Finally, Manoquet drew breath, and looked around with wild eyes.

"That's right…that's right," he murmured, in a halting voice. "We're in his home…!"

"Whose home, my friend?" said Madame Manoquet, trembling, dismissing everyone with a gesture, including her daughter.

"You didn't see him, then, coming toward me through the drawing room mirror, as if to do me he honors of his house?"

"In the name of Heaven, my friend, who? Who do you see in all mirrors, in all glassware, everywhere?"

"Him!"

"But Who? Who, then, once again? You're killing us with your terrors…have you lost your reason? Who?!

"Him! Mornaix!" replied the unfortunate, with a mad gaze.

Madame Manoquet threw herself upon her husband in order to stifle his speech.

"Shut up, shut up, wretch!" she cried. "For your daughter, for your life, for all of us…"

"What? What have I said?" Manoquet said, suddenly, brought back by his wife's fear to a sentiment of reality.

"Nothing, my friend," the poor creature replied.

From that day on, until that of the scene that we described at the Café de la Mairie, the life of those two beings was infernal. Manoquet sensed madness gripping his cranium in spite of his combats, in spite of the energy of a will that had become terrible. His wife waited, her heart wrung by anguish at every twist and turn of the criminal investigation, warding off scandal by supreme efforts.

At any price, she wanted to deflect attention away until winter, in order to take Manoquet to Paris without causing too much astonishment; but every day, new scenes rendered deception impossible; every day the catastrophe became more imminent. The wife and mother saw it, inevitable, terrible and menacing, ready to make the edifice of so much play-acting and lies collapse.

There are unknown devotions and unmerited expiations that ought to have the power to redeem crimes. During the two months that had gone by since the murder, Madame Manoquet had suffered a horrible martyrdom. In consequence, she seemed to have aged ten years. Her hair went white, her face paled and became deformed; but she did not want anyone to notice those changes, which would have attracted attention to her interior. Almost dying, she dyed her hair and put on rouge.

She tried to keep her husband at home under a thousand pretexts; one day it was a head-cold, another aching joints: indispositions that prevented a patient from exposing himself to the inclemency of the weather but did not require the assiduous cares of a physician.

Manoquet was only too well aware of the derangement of his faculties; he was too fearful of having his visions outside not to support his wife's precautions. But if it was necessary to avoid, above all things, letting the anguish and the terrors of the criminal be seen, it was equally necessary not to astonish the unquiet spirit of the little town by an absolute retreat. The tyrannies of provincial life came continually to subject that struggle to further proofs. Sometimes there were cruel reflections that were circulating, sometimes indiscreet visits that came to interrogate the domestic hearth. And if the rich landowner missed a dinner or a fête, the whole village came the next day to obtain news of "poor Monsieur Manoquet."

Madame Manoquet was obliged to intimate to the domestics the order to keep silent about their master's mental derangement. The position became intolerable.

It was, therefore, with an anguish impossible to describe that the poor woman waited for her husband on the evening when he had gone out with the maire. But when she saw the hours going by without Manoquet reappearing, her anxiety no longer knew any bounds. She made her daughter and all the domestics go to bed and waited, walking in the courtyard, for the moment to open the door to the criminal pursued by the furies. The honor of her daughter and her household in danger, the life and fortune of her husband menaced by the law, had made a heroine of that bourgeoise, futile and feeble before fortune and success.

She had hardly had time to close the gate again when Manoquet, mad and trembling, his eyes haggard, launched himself into his bedroom and threw himself down on his bed.

"My God, what's the matter?" she cried.

"All is lost!" murmured the unfortunate, with a gasp that seemed to be that of agony.

"Explain yourself, explain yourself…what have you done, what have you said?"

"I'm dying…"

"In the name of Heaven!

"They took me to the Café…to the Café de la Mairie, all lined with mirrors; do you understand? I saw him everywhere… in every corner… in all the faces…playing when I played… speaking when I spoke, drinking when I drank. I saw him beside himself, furious, as terrible as a fugitive from Hell, multiplying himself a thousand times, when I fought back, breaking the mirrors... I uttered horrible screams... Vanvré is on the track; Vanvré suspects, and is casting suspicion everywhere..."

Madame Manoquet washed her husband's temples with fresh water, helped him to undress, and then take a calming potion. She sat down beside his bed, prey to unspeakable terrors. Every footstep she heard striking the pavement of the street seemed to announce the arrival of disabused justice. She spent the night putting mustard plasters on the invalid's feet and cold compresses on his head.

Finally, toward morning, he seemed more tranquil.

"Listen," she said to him. "It's necessary to save us all, and we're on the edge of the abyss. You can no longer hide your condition. It's necessary to allow belief in the madness but to hide the cause at all costs. There can't be any hesitation any longer; it's necessary to give our daughter to Vanvré, with Les Barbettes for a dowry. Here's an invitation to dinner for him; it's necessary that he has it this morning, in order to stop his evil tongue..."

"But..."

"It's our only hope of salvation. If you're interrogated about yesterday's fury—and my God, you will be interrogated—nothing can prevent that!—confess that mirrors fill you with horror because, for some time, you've seen a specter therein...that of...your father, for example! The explanation of your terror has become necessary...and after all, it's necessary to have you cared for; you're very ill."

The unfortunate did not respond, for he was, in fact, suffering horribly. The excitation of the fever was diminishing, but the atony that followed the crisis was horrible. He seemed to sense his brain melting within his fiery skull, his ideas dispersing and becoming incoherent, while his vision took on veritable substance and came to life. Sounds only arrived at his ear confusedly, spoken works lost their meaning in his mind, objects vacillated before his eyes, taking on bizarre forms. He felt his will dissolving and his reason escaping him.

Contrary to her expectation, Madame Manoquet did not have to submit to the torture of the curious visits that ordinarily came to interrogate each of her frowns in order to formulate a text and commentaries. No one came to ask for an explanation of the previous day's crisis—no one, not even close friends.

That deathly silence, that general abandonment, redoubled the poor woman's terror; the further the day advanced, the more anxiously she awaited a strange face, on which she would be able to read impressions originating from outside. The questions that she had dreaded so much in the morning she now desired with a violence that became more intense by the minute.

The dinner to which she had invited Vanvré was arranged for the following Sunday. She wrote further invitations and sent her domestics to deliver them, recommending them to bring back the responses.

No response was affirmative, however; some people were in the country, others absent or ill. She sensed a formidable storm building.

Toward midday, the wife of the maire, who had asked Mademoiselle Manoquet to come and give her an opinion regarding some new purchases, asked to be excused that day.

By three o'clock, the waiting had become the horrible torture that only those who have been suspended between life and death at some point in their lives can understand.

"What's the matter, Mother?" Élisa said. "You're very pale. Is my father's indisposition dangerous?"

"Madame," asked the domestics, "is it necessary to go and fetch the doctor for Monsieur?"

And the poor creature tried to hide her torment, and ordered preparations for the fête.

Finally, the bell at the gate rang.

Madame Manoquet ran to the window, and saw a black silhouette through the foliage. She put her hand to her heart in order to compress its beating. Was it the examining magistrate?

"Madame," said a domestic, "it's Monsieur Garraudot."

Monsieur Garraudot was the local physician, who had come without being summoned. He had learned, he said, of the sudden indisposition of Monsieur Manoquet and he had come to offer his habitual cares.

That visit was, for Madame Manoquet, simultaneously a relief and an anxiety; she trembled to put her husband to the proof of the doctor's questions; however, she could not refuse to introduce him without that refusal seeming suspect. Every incident might acquire a decisive significance in that struggle, in which everything was a trap and a reef.

"My husband is in bed in his room, doctor," she said. "Be welcome—I was going to send for you, because"—she added in a low voice—"I've very afraid that the poor man is mentally ill."

The physician went through the drawing room in order to reach his client's bedroom. Madame Manoquet went in with him and opened a gap in the curtains of the bed.

"My friend," she said to her husband, looking at him with the fixed state that subdues madmen, "here's Doctor Garraudot, who has come to see you.

Manoquet lifted himself up on to his elbow with a fearful movement, "Why?" he demanded, in a hesitant voice. "Send him away... I... have no need of a physician."

"Come on, my friend, allow yourself to be cared for," she said, putting her hand on the invalid's shoulder, in order to make him sense the authority behind her plea. "It's his head, Doctor!"

Garraudot approached, palpated Manoquet's burning head and took his pulse.

"What a fever!" he said. "There's reason to fear derangement of the brain or apoplexy. What are you doing for him, Madame?"

"Eh! How do I know what to do, Doctor?"

The physician sat down. "Monsieur Manoquet," he said, "You're very ill. A physician is a confessor, you know. Now, if your malady has a mental cause, whatever it might be, it's necessary for me to know it."

That direct, positive interrogation—brutal, even—caused the moribund to start, utter a cry and hide his head under his bedclothes. It seemed to him that the piercing gaze of the practitioner was about to see his crime in the depths of his conscience, or even to distinguish behind his face, as if behind a mask, the terrible and accusing face of his victim.

Madame Manoquet gathered all her courage. "Doctor," she said, "My husband is pursued by a vision. For several weeks, in all mirrors and all surfaces that reflect his image, he sees the specter of his father."

And she leaned toward the moribund, placed her hands on his forehead, fixed her gaze once again upon the man's haggard and mad eyes, in which she wanted to retain the last glimmer of reason by means of a supreme magnetism, and said: "Isn't that so, my friend?"

But Manoquet writhed like a worm under that gaze; his hands trembled, his teeth chattered and his lips agitated, murmuring words that stuck in his throat.

And the more he was gained by vertigo, the more his wife darted her gaze and pressed with her hands, as if by squeezing that errant head, she could defend him from madness.

A strident cry finally emerged from Manoquet's breast.

"Go away... go away," he said. "Your eyes... your eyes are also mirrors!" And he fell back, as inert and stiff as a cadaver.

She stood up, and let the curtains fall back over the distraught face of her husband. Tears of despair rolled down her cheeks, She was vanquished.

"Well, Doctor?" she said.

The doctor paced back and forth in the bedroom, his forehead pensive, his eyebrows furrowed.

"Well, Madame, I'll come to bleed him tomorrow..."

He picked up his hat and took a few paces to leave, but then he turned back. "Madame," he went on in a whisper, but loudly enough to be heard by the invalid, "there has been much talk in the town about Monsieur Manoquet's visions, and—ought I to tell you?—some people, doubtless also visionaries, in looking at his distressed face, think about another head... Adieu, Madame."

When Monsieur Garraudot had gone, the poor woman, at the limit of her strength and courage, let her sobs burst forth, understanding all her impotence against death and dishonor. She ran to Élisa's room and threw herself into her arms.

"My child," she cried, "pray for your father, and may God save us!"

What happened in the brain of the criminal between the doctor's last words and nightfall? What springs finished uncoiling, what strings broke? No one ever knew, for no one was observing him at the precise moment when madness installed itself there victoriously in pace of the lost common sense.

He was alone; it was dark, and it was two months, to the day and the hour, since he had quit his house by a hidden door to go and carry his evil thoughts into the country.

Without making any noise, but mechanically, as if moved by a spring, he got dressed, climbed out of a window, into the garden, and then into the street.

As ten o'clock chimed he went into the Café de la Mairie.

The town seemed to have arranged to meet there, amid the debris of the previous night. Each society, united in a group, forgot the time, drawn by the heat of the discussion. Gaujac, the maire, Hannequin, Vanvré and the physician formed the most animated of those groups.

At the sight of Manoquet, they all uttered a cry of astonishment and recoiled.

The latter advanced, looking in all directions at the mirrors and the debris, without astonishment and without terror, but with wild eyes.

"Yes, yes, Messieurs," he cried, "you're right to recognize me. I'm Mornaix, and it's natural that the sight of me astonishes you. But have no fear; I don't mean you any harm. It's Manoquet that I'm searching for.

"For Manoquet is a murderer, Messieurs! He entered my home like a thief, like an assassin. He surprised me counting my gold, my wealth, my life. The struggle was terrible…and as he was the stronger, and he had knocked me down, he thought that he had killed me. And as he carried away my casket, he thought that he had robbed me. But no! No! It was me—me, Mornaix—who had killed him, for I had snatched his conscience! It was me—me, Mornaix—who had robbed him, for I had stolen his soul, for I had imprisoned him in my body…in my miserable and old little body!

"You haven't seen that yet, because I wanted to make m suffer for longer…but he, who sensed that he was double, saw my reflection instead of his own in all mirrors. Today, you all recognize me, because the hour of vengeance has come… Go and look for Manoquet in his beautiful new house. Go and snatch him from his opulence and drag him away, to prison first and the guillotine afterwards. Go! Go!

"You're afraid, Messieurs? Phantoms frighten you… Avenge me, then! Avenge me, then, and quickly, if you too don't want to see me everywhere, demanding vengeance, if you don't want to recognize me, with terror, in every mirror, and rediscover my hideous face in every image that shiny surfaces sent back to you. Kill what remains of my murderer! Blood summons blood! Kill him, for he has my reflection as an indelible seal, and while he lives, you will see my phantom… Kill! Kill! To the executioner, Manoquet!"

And he fell down, his limbs stiff, his lips foaming, his eyes bloodshot.

When, after a moment of stupor, they dared to approach him in order to lift him up, he was no longer anything but a cadaver.

"Of what did he die?" asked the curious.

"Of a devastating attack of apoplexy," replied the physicians.

The Slab

On the evening of 20 December 183*, there was a fête at an old town house in the Rue Saint-Louis, in the Marais. A file of carriages was stationed outside the door. As the weather was foggy and the pavement wet, carpets had been laid out in the courtyard, and twill awnings extended as far as the extremity of the perron to protect the ball gowns. All the windows were illuminated; the music of waltzes and square dances was audible in the street. The steps of the staircases and the railings of the balconies were decked with flowers. Liveried valets were opening the doors of the carriages and introducing the guests.

The marriage was being celebrated of Madame de Marneroy, the widow of General Comte de Marneroy, with Monsieur Adolphe Rouvières.

The assembly was numerous: on the side of the bride, an aristocratic society had come, or chosen from the ranks of the administration, the magistracy and the army; on the side of the husband, a few députés of the center left, as one said then, many candidates for all social positions envied by those who did not have them, a few artists, and people celebrated, by whatever entitlement, in the Parisian zone that extends between the Odéon, the faubourgs Montmartre and Poissonnière, the Porte Saint-Denis and the Madeleine.

The bride was a young and gracious person, scarcely twenty-six years old; more agreeable than pretty, more elegant than well-made: a true Parisienne, mediocrely provided by nature, but of whom society and education had made a delightful woman. She seemed sovereignly happy in the new union that she had just contracted, and to be having difficulty veiling the frankness of her happiness under the smiling and tranquil mask of a mistress of a house that was receiving guests.

Monsieur Rouvières was coming and going in the drawing rooms, mingling with all the groups and talking to everyone, like a man taking possession of his house and his society, and a position perhaps long desired. He might have been thirty or thirty-five years old. He was neither more handsome nor uglier than social convention permitted a man to be; his face was intelligent and his manner distinguished. Half-advocate, half-litterateur, occasional poet, sometime philosopher and always a witty talker, it was easily imaginable that he might please and that Madame de Marneroy would renounce for him her liberty as a widow.

In the midst of the dancers and on the knees of dowagers, a third individual was circulating, who seemed to be the monarch of the fête to judge by her noisy and communicative joy. She was a adorable little girl of five or six who was running from one person to another, kissing and congratulating everyone, receiving a bonbon here and a kiss there.

Marguerite de Marneroy was jumping with pleasure at being at a ball like a grand demoiselle, seeing her mother in her ball gown and having a papa. Hers was a happy nature, the most charming of childish natures. She gave her stepfather a thousand caresses and smiled at the new life that her mother's marriage made for her, as she would have smiled at any change, because she could not conceive of the idea of unhappiness.

Pretty Marguerite had curly hair of an admirable ash-blonde, an extremely white skin, lips as red as ripe cherries and dark eyes and eyebrows. That opposition of hair and eyebrows gave her infantile beauty a singular animation and a strange cachet that fixed her pert little head in the memory.

She was known as Pâquerette[22] while waiting for her to grow up, and age had made her a flower queen of the little spring star, and certainly, said the old folk, she was well named, for her young smile and the frank gaze of her eyes rejoiced like April flowers.

While the ball was at its greatest animation, the insouciant child was the subject of all the conversations of dowagers and wives who, for one reason or another, were "doing tapestry."

"That's a pretty girl," said one, "who is welcoming her misfortune very cheerfully!"

"And who smiling prettily at the man who the force of circumstance will make her enemy!"

"Oh! Why her enemy?"

"Well, my God, every cause has its consequences. Monsieur Rouvières is glad, today, to marry a woman whose position permits him to aspire to everything and whose present fortune might sustain many pretentions; but when it's necessary to render to Pâquerette accounts of guardianship, his situation will change considerably. And do you believe that, in seeing the child grow up, he will not fatally think of the day when she will take from him, first this house, then the Château de Marneroy, and also some thirty thousand livres of income..."

---

[22] *Pâquerette* is, in essence, a synonym of Marguerite, both being common names of the flower known in English as a daisy.

"But will nothing remain to Madame Rouvières?"

"Scarcely fifteen thousand livres of income, for in remarrying, she necessarily loses her pension as the general's widow—and when one is habituated to lead such a grand existence, that's very little. It's the budget of a widow who can cut a figure in society without conserving an established house, but it's not what Rouvières needs, who wants to become and remain an important person."

"Mademoiselle de Meillac had no dowry She was well-connected, pretty, raised in a fashion to make an accomplished woman of the world; Monsieur de Marneroy was no longer young, the possessor of a nice fortune; he married her because she combined all the advantages he was looking for. In the contract he assigned her a dowry of fifteen thousand livres if he left children, and Pâquerette was born. That's why Monsieur Rouvières has scarcely twelve years to be rich!"

"Bah! He'll take advantage of those twelve years to become a député, a Councilor of State, or even a peer of France..."

"Yes, that will be the best thing for him to do...but between us, I don't believe that he's very strong. He's thought to have the gift of the gab rather than genuine ability, more ambition than talent. And then, peers of France and Councilors of State require more than fortune!"

"He'll undertake speculations on the Bourse!"

"In sum, he'll get by, that goes without saying...but it will still be necessary for him to renounce the usufruct of Mademoiselle de Marneroy's fortune!"

"How pretty she'll be, Pâquerette! What lovely dark eyes and what vivacity of movements; how healthy and fresh she is!"

"Her grandmother is mad about her. Look at Madame de Meillac in her armchair by the fireside. She's devouring her with her eyes."

In fact, it was curious to observe the exalted tenderness that was depicted in all the old woman's movements for the little creature who was rolling at her feet, climbing on to her knees, adjusting a flower in her bonnet or a curl of her white hair.

"You're going to have a charming little daughter," one of Rouvières' friends, a painter, said to him.

"Yes," he replied, in a distracted tone. "But very noisy, very spoiled..."

A moment later he went past the fireplace in order to introduce an influential député to his mother-in-law. Pâquerette seized his legs, calling him "Papa" and bursting out laughing.

Madame de Meillac raised her eyes to look at her son-in-law and perceived a slight sign of impatience, suppressed beneath the agreeable mask that he was obliged to adopt in order to kiss the little girl.

She sighed, and launched a suspicious gaze at the man who was about to become the severe master of the adored child, and kissed Pâquerette yet again. *As long as he doesn't make her unhappy!* she thought.

"There's a little scamp whom our friend will have put in a boarding-school within six months," said the painter to the député.

"Do you think so? In fact, it's said that all of Madame Rouvières' fortune will revert to Mademoiselle de Marneroy, and, perhaps without admitting it, Rouvières already hates the child who will one day take back that so much envied ease...for between us, he's 'eaten the mad cow,' as the vulgar saying has it; he doesn't get cases every day and often pleads for the glory of it. For

253

myself, I know pertinently that for ten years he's been trying to sell his soul to the devil, and..."

"And the devil doesn't want it? A bad sign, my dear for an ambitious man like Rouvières. And it's that poor Madame de Marneroy who's made the bargain?"

"Which is to say that she'll pay the expenses. Don't worry, now that he has an income of fifty thousand livres, beautiful landed properties and an influential salon, he'll find an acquirer..."

"And then, the child might die," added the painter.

The ball finished as brilliantly and joyfully as it had begun. Gradually, the guests withdrew, and at about two o'clock in the morning, no one remained in the drawing room but the four residents of the house: Monsieur and Madame Rouvières, Madame de Meillac and Pâquerette, who was asleep on her grandmother's knees.

II

Two years later, there was another celebration at the house in the Rue Saint-Louis, less noisy this time. There were no carriages at the door, no music in the drawing rooms. It was an intimate fête, the splendor of which did not extend beyond the family circle.

It was a baptism.

Ten days before, Madame Rouvières had given birth. She got up for the first time and, half-lying on a sofa, she was taking part in a family dinner served in her boudoir.

She was resting her languid head on her cushions; the domestics, whose footfalls were muffled by the carpets, where carefully avoiding clinking glasses and silverware. Monsieur Rouvières was speaking in a low voice in order not to fatigue her and Madame de Meillac was lavishing abundant cares on her.

The guests from outside the household were Monsieur de Meillac, Madame Rouvières' paternal uncle, and Madame Aydie, her maternal aunt, who had come to hold the newborn over the baptismal fonts.

Pâquerette was no longer there.

Had she been put in a boarding-school, as Rouvières' friends had anticipated, or had she simply been distanced momentarily in order that her babble should not deafen her mother. Or…?

"You wouldn't believe, my worthy uncle and my dear aunt, how happy I am to see you become godfather and godmother of my second daughter, as you have been of the first," said Madame Rouvières, in a voice that was still feeble and somewhat plaintive. "At the moment, when I close my eyes, it seems that I'm going back eight years; I believe that it's the day of my poor Pâquerette's baptism all over again. I try to forget the past…oh, if only I could succeed in believing that I've had a long dream, that the admirable child I saw for six years so alive, so cheerful and so pretty were only coming into the world today!"

A few tears ran down the pale cheeks of the recumbent woman.

Madame de Meillac rang to ask for the child to be brought. She thought that the sight of her might console the poor mother, whose heart was torn by poignant memories—and then, she too needed to stop tears that were ready to flow.

A beautiful nurse entered, giving her breast to a baby enveloped in embroidered swaddling-clothes and lace. She presented Mademoiselle Pauline-Marguerite-

Henriette Rouvières successively to each member of the family.

Madame Rouvières propped herself up on her bed, took her child and examined her for at least the twentieth time in a week.

"See, Maman," she said to Madame de Meillac, "what little black eyebrows she has. And her eyes, which she can already open very wide, I find that she has a strange resemblance to...the elder. We'll call her Marguerite, like her, and also Pâquerette, as long as she's small..."

"I beg you, my dear, not to enclose yourself in your dolor like that," cried Monsieur Rouvières, who seemed annoyed by that idea. "And above all, don't try to render a sad memory perpetual, by making it ever-present. Let's call our daughter Pauline or Henriette, but not Marguerite!"

"What does it matter if, on the contrary, that name deceives the regrets of your wife, like the resemblance that is already visible for everyone," said Madame de Meillac.

Monsieur Rouvières furrowed his eyebrows violently. "Come on, dear Maman," he said, in a low voice, leaning toward Madame de Meillac, "don't encourage these follies!"

"Pâquerette! Pâquerette!" murmured Madame Rouvières, smiling and weeping while rocking her baby.

Monsieur Rouvières got up from the table and paced back and forth in the boudoir to contain an evident malaise.

"But my dear friend," he said, after a few moments of silence, "Pâquerette, our dear child, isn't dead... at least, we have no proof of her death. She has disappeared, but we'll find her again. The entire police force is searching for her, and can't fail to have news of her one day. It isn't in a civilized country like ours that children are abducted like that, never to be seen again."

"Pâquerette! Pâquerette!" repeated Madame Rouvières, without paying any attention. She seemed to have forgotten the real world in order to take refuge in an imaginary one. "Yes," she went on, as if in a dream, "this is the way she was when she came into the world. I can see her, in her swaddling clothes... in her long baptismal robe, which I embroidered to make her beautiful... Then she grew...I remember the day when her first teeth came though...my anxieties...my joy when she walked on her own and said 'Maman' for the first time...then the day when I consecrated her to white...."

Monsieur Rouvières had resumed his pacing, having great difficulty restraining the outbursts of an emotion that seemed to participate simultaneously in anguish and anger. Madame de Meillac stifled her sobs with her handkerchief. Monsieur de Meillac and Madame d'Aydie were also weeping.

"She was two years old," the invalid continued, still prey to a sort of somnambulism. "I made her a little white robe in muslin...a short and bouffant little robe...low-necked. Maman, do you remember that you put around her neck than coral necklace, which made her resemble the pâquerettes of the field? I was annoyed, because after my vow, she wasn't supposed to wear red..."

This time, Madame de Meillac could not retain a cry, and the poor mother shivered as if she had been woken up with a start.

"No, no!" she cried, kissing the newborn, "all that isn't true! This is Pâquerette, who is coming into the world, who has no teeth yet, who can't speak, who doesn't smile, but who will grow!"

Monsieur Rouvières took the child from his wife's arms and returned her to the nurse. "Take the child away," he said, in a tone of contained authority. My dear," he added, taking his wife's arm, "my dear, you're suffering, and in your condition such excitement might be dangerous. Go to your room and rest. Come on, come with me."

Madame Rouvières got up and followed her husband. When they had both gone out and the nurse had left the boudoir, the three old people looked at one another, weeping.

"My poor daughter will never be consoled," said Madame de Meillac.

"But after all, the child will be found, dead or alive!" cried her brother-in-law. "All the police in the realm won't remain impotent before that extraordinary abduction..."

"A child six years-old who knows her name and address doesn't disappear like that," added Madame d'Aydie.

"There's some horrible catastrophe underneath this, murmured the grandmother, shaking her head. "My poor child is dead!"

"Dead! Reflect on what you're saying, my sister. There's been a murder, then? And who in the world could have an interest in the death of Pâquerette?"

"Oh, a murder... no, that's impossible. It was the day of our return from Marneroy. We were settling in here for the winter; all the doors were open, and the child must have slipped out..."

"But then, someone would have brought her back... even if she had left the house, the street, the quarter...

unless we believe in fairground performers who steal children."

"Eh! That's still seen!"

"The poor child might have been playing in the courtyard, the rim of the well had crumbled; she might have fallen in while no one was watching her."

"The well was excavated for a week."

"A child who is lost in Paris, after dark, might fall into a drain, into the ventilation shaft of a cellar, into the foundations of a house under construction..."

"The cadaver would have been found!"

The old folk fell silent, not daring to go any further forward with investigations renewed a hundred times.

Monsieur Rouvières returned to the drawing room, still somber and agitated.

"Madame," he said to his mother-in-law, "watch out, I beg you, that my wife doesn't conserve foolish ideas. Don't let her give our child a name of such sad memory."

"Why constrain my daughter to renounce an illusion that consoles her?" replied Madame de Meillac

Monsieur Rouvières added nothing more. He appeared to be extremely discontented, but reluctant to let his discontentment show. After a moment of embarrassed silence, he left the room. Madame Rouvières named her daughter Pâquerette in spite of the muted opposition of her husband, and the grandparents did likewise.

That was not bravado, for no one would have resisted a desire frankly expressed. But the more the child developed, the more it seemed, in fact, that her resemblance to her sister became striking.

Her large eyes, and above all her dark eyebrows, already well-arched, gave her the singular expression that had made Marguerite de Marneroy remarkable. And then, tiny as she still was, Madame Rouvières and Madame de Meillac claimed to find an extraordinary analogy of gestures. There was nothing, including her infantile sufferings, that was not compared to those of the first-born. That strange resemblance was pointed out to all the friends of the household.

"It's my Pâquerette," said the mother. "The elder is dead, but God has had pity on my sadness, and has sent her back to me. The soul of my cherished child has passed into this little body; I recognize her gaze, her smiles..."

Every time the conversation took that course, Monsieur Rouvières left the drawing room with a slight shrug of the shoulders.

"You hated Monsieur de Marneroy's daughter, then?" Madame de Meillac said to him one day, plunging a clear gaze into the depths of his eyes.

Rouvières shuddered. "Me, hate Marguerite? A child who had become mine? I've wept for her as much as you. Oh, Madame!"

"Then why are you so afraid that your daughter might resemble her?"

"Afraid? In truth, Madame, I no longer understand you," said Rouvières, having gone pale.

"If that resemblance and the illusion that it procures your wife were not so odious to you, you would welcome with as much joy as us this second Pâquerette, who is reflowering in the broken stem of the first."

"Madame, that semi-mystical poetry is scarcely accessible to me, I confess; and if Madame Rouvières finds a singular consolation in hallucinating herself with regard to a still very contestable resemblance, I cannot see without displeasure a name imposed on my daughter that

I had not chosen. I regret above all only seeing her loved by way of memory."

The child reached the age of two.

As long as Monsieur Rouvières was able to persuade himself that his wife and his mother-in-law were mistaken, he shook off his painful impressions, and succeeded in dissimulating the terror that agitated him at times; but when the little girl walked and talked, there was no longer any means of refusing the evidence. She was Pâquerette, and no mistake; it was Pâquerette such as the entire residents of the house, all their friends and all the domestics had known her, who protested the fact at every one of her gestures.

Then Rouvières became somber. Since his marriage, he had not ceased to receive luxuriously and open his house to powerful or celebrated people; gradually, he abandoned his interior. He went out earlier and returned later. Often, he dispensed with going to see his wife and kissing his daughter. One might have thought that the child, so much desired by him and initially welcomed with so much joy, had become dolorous for him to see.

When the name of Pâquerette resounded in the stairwells and the corridors, he shivered as if under an electric shock. When the force of circumstance put him in the presence of his daughter, he was obliged to constrain himself to submit to her caresses and to return them.

Outside, he led a noisy life in order to stun himself. He frequented theaters, clubs, cafes, and madcap societies where one forgets for a time the sufferings of intimate life.

However, the more time went by, the more his mysterious anguish was augmented. It was in vain that his wife tried to calm him, to retighten the bonds of the household precisely by means of the presence of the child who ought to have been the joy of the family. He had fits of black melancholy and strange abruptness.

Once, Madame Rouvières asked him if the name of Pâquerette, given to her daughter, was truly painful for him to hear, and whether it was necessary to change it.

"No, no!" he cried, precipitately, and changed the subject.

Nevertheless, they tried to call the child Pauline, and Madame Rouvières avoided comparisons and memories in his presence.

But then it was no longer the visions of others that tortured him; it was his own. Whether the little girl had one name or another, for him she was always the same, and when the residents of the house shouted "Pauline! Pauline!" the testimony of his ears and eyes responded "Pâquerette! Pâquerette!"

With the months and the years she became even more similar to the vanished child. They still had a portrait of Marguerite de Marneroy, made a month before the unknown catastrophe that had removed her from her family, and not one stranger entered the drawing room without recognizing the child that he saw rolling on the furniture or running in the corridors. Among the former friends of General de Marneroy people ecstasized about that incomparable similitude, and the rumor of the phenomenal resemblance soon spread. It was cited in drawing rooms; Rouvières could not go anywhere where it was not mentioned.

Either because that caused him real pain or because he was prey to a kind of unhealthy superstition, he became even more depressed and excessively irritable, and at times, could not contain movements of hatred and terror at the sight of his daughter. He had an inexplicable repulsion for certain costumes, for some of her gestures, and for particular inflexions of her voice.

Now it was him who discovered more analogies every day. It was him who called her Pâquerette without being able to resist the force of the evidence.

"My friend," his wife said to him, "I don't understand why that resemblance seems to make you unhappy. Since Providence wanted to take our first child, is is not, on the contrary, a consolation to see her again in this one, as if Heaven, touched by our regrets, wanted to return her to us? Personally, I try to forget…and I sometimes succeed. And I'd like to believe that Pâquerette has merely changed her name, like her mother."

"Yes, you're right," replied Rouvières, with embarrassment. "But I'm not unhappy…you're mistaken."

And yet, every day his face deteriorated, his eyes hollowed out in their orbits; he no longer valued anything, neither the fortune nor the honors. He would have liked, at any price, to flee the conjugal house or send away the child; but he did not dare. Finally, his malady took on all the characteristics of hypochondria.

There was a room in Madame Rouvières' apartments, once little used, of which the little girl was especially fond, because it had been given to her to store her toys. It was known as "Pâquerette's room," and her mother and grandmother became accustomed to bringing their needlework there in order not to quit the cherished child. They spent several hours of the morning and evening there. When Madame Rouvières had her door closed to visitors she sometimes spent entire days there, and when she was not expecting her husband she took her meals there.

That room was particularly displeasing to Rouvières, and he avoided going into it every time he could do so without affectation. Evidently, if he had asked his wife to sit elsewhere, she would have hastened to return to her habitual boudoir; but he feared above all letting her see his horror for that part of her house, and if a shiver escaped him on the threshold he immediately found a means of explaining it by the cold, a draught or a feverish disposition.

In front of the fireplace there was a large white paving-stone, and in the middle of that stone slab there was a black incrustation that resembled a Greek cross. When Madame de Meillac and Madame Rouvières were each sitting to either side of the fireplace, Pâquerette—for that name had finally prevailed for everyone—continually came on to that stone in order to leap on to the knees of her mother or those of Madame de Meillac. Those games were insupportable to Rouvières, who tried to draw his daughter into other parts of the room, or even to pick her up abruptly, under the most unexpected pretexts.

One day, Madame d'Aydie had come to spend the evening with her relatives and she occupied the middle of the hearth. There was only a small fire, because it was scarcely autumn. In the space encompassed by the three women Pâquerette was crouching on the paving-stones, trying to draw a daisy on the black stones with white chalk.

When he came in, Rouvières did not see her at first. "Where's Pâquerette?" he asked, after the usual salutations.

"Here," said the mother, indicating the hearth with her gaze.

There was only one lamp lit, and, as it was hooded with a lampshade, it cast a circle of bright light on the work-table and left everything else in obscurity. Otherwise, it would have been possible to see Rouvières' eyes become fixed and his hair stand on end.

But at the same moment the little girl got up and ran to her father, laughing, with the good, frank laughter that everyone recognized so clearly.

"Papa, Papa," she cried, "Come and see how I've made my portrait."

And she dragged the unfortunate, whether he liked it or not, directly in front of the fireplace; then she knelt down on the stone again and touched her drawing with her finger, while her blonde head, leaning over her work, resembled the golden heart of the spring flower.

"Here I am! Here I am!" she cried, in a burst of infantile joy.

This time, Rouvières collapsed, and lost consciousness.

He was picked up, made to inhale salts, and transported to his bed.

"Decidedly," said Madame Rouvières, "my husband has an unknown malady, with which I ought to occupy myself. It's necessary to put him in the hands of the doctor."

The next day. in fact, Rouvières had an ardent fever, and became delirious.

Doctor ***, celebrated in the medical world for his aptitude in treating mental illnesses, was summoned. After having examined the invalid over several days and prescribed calming potions, he told the family that Monsieur Rouvières' intellectual faculties had been disturbed and that it was necessary to avoid emotions. Then he investigated, with a skill and a tact well-known to his clients, the causes that might have produced or influenced that derangement.

Several inductions that became clear subsequently, however, were then very confused in the minds of the residents of the house. The facts had not been grouped together, or a host of small details remarked. That is why the illustrious practitioner only learned vaguely the story of Marguerite de Marneroy's disappearance and the strange resemblance of the two Pâquerettes. While carefully conserving all the indications that he could collect, he did not appear to attach any great importance to them, for fear of awakening ideas that he was still repelling himself.

However, the more he studied the aberration of his patient, the more his suspicions took a fatal direction. Evidently, it was terror that provoked ravages in that sick intelligence; but what terror? Was it that of a weak mind dominated by superstition, or that of a guilty man pursued by remorse?

Since the scene that we have described, the delirium had not ceased. As the doctor had observed that the invalid was particularly exasperated by the sight of his wife and daughter, he had ordered that they not enter his room frequently. He therefore often remained alone with Rouvières, and in the moments when he did not fear any indiscreet ear, he tried to bring him to a confidence or a confession—but he only obtained inconsequential phrases without any precise meaning.

"It's a specter," said Rouvières, with wandering eyes, "It isn't my daughter... Doctor, it's a deceptive apparition... Don't believe that that child with dark eyebrows and blonde hair is a living creature... No, no! Don't believe it..."

One day, however, the madman appeared to enter into a calmer period. He leaned toward his physician and seemed disposed to confidence.

"You see," he said, "before, she was so badly brought up! She made so much noise! Doctor, you can't imagine how insupportable she was! That day, she was playing on the stairs and she was shouting! She was shouting to penetrate the brain. I pushed her... she fell all the way down... I heard a dull thud... I ran... quickly... quickly..."

The madman stopped suddenly, looking around fearfully.

The doctor listened with his mouth slightly open and his hands trembling; but he did not want a surge of fear to interrupt the story commenced. In order to overcome the sick man's hesitation he repeated his final words,, mechanically: "I heard a dull thud...I ran...quickly...quickly..."

"Yes!" said Rouvières. "Her head was split, and she was gasping...horribly. I took her away...to care for her... She was still gasping... Everyone was going to come...I took her by the neck to make her shut up...and I squeezed, mechanically... She didn't cry any more. But I saw the blue marks that my hands had made...Then what would become...? I was scared, Doctor, I was scared, and I hid her... How was she able to come back?"

The doctor shivered under the weight of that horrible secret, and he felt a sharp pain in his heart in thinking about the mysteries of blood and infamy that he had already collected and that he had to retain there, as if in a tomb.

The heart of a physician, that of a notary and that of a confessor: what abysms!

Doctor *** tried to calm the effervescence of the madness, but he dared not combat it in its principle. Meanwhile the refrigerants acted sufficiently to extinguish the fever and to lead the invalid to a kind of atony.

Then he proposed to Madame Rouvières that he take her husband to a sanitarium in order to bring about a complete cure. But the young woman could not believe in such a grave danger. She was convinced that her husband's apparent calm was the commencement of a cure, and refused to let him leave. His condition was only known to the family, and would not sending him to Doctor ***'s establishment confess to the world that he had lost his reason?

On the contrary, as soon as Rouvières was convalescent, she installed herself in his room and tried to recall his memories.

However, the doctor obtained a temporary removal of Pâquerette, who was taken to the country by her grandmother.

Madame Rouvières was incapable of suspecting the husband she loved of a crime. She even accused herself of having aided his aberration by her continual allusions to the resemblance between her two daughters, whom she took pleasure in making only one. So she surrounded the invalid with cares and tenderness, and only thought of recalling him gradually to the sentiment of real life.

Hearing no more mention of Pâquerette and no longer seeing her agitating around him, Rouvières calmed down more every day. Finally, he could sustain a conversation and receive a few friends. His wife thought that he was saved, and ceased making him remain in his room. Soon, he was well enough to resume his habitual life. He went out; he went into society and received in his home.

By virtue of one of those irreflective habits that often govern us without our being aware of it, Madame Rouvières continued to inhabit Pâquerette's room, for the physician had not made any prescription in that re-gard.

The first time that Rouvières went into that room, his eyes fixed wildly upon the stone slab in the fireplace. The he looked around anxiously. Only seeing his wife, whose eyes were lowered over her embroidery, he suc-ceeded in vanquishing his emotion, or at least in not manifesting it. Madame Rouvières did not perceive any-thing.

After a few months, the last traces of the madness had disappeared, and Rouvières' health became excellent again. He wife believed him to be absolutely cured.

Then she wanted to see Pâquerette again, and she wrote asking her mother to bring her

Rouvières had never mentioned the child since his recovery, but he had often asked for news of his mother-in-law, whom he was astonished not to see.

When Pâquerette had returned to the house with Madame de Meillac, Madame Rouvières wanted to pre-pare the convalescent to see her again with precaution.

She was sitting by the fire in that terrible room and her husband was facing her, reading.

"My friend," she said to him, "Don't you think that we're rather lonely, and that it's time to recall our fami-ly?"

"Yes," he replied indifferently. "Solitude doesn't frighten me, with you," he went on, trying to smile, "but I'd be glad to see your mother again. Is she still at Marneroy?"

"She's going to come back with your daughter."

"You know very well, my dear, that we no longer have a daughter," said Rouvières, with a sinister smile.

Madame Rouvières raised her eyes to look at him, fearfully. She dreaded the return of the madness, and threw herself into his arms.

"My friend, I beg you, I implore you," she exclaimed, "Don't deprive me any longer of Pâquerette, of our child... return to yourself."

Suddenly, however, Rouvières had resumed his fixed and somber gaze.

"Pâquerette is dead!" he said.

At that moment, the little girl, who had escaped from her grandmother, appeared in the room and launched herself at the slab between her father's legs.

At that sight, Rouvières fell back in his armchair, prey to a violent nervous attack. He uttered inarticulate cries; white foam flecked his lips.

His wife hung on the bell; everyone came running; they hastened around the fire and threw cold water in his face while a domestic ran in all haste to fetch the doctor.

"Rid me of that specter," he murmured, as soon as he had recovered the power of speech. "I no longer want to see the dead!"

"But it's your daughter, my friend—she's quite real, alive. Pâquerette, kiss your father, tell him that you love him and that you don't want to die."

Pâquerette climbed on to Rouvières' knees, opening wide astonished eyes.

He leapt up, threw the child to the floor, at the risk of injuring her, and uttered a savage cry.

"Pâquerette is dead! I killed her! She's there!" he cried, falling on the slab like an inert mass.

They only picked up a cadaver. A few months later the paving-stone of the fireplace was taken away, while a priest recited the mass for the dead; and a family in mourning conducted the skeleton of a child to the cemetery.

www.ingramcontent.com/pod-product-compliance
Lightning Source LLC
Chambersburg PA
CBHW030359020726
47493CB00003B/881